BETTER

LEFT

BURIED

BETTER LEFT BURIED

MARY E. ROACH

HYPERION

LOS ANGELES   NEW YORK

First Edition, August 2024
10 9 8 7 6 5 4 3 2 1
FAC-004510-24165
Printed in the United States of America

This book is set in Adobe Caslon Pro/Adobe
Designed by Phil Buchanan

Library of Congress Cataloging-in-Publication Data
Names: Roach, Mary E., author.
Title: Better left buried / by Mary E. Roach.
Description: First edition. • Los Angeles : Hyperion, 2024. • Audience: Ages 12–18. •
    Audience: Grades 10–12. • Summary: Told in alternating voices, teenagers
    Lucy and Audrey investigate a town full of secrets, a family full of mystery,
    and an abandoned amusement park where people keep turning up dead.
Identifiers: LCCN 2023032369 • ISBN 9781368098403 (hardcover)
Subjects: CYAC: Mystery and detective stories. • Murder—Fiction. •
    Secrets—Fiction. • Mothers and daughters—Fiction. • LCGFT: Detective
    and mystery fiction. • Thrillers (Fiction) • Novels.
Classification: LCC PZ7.1.R57747 Be 2024 • DDC [Fic]—dc23
LC record available at https://lccn.loc.gov/2023032369

Reinforced binding

Visit www.HyperionTeens.com

TO ANA FRANCO,
WHO DESERVED TO HAVE
HER NAME IN A BOOK

BEGINNING.

AUDREY
FRIDAY.

THE LETTERING ON MY FATHER'S GRAVE IS CHIPPED in the right corner, the curve of the *n* at the end dulled. That is the first thought running through my head as I crouch in the dewy grass at the edge of the cemetery.

He is one of the last people to be buried here, not because this town stopped hemorrhaging its own, but because the shiny amusement park was too close by, and nothing drives away visitors faster than the sight of the dead.

Now Anselm Amusements is closed and abandoned, the twisting arms of the empty roller coaster framed against the moon, the shadows from the beams bisecting Dad's grave.

Audrey Nadine, he'd say if he were here, his voice gentler than I ever am with myself. *Did the wander bug bite you again?* He would talk the way he always did when I was little and snuck out into the backyard or onto the roof when I needed some space. He wouldn't make me go back, not right away. He'd just tuck his flannel around my shoulders and wait with me until I was ready to go home.

But Dad is gone, and all I have is the memories and the texts in my phone from Pierce Anselm himself. The one that says, *I didn't mean for any of it to happen.*

And then another, hours later.

Meet me in the park.

I have that, and Dad's old flannel, still loose at my shoulders and long for my wrists.

And I have the knife tucked inside my boot.

Just in case.

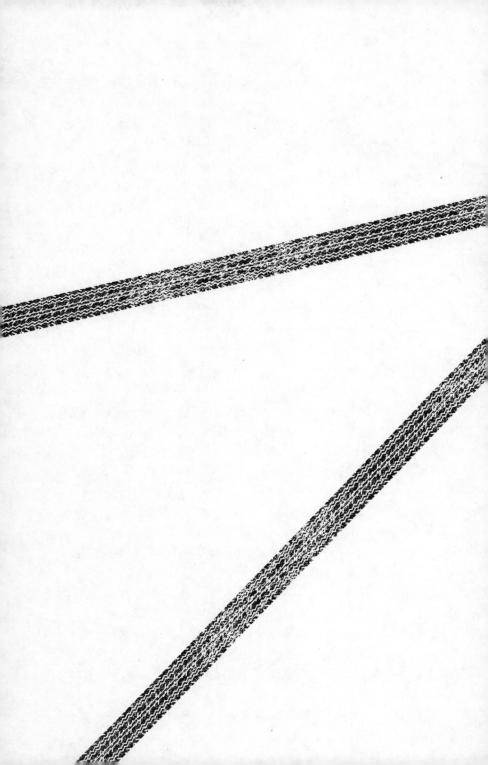

DAY ONE: FRIDAY, MARCH 22

CHAPTER 1

LUCY

8:43 P.M.

SOME MOMS TAKE THEIR SIXTEEN-YEAR-OLDS ON road trips to a music festival, a national park, or to see faraway family for spring break.

My mom?

Well, my mom is taking me to a crime scene.

Jules and Amy and Nora are all going on spring break trips somewhere warm and sandy and distinctly crime free. *Their* moms bought them plane tickets and new swimsuits.

Not mine, though.

No, *my* mom announced when we were halfway to Dad's—where I am *supposed* to be spending spring break—that she needs to make a pit stop. For an investigation.

So that's how we end up in her brand-new Jeep Wrangler, driving six hours north out of our way to some backwater town I've never heard of.

Haeter Lake, Tennessee.

"So, Katy," I attempt again. "Remind me why you couldn't just drop me off at the airport?"

She doesn't respond, just keeps her dark eyes fixed on the road ahead of us.

We're winding through yet another endless stretch of trees. I've been nagging her—about this, and any other topics of conversation I can think of—ever since we passed Nashville an hour ago.

It's been nothing but thick, tangled forest and arguments ever since.

Or at least I'm *trying* to get to the part where we argue, but currently Mom is keeping me firmly stuck in the I-ask-annoying-questions-and-she-gives-one-word-answers stage we have to cross before we get to the arguing part.

Another hour with nothing but mostly leafless branches to look at—not even mountains or coast or something *interesting*—and my last remaining brain cells are going to melt right out of my skull. "Can I at least know *why* we're driving six hours to the middle of nowhere for this guy?"

"*This guy* has a name. Pierce Anselm is a personal friend, Lucille."

Oof.

Straight to *Lucille*.

She sounds tired of my bullshit already, which does not bode well for all this extra time we're apparently destined to spend together.

She's looking straight ahead, her jaw set, not a strand of dark hair out of place. Her skin is a soft brown, while mine is as pale as my dad's. Today, her brow is furrowed with anxiety, which is rare for her.

Usually, she's difficult to fluster, forever holding on to the rock-solid calm it takes to sit across from a United States congressman and intimidate him into confessing to murder.

It's why people fly her out all over the US to solve cases for them that the cops can't.

It's why she sometimes feels a million miles away from me.

So even if he *is* a friend—and Katy doesn't really *do* friends—I don't get why we're driving out to the middle of goddamn nowhere, Tennessee.

"Is he rich?" I ask, drumming my freshly painted pastel-green nails on the armrest.

"That's enough." Mom's hands tighten around the steering wheel, her knuckles turning white. The sleeve of her blazer has inched up, revealing the tattoo on her forearm that she refuses to talk to me about.

Memento vitae.

"But if you *know* him," I persist, "isn't that breaking one of your rules? Investigating a case you have a personal connection to?"

It has always been the rule—she can't be too close to a case because she *has* to be detached. Objective. Cold.

And maybe that's why I'm pushing for answers now.

Usually, even when I travel with her, I leave her cases alone.

But maybe I'm pushing because there are so few people she calls *personal friends.*

"Like I said: Pierce is a close family friend," Katy tells me stiffly. "And he requested a private investigator. Specifically me."

"When did he ask you to come?" I glare suspiciously at her. "Did you know before we left? Katy, I could have just *flown.* Then I wouldn't be stuck on a road trip to the backwaters of Appalachia, and *you* would have some peace and quiet."

She sighs. "No, I did not know," she answers. "And I'm sorry you have to come with me. I got a very urgent text just after we left, and I haven't . . . I haven't heard from him in a long time. But if all goes well, I'll be able to help Pierce sort out whatever's bothering him and we'll be on the way again tonight. By morning at the latest."

"There isn't *anyone* you drop everything for," I say.

Not even me, though it doesn't seem particularly helpful to point that out right now.

"He's a family friend," she repeats.

"*I'm* family," I say. "And I've never heard his name before. Also, that's a weird request. Is he a weirdo? I really don't want to waste my spring break investigating some creepy family in some creepy little town."

"Pierce isn't a weirdo. And I haven't seen him or his family in years, not since before you were born," she answers finally. Her shoulders are tense, and she rolls them and then tilts her head, neck cracking. "It's a bit complicated."

Complicated is Katy's favorite way to end any conversation she doesn't feel like having, whether that's about what happened between her and Dad, or about their custody agreement, or about anything else in her life that happened before I was born, really.

"So, what kind of case does this Pierce guy want you to solve? And please say I won't be wasting my *entire* spring break helping you solve it."

"No, Lucy, we'll be on our way soon," Katy says wearily. "I'm sure this will be quick, and you'll be at your dad's place in no time."

It's dark by the time we turn off the main highway, first down a narrow county road with thick trees and no streetlights and then down an even narrower paved road. There are a few gaps in the trees, houses with a single lamppost outside and some with nothing, gaping voids in the dark.

"Katy." My voice sounds smaller now, even to me.

She looks over at me, her own face cast in shadow.

I'm scared, I was going to say, because it isn't like Mom to act like this, and because I don't like the dark and the quiet out here. But how do I say that to a woman who has never been scared of anything?

"You okay?" she asks crisply. "We're almost there if you need a bathroom."

I have to pee every forty-five minutes—excuse *me* for being well-hydrated—but that isn't it, not this time.

Okay, yes, maybe I do also have to pee.

Anyway.

All this freaks me out, if I'm being honest. But there isn't anything I can do about that now, and besides—what would Katy do if I told her I wanted to get the hell out of here? She has a case to solve. So all I say is:

"I'm okay."

Katy slows the Jeep as we pass a faded green sign that reads HAETER LAKE, POPULATION 1,376. The main street is wide and dimly lit, just one flickering streetlight outside of a café and another at the end, outside of the bank, the only building on the street that looks as if it has been updated recently.

We wind our way back up into the mountains north of town, the curves of the road sharp. In the rain this would be dangerous—maybe it's dangerous in this darkness. And if someone took a turn too wide and there was another car coming, there would be no time to slow down, no time to swerve.

A shiver snakes down my spine.

"Pierce's family lives up this way," Katy explains, though I didn't ask. "But we're meeting at his business."

"This late at night?" I stare at her. "Mom, this is *weird*."

"I think something has him spooked," she admits, the click of her blinker the only sound in the sudden silence. "But I can take care of myself, Luce, and—you called me Mom."

The car slows, and she turns to look at me, her eyes piercing.

I look away, shrugging one shoulder uncomfortably. "Would you prefer I called you Katy *all* the time?"

"You only call me Mom when...when you're scared," she says, and then she stops and shakes her head.

"I'm not *scared*," I snap, a little too sharply to be convincing. "This is just weird. And not like you."

She sighs. "You're right. And I'll be quick, honey, I promise. I'll calm Pierce down and help him sort things out and—"

The trees fall away, opening out before the vast outline of a theme park—a Ferris wheel, a carousel, and silhouetted against the dark, barely moonlit sky, a roller coaster curving and twisting.

"It's— I didn't know they closed this place." Katy's voice is so soft I can hardly hear it.

"I can't believe you took me to a creepy abandoned theme park," I huff. "Happy spring break to me."

"You can stay in the car," she says shortly. "And no, Lucy, I'm not asking."

"Pssh. As if I would get out and walk around. I've *seen* horror movies,

Mother. I know better than that." I hesitate when she parks, hand lingering on the steering wheel as if she is trying to steel herself for . . . this. Whatever *this* is. "Are you gonna be okay?"

"Of course I am," she says firmly, and then we see it at the same time, illuminated by Mom's high beams.

At the base of the rickety old roller coaster, a man is lying facedown in a pool of blood.

CHAPTER 2

AUDREY
9:58 P.M.

HE'S DEAD.

Pierce Anselm is dead, his blood seeping into the ground of this cursed fucking park.

The knife is clenched in my fist as I sink back into the shadow of the trees, my hands trembling. The beams of the roller coaster look as sharp as blades where they are silhouetted by the moon, vines choking it as they climb up toward the dark sky.

I find that my legs don't move the way I want them to once I reach the cover of the trees outside the park. I am shaking badly. I cannot *breathe*.

And then the lights of a car cut the dark, so close to me I have to stifle a scream. A car, one I don't recognize.

And then two people, a woman close to Mom's age, who runs toward the body. She is too late, too late to save him.

She makes a noise in her throat, something like a cry or maybe like a scream.

I recognize the sound. I made it here, in this park, five years ago, on the worst day of my life.

But the girl stays outside their Jeep. She is my age, curvy and red-haired and wearing a soft yellow sundress that looks out of place in this graveyard we find ourselves in.

And then she turns.

Her eyes meet mine, sharp and piercing even from this distance.

For half a moment, neither of us makes a noise, both of us frozen in horror. I am close enough to see the goose bumps trailing down the bare, freckled skin of her forearms.

She is close enough to see—

Me.

And then she screams, the sound shattering the night, just as the red-and-blue lights of the sheriff's car light up the parking lot.

I do what I should have done long ago.

I turn and *run.*

LUCY. 10:03 P.M.

There's a person out there in the woods. There *is.*

Katy is holding me tightly against her chest, and that's how I know things are bad. Like, *bad* bad.

"What is it, honey?" she asks. "What did you see?"

I point wordlessly into the dark forest, where just a moment ago I saw—wide, dark eyes. Mud on her jacket. The sharp glint of a *knife.* "I saw her," I say. "Or him. I don't know. They had a *knife.*"

Katy's heartbeat thunders against my ear, her grip only tightening as the cop car pulls up next to us, its lights flashing but its sirens quiet.

"Mom?" I whisper.

And okay, fine, so maybe I only call her that when I'm really, really scared. I'm grown enough not to need her most days. But I've never been at an actual crime scene and seen—seen a *body* before.

"Don't say anything to him," Katy whispers into my hair. "Okay? Don't say anything to anyone."

"Mom?" More urgently. I can hardly breathe.

My chest hurts, and there's a dead body, and a creepy, abandoned theme park with towering trees and a rusted-out slide with a trunk growing through, and giant teacups that used to spin guests but now just creak and groan as if they are crying for the man who is dead.

The man who was somehow connected to my mom.

"*Promise* me," Katy says fiercely. She pushes me back to arm's length, her hands digging into my shoulders so tightly it hurts.

"I promise," I say quickly, and she lets me go.

The sheriff gets out of his car, which is parked so close to Katy's that I may not be able to get back in my seat without scratching his door.

He looks like he's in his late fifties, though it's always hard for me to guess when it comes to old people. He has yesterday's stubble, as if he gave as much attention to his appearance as I did this morning. The man stifles a yawn as he raises a hand to wave to Katy.

"Please don't say *fuck the police*," Katy whispers. "Please? Just this once?"

I choke on a laugh that would have sounded near hysterical.

When she steps away from me, I shiver suddenly with the cold.

She moves toward him and—he pulls her into a hug.

A *hug.*

Wait.

Am I still in Katy's Jeep, dreaming this?

Because other than, like, just now, in proximity to a dead body, Katy doesn't even really like to hug *me.*

"Katy?" I blurt out, my voice loud and shattering in the horrible quiet of this parking lot. I scuff my boot against the buckled asphalt we're standing on. "*What?*"

This guy just *hugged* her, and she didn't respond by knocking him out.

"You must be Lucy." The sheriff smiles, just a little, at me as he releases my mom. He steps forward, hand extended to shake mine, and I take a tiny, involuntary step back. He raises an eyebrow but doesn't comment.

Don't say fuck the police.

Don't say anything.

To anyone.

Katy's words echo in my head, sharp and painful in contrast to the warm hug she just gave this man she asked me not to trust.

Finally, I reach out and shake his hand, my grip firm, just the way Katy taught me.

"I'm Cliff," he says, squeezing my hand with a sympathetic look. "Terrible circumstances, of course. But everyone in Haeter Lake has been dying to meet you. We've missed your mom a lot."

The use of the word *dying* feels wrong and cruel and horrible. I reach out a hand and steady myself on Katy's Jeep, my stomach tightening.

Haeter Lake, Tennessee. A family friend. A body by the roller coaster.

A cop who knows my mom.

These people are dying to meet me? They *know* about me?

I shiver again.

The sheriff—Cliff—is smiling, friendly, kind. Hugging my mom. All of that is discordant and strange and surreal.

Why does this town *know* me?

Katy barely looks at me, but I already know better than to look for answers there. "He texted me today," she says finally. "It's Pierce, Cliff. Pierce Anselm is dead."

Cliff's eyes dart to the body, his face pale.

Behind Katy's car, there is a sharp *crack*.

I scream again, high-pitched and fierce.

Katy's hand clamps down on my shoulder. "Lucille."

"Just a rabbit," Cliff says reassuringly, but the sound of his voice makes my stomach hurt.

It's too big to be a rabbit, I want to say, but Katy said not to say anything. Anything at all.

Not even about the person I saw in the woods?

I look at her for answers, but her gaze is fixed on the roller coaster and the body. The body I can't look at.

"Christ." Cliff shakes his head. "I thought— Well, when you called earlier and said he'd reached out, I called the house and asked if he was all right. He seemed in good spirits then, Katy."

He hesitates, his gaze flicking to me.

I want Katy to say, *No, don't talk about this in front of my kid*, but I also want our spring break trip to Hawaii. Some wants stay wants and nothing more.

"What is it?" Katy asks. She shifts slightly, placing her body between me and the park.

"Do you think he jumped?" Cliff runs a hand over his beard. "I— I'll call the medical examiner and the deputy to help with—*God*—to help with the body."

Mom hesitates for too long at his question. "I don't investigate the dead," she answers finally.

Both of those things—her silence and her answer—sound like *No, nope, it was definitely murder, no jumping happened here.*

Comforting as she always is.

"Katy." I say her name snappishly, because that's usually the only way to get her attention when she's gone cold and distant like this.

Her eyes snap to mine, startling a little bit as if she had forgotten I was there. She settles a hand on my shoulder, her grip tight.

"We should *go*," I say.

It's selfish, and wishful, and Mom isn't going to leave. I can already tell by the grim set of her jaw.

She squeezes my shoulder, almost gentle for a moment. "I know," she says.

"Katy," Cliff says. "The—the family. We have to tell the family."

He says *we*, like it's not just his job.

But Mom is nodding. "I'll come with you," she says. "Call Veronica first. Tell her we're coming to their place now."

Mom must realize how tightly she's holding my shoulder, because her hand opens, her knuckles nearly white from the pressure. "We'll go to our motel after," she tells me quietly. "We'll know more in the morning. Cliff can handle it from here."

"Veronica will want you to be part of this," Cliff says. There is regret in his voice as he says it. "Especially since Pierce asked for your help."

Katy's hand spasms on my shoulder.

I lean into her, because she is warm and strong and if I am not right beside her, so close we're touching, I will disappear right into the forest, vanish behind those bushes that sway, those trees that lean close enough to nearly touch me. That girl with the dark eyes and the knife in her hand—the girl I might have imagined—will find me.

"Can we go home?" I ask Katy.

If she notices that I sound close to tears, she doesn't react.

She shakes her head. In the sharp light of the moon, her pupils look dilated. "Not yet, baby," she murmurs. "Not yet."

"I hate to keep you out any later for this," Cliff says, not at all sounding as if he regrets it. "I'm going to—" He clears his throat, looking at me again. "I've got to secure this scene and make a call to the medical examiner. Why don't you head up to the big house and talk to the family? I'll send my deputy with you."

Katy deals with the police often, and she rarely does as she's told. She usually fixes them with that cold, unimpressed look that says she won't be doing anyone's plan but her own.

But now, she nods woodenly. "Of course," she says softly. "I'm happy to help."

Cliff hugs her again. "I'll stop by the house after I'm done here," he tells her, and then nods to me.

Katy puts her hands on my shoulders again and guides me back toward the Jeep, her posture tense.

She breathes out once we're in the car, but when I open my mouth, she holds up her hand. "I know you have questions," she says.

I have *always* had questions. I've gotten vague answers out of her in the past—I knew she had lived in Tennessee when she was younger, though I had assumed a city like Nashville, not a small rural town at the edge of nowhere—but now I have a hundred more, swirling around in my brain. "Of course I have some fucking questions—"

"Not now." She is back to the version I know: calm and commanding and utterly in control of herself.

But as she drives the Jeep out of the parking lot, away from the body, up, up, up into the darkness of the mountains, I watch Katy's face in the rearview mirror. And now that we are out of Cliff's sight, she doesn't look calm at all.

Her eyes are wide, pupils round, and her chest is heaving as if she is trying and failing to catch her breath, one breath away from a panic attack as if she is, for the first time, just like me.

AUDREY. 10:47 P.M.

I stagger off my motorcycle—well, Dad's old motorcycle—in the dark gravel path outside our home, the small trailer at the edge of the trailer park. My hands are shaking, dirt caked beneath my fingernails and embedded in the soles of my new running shoes.

Dirt everywhere.

And Pierce Anselm is dead.

Pierce Anselm is dead.

And I shouldn't feel relieved, but when I swing my leg over my motorcycle, *Dad's* motorcycle, it feels. Good. And terrible. But good, too, and that scares me more than the body did.

Our one little streetlight flickers, its yellow dome a halo—for Mom. She is standing outside in her work shoes, her arms folded, her brow furrowed.

Fuck.

She's in her scrubs, her black hair pulled into a ponytail. She's not wearing makeup, and the dark circles under her eyes are even more pronounced than usual. "Audrey Nadine," she says. "Where the fuck were you?"

I can't even pretend I was with my friend Chris, because he already dipped to spend his spring break with his grandparents in Arizona.

Before the accident, before everything, I wouldn't have made it to the Friday before spring break without at least half a dozen invitations to hang out at bonfires or cabins or down at the lake.

But now, with five bitter years stretching between me and the accident, and more than a few fistfights, after asking everyone and anyone to *choose*, to choose a side, to choose *me*, they have all drifted away.

"I—I just wanted to go out for a bit," I say. The Post-it note that was stuck to my locker earlier is still crumpled in my pocket, the scrawly handwriting with its lie. *I swear I didn't know*. "Just drove around a bit on the bike."

Her eyes flash, and for a moment I wait for her to call me on the lie. But then she tilts her head, considering something. Finally, she says, so softly it sounds that much more dangerous, "It's past curfew."

"Sorry," I mutter.

We're talking about curfew, and Pierce Anselm is in a pool of his own blood back at the park.

"Did you expect me to be at work?" Mom's voice sounds tense. She's not usually that strict, at least not about curfews, because I can handle myself, because Chris is steady and kind and watches my back. Because I grew up too fast to act like the other dumb teenagers from Haeter Lake. But tonight, the worry in her voice is unmistakable. "I had tonight off," she says when I don't answer. "But I just got a call. They need me."

"Why?" I swing my leg off my bike and knock the kickstand into place. When I try to move past her, she adjusts her stance, blocking my path.

"Who were you with?" she asks. "I *know* Chris is out of town."

If it were any other night, I would be both devastated and angry at the implication that Chris is the only person who would hang out with me, but she's right.

Chris said as much before he left, said, *I'm sorry you're spending spring break—*

And I'd cut him off, said, *Don't say* alone. *Don't say it. Don't say it.*

"I was alone," I tell Mom.

Her eyes drop to my shoes, to the mud caked there.

And mine drop to hers.

Her work shoes, sensible, slightly worn gray runners, are caked in dark, muddy clay.

Mom's gaze snaps to mine. "They called me in," she says quietly.

"Because someone found a body." Her dark brown eyes are intent, piercing, like she's searching for something when she looks at me.

I drop my eyes. Back down to that packed mud. "A *body*," I repeat.

After a long moment, she steps back, a little bit of the mud from her shoes falling from her shoe onto our front step. "Come inside."

I huff as I toss open the metal door to our trailer and kick my muddy shoes off inside. My knife is still tucked in my sock, hidden away, and there's—there's no blood on me. Or at least I couldn't see any under the light of the moon when I left the park behind. So there's no way. No way Mom can know.

I toss my leather jacket over the back of my chair, and something flutters to the ground. The Post-it note, the one from my locker. I pick it up and catch Mom looking at me.

Her stare is still intent.

"Someone left a note on my locker today," I tell her, though she didn't ask. "Don't know why I kept it."

Mom is like that. She'll wait long enough, quiet and sure, and you'll find yourself spilling your secrets before you can stop yourself.

Most of your secrets, anyway.

Her gaze flicks to my mud-caked shoes and then back to me. To the Post-it note.

My heart thumps inside my chest.

"I'm really not hungry," I mumble. "Can I please go to bed? I'm sorry I missed curfew."

After a long moment, she sighs. "Yeah, baby," she says finally. "Yeah, okay. But you stay here tonight, you understand me? If I find out that you've gone out again tonight—" She glances at the shoes, her gaze so intent I think she might burn a hole right through them.

"I won't," I promise quickly.

I disappear into my room and crawl into bed as quickly as I can. I lie there trembling for a long time, my body shaking so hard that the bed itself wobbles.

Sundress *saw* me. I know she did. I don't know her, or why Sundress and her mom were there, or what they might have wanted with Pierce Anselm, but she *saw* me. And Mom—I don't know what Mom knows, or thinks she knows. Or wonders.

There is a *thud* behind the trailer, in that gap of dead grass between our trailer and the forest. It's an empty space mostly, something that could be called a backyard only if you were being generous.

I jolt upright.

There is another, softer rustle.

And then the sound of water running.

I hook one finger on the blinds where they are already bent from the old days when Dad was here and we'd sit together and peek out at the stars or the moon or the forest together. Now, alone, I peek through.

Mom is back there, her face illuminated by her phone's flashlight, and she is hunched over something on the ground.

A pair of shoes. No, two.

She is running the hose carefully over the bottoms of the shoes, scrubbing roughly at the mud caked there, glancing over her shoulder every few seconds or so, even though no one lives close enough out here to see. In the harsh light of her phone flashlight, her eyes look hard, determined, fierce as the day she stood toe to toe with Pierce and Veronica Anselm and said, *You will pay for my husband's death.*

A moment later, Mom kills the light completely, and then it's just the gurgle of the hose and the soft scrape as she scrubs the mud from both our shoes. And I just lie there, trembling, wondering what exactly Mom knows—and what she is covering up out there in the dark.

CHAPTER 3

LUCY

11:14 P.M.

KATY PULLS OVER AT THE END OF THE ROAD IN front of a gate—and looming behind it, a mansion bigger than any house I've ever been this close to—and waits until the deputy joins us.

"Katy," I say shakily. "Why do *you* have to do this?"

She squares her shoulders and looks past me, her face illuminated by the red-and-blue flashing lights of the deputy's car and the lights along the private road leading to the mansion.

"I don't need questions right now, Lucille," she says, in that I'm-on-a-case voice that means she doesn't have time to entertain me.

"Mom," I attempt. "I'm *scared*."

She turns to me suddenly, her body jarring when I call her Mom.

"It's going to be okay," she says woodenly, but she is at least looking at me now. "I'm sure you've got questions, but I need you to do something for me, Luce. I need you to wait until we've left Haeter Lake in the dust before you ask me any of them."

And then she's driving again, the mansion looming through the twisted branches up ahead, distant and magnified at the top of the hill. The lawn that slopes toward the house is well groomed, the grass close-cropped and well maintained.

A pool, still covered for the winter, stretches out behind the house, and then wooden steps lead up to a deck high above the ground with a covered pavilion, lawn chairs, and a grill. Beyond all of that is the long, low silhouette of a building, something that could be a greenhouse, and then past that a path winds its way into the forest.

When we get out of the car, I follow Katy so closely I nearly step on the back of her heel, something that always annoyed her when I was young and clingier.

Katy pauses for a long moment before she knocks, again waiting until the deputy joins us before she lifts her fist and knocks.

The sound makes me jump, but I force myself not to lean close to Katy.

We are on a case. We are professionals. Well, she is. And me clinging won't help anything.

The woman who answers the door is tall and silver haired, and though she looks as if she's ready for bed—silk pajamas, her hair loosely pinned, her glasses on—she looks elegant all the same.

She is—

Regal.

That's the only word I can think of.

She pauses and then gasps, putting her hand over her mouth. The gesture feels practiced; the emotion only allowed after she weighed it and decided it was acceptable for public display. "Katy?" she says. "Oh, darling, what are you doing here? Is everything all right?"

A hundred emotions pass across Katy's face and then she steps forward and wraps her arm around the woman. "Veronica," she says. "Veronica, I'm so sorry."

The deputy ushers me backward, a short way away so that I'm standing at the bottom of the steps. She tells me, very kindly, that I shouldn't have to hear all of this, and that it's law enforcement business, and I manage not to say anything rude about the police.

I do still watch all of it unfold.

This Veronica, who calls my mom *darling*, who my mom hugs—this woman does not fall apart at the news that her husband is dead.

She stands very still, in a way that looks as if she is trying to contain everything that wants to spill out, and then she presses her hand to her mouth and steps back inside, face crumpling into grief.

Katy follows, as if I am forgotten here.

The deputy does not glance back either.

The door shuts, and I let it, and then I am alone in the dark on the steps of the mansion, shivering against the wind and wondering what else is just beyond the ring of the lamppost that illuminates the steps.

I am frozen there—making no move to knock or go inside, imagining the flash of eyes I saw in the forest, the glint of steel, the panicked look of a girl, a *girl*, I know I saw her, before she turned and ran.

And then the door swings open with a *bang*, and Katy descends the stairs, her eyes fierce. "Get your bag. Come *inside*," she says sharply. "Don't linger out here."

Her hand is heavy on my shoulder, fingers digging in, but I don't complain.

The light of the entryway is welcoming and warm. Veronica is crying, her well-manicured, ringed hands still pressed against her face, and there is a boy next to her now, a kid close to my age with high cheekbones and a shock of wavy blond hair. He looks pale and scared, and he is holding tightly to Veronica's hand.

"Stay close to me," Katy hisses in my ear.

Finally, Veronica stands, her hands a little shaky. She squeezes the boy's shoulder once and then her gaze settles on me.

"Katy," she says in wonder as she takes in the sight of me for the first time. "Oh, Katy, this is your baby girl. I've wanted to meet her."

She cups my face in soft, wrinkled hands, though her eyes are sharp when they take me in. "She looks just like you."

And that is how I know Veronica Anselm knows how to lie, and does it well.

No one has ever accused me of looking like my mom—or even, really, my dad. Mom is tall and lean and muscular, hard in every place where I am soft.

I, on the other hand, am short and curvy and almost always out of breath. Plus, I have red hair to Mom's dark brown.

"Thank you." Mom puts a hand on my shoulder, drawing me gently back. "Veronica, do you need anything tonight? I'd like to get my daughter to bed, but then I am ... I am at your disposal."

"Of course, of course." Veronica steps back and pushes a button on a sensor on the wall. It looks like climate control, but one of the fancier, newer models, the kind that monitors every aspect of temperature and lighting. The mansion looks old on the outside, stately and grand, but inside everything is sleek, modern, updated to prove how much money they've got. "I can never figure out how to do this from my phone, no matter how many times dear Gussy shows me."

Mom hmms politely in response.

Veronica's hand trembles, just a little, as she sets the temperature. "Well, then." She clears her throat, a mask settling back over her face, emotion controlled. "How would you like to stay in your mom's old room tonight? We've kept it just the way you liked, Katy. Even the old Avril Lavigne posters."

I'm not quite sure who that is, but I can't imagine Mom as a kid, period, let alone a kid *in this house* who left posters on the wall in her bedroom. I open my mouth, but shut it again, remembering Mom's panicked request to say nothing to anyone, to wait until we are gone before I ask my questions.

"Oh, we couldn't possibly intrude at a time like this," Mom says smoothly. "And this is Gus? He belongs to—"

"Blake," Veronica answers, while at the same time the boy—Gus, apparently—says: "Curtis."

Katy's head swivels back and forth between them, taking in something I don't quite understand. But I know enough to know she looks *scared*.

"Well, Curtis's son, of course," Veronica says after a pause. "Of course. But my son has decided not to be a part of our lives. Oh. Oh, we'll have to tell him. He was always closer to his father than Blake was. But yes, Katy darling, Blake has been raising our sweet Gus."

Gus, to his credit, does not give her the sort of eye roll I would give someone for Veronica's tone, but he catches my eye, just for a moment.

I almost open my mouth to ask more about this past tension, because Katy usually would be nosing around for things like motive and sources of conflict, and she's *not*, and that's unsettling. But she has been off-kilter and quiet and strange—and the mention of Curtis's name made her look like she wanted to run.

"Anyway," Veronica says, wiping at one last tear with one delicate hand. "This is all very horrible, but we must get some rest. Cliff has assured me that he's handling everything. You'll stay here tonight."

She waves us farther into the mansion, leading us up a wide spiral staircase, her footsteps slow and measured. "Katy, darling," she murmurs. "Why did you come? How did you know to come back?"

Katy pauses at the top of the stairs, quiet for a long moment. "You don't know, V?"

For a moment, she's there, the mom I knew before we entered Haeter Lake. She looks like the woman I always knew her to be, formidable and smart, teasing secrets out of people who want desperately to keep them buried.

"He didn't tell you?" I blurt at Veronica.

For a moment, the expression on her calm, almost expressionless face darkens.

But then it clears, storm clouds flitting away and replaced by perfect stillness.

"Tell me what, sweetheart?"

"Pierce texted me," Katy says. "But no matter. Let's get to bed. What an awful night for you, Veronica. I'm so very, very sorry for your loss."

Veronica acknowledges her with a dip of her head, silver hair remaining perfectly in place as she does. She leads us down the hallway on the second story, past an ornately decorated bathroom to a small bedroom that looks out of place with the rest of the house.

"Just as you left it," Veronica tells Mom meditatively. "As if you'd never gone away. Lucy, you'll stay here."

Just as you left it? Who *was* Mom to these people?

Mom barely looks at me, so there won't be any answer there.

I want to grab her stiff shoulder and drag her back out into the misty midnight air.

Who are they to you? I want to scream at her. *Who are they to* me?

Home has been a gap in my chest my whole life, an absence, an ache. Home was me following Mom on her cases, traveling more than we stayed any one place, asking questions about where she was from and never getting any answers.

Home was something I had invented in my head.

"I'll just say goodnight to—" Mom begins.

"And you'll have the room down the hall," Veronica says crisply. "Goodnight, Lucy, dear. I'm so sorry to meet you under such awful circumstances. Sleep well." She shuts the door between Mom and me before I can say anything.

I look around the room. This room, unlike the rest of the mansion, seems as if it has not been updated in years.

I never expected home to look like this.

There is no hint of dust, but otherwise the room looks untouched— the only carpet of any kind I have seen in the house, an old dark-green rug beneath the narrow bed. The nightstand has chipped white paint, and the dresser beside it is covered in mock-trial trophies. Veronica was right about the posters, too—Avril Lavigne, a singer apparently, has her place on the wall beside Shakira and Britney Spears. The Britney poster is signed.

Cross-country, track, and debate trophies line one of the shelves.

Of course Mom was her own kind of champion in school.

In *school*. Because this town is where she went to school.

It's too much for one day, the trip up here, the dead body, the creepy preserved bedroom, the news that *my mom is from here*.

I set my bag gingerly down on the bed, but before I have the chance to process anything, or to look around further, there is a creak and a groan and the wall behind my bed fucking opens.

Katy steps through, ducking her head, and moves so fast she nearly knocks me over as she catches my scream with her hand placed firmly over my mouth.

"Shh," she says sharply.

There is the mom I know, a badass who has no time for drama. Especially mine.

"I'm sorry to scare you," she whispers, removing her hand from my mouth.

"There's a *secret passageway*?" I stare up at her, and then back at the—well, not the wall. The door, I suppose. *"You can walk around in the fucking walls?"*

"Be *quiet*," Katy hisses. "I'm not in here, and you didn't see me. Veronica doesn't know all the passages. Definitely doesn't know about this one. They were old servant corridors a hundred years ago. Pierce had them sealed off because he—he was proud of how progressive he was, letting the servants use the main entrances and hallways. Said these were all a safety hazard anyway. But I found them."

"For fuck's sake," I whisper. "Katy, what's going on?"

"I don't have time to explain," she says firmly. "I'm being watched. I will be watched as long as I am here. Baby, I don't know what happened, but I need you to know that you can't trust these people. Don't tell them anything about yourself or about me or about your dad. Don't tell them about Pierce, or what he texted me, or what you saw at the park. Don't tell them *anything*."

I shiver, and Katy pulls me close.

"Katy," I whisper. "Are we in danger here?"

Katy hesitates.

In the stillness, I can hear the creak of the old house settling. Despite all the updates, the bones of this house are old. Old money, old secrets.

"Who's Curtis?"

Katy stiffens. Says nothing.

"Did he—" I stop, my voice snapping as if a thread has been cut, as if the house itself sucked the breath out of me.

"He's Veronica and Pierce's son," Katy answers finally. "He's not in Haeter Lake—or he shouldn't be—and he's not your problem. If he is in Haeter Lake, he's someone to stay away from. Do you understand?"

I don't understand anything, but there doesn't seem much point in saying so.

"Katy," I say when she doesn't press me on it. "Can we leave tomorrow?"

"Baby, I'm sorry," she says. "Because I found the body, I—I have to stay in town for a few days. Just until everything is squared away."

I spring back from her. "Are you—are you a *suspect*?"

"I won't be," Katy answers. "Once they clear up time of death and we have my alibi from the gas station cameras outside of Knoxville, I'll be just fine. It's just a precaution. Cliff and Veronica both know I had nothing to do with it. And they know I'm too smart to let this get pinned on me."

I drop onto the bed. "Katy, holy shit. Who were these people to you?"

"Family," she says. "Kind of. But it doesn't matter now. The less I tell you, the less you ask, the safer everybody will be. Okay? I've got to get back to my room now because Veronica will check any minute. The bedroom door bolts, okay? Make sure you bolt it tonight. And keep this under your pillow." She pulls a small knife from her pocket and presses it into the palm of my hand.

And then she turns and ducks out into the narrow secret corridor, the wall sliding back into place.

I stare down at the blade in my hand.

I'm in my mom's childhood bedroom, in a mansion full of people who may love her or may hate her or something more confusing than either of those things.

And my mom is a suspect for murder.

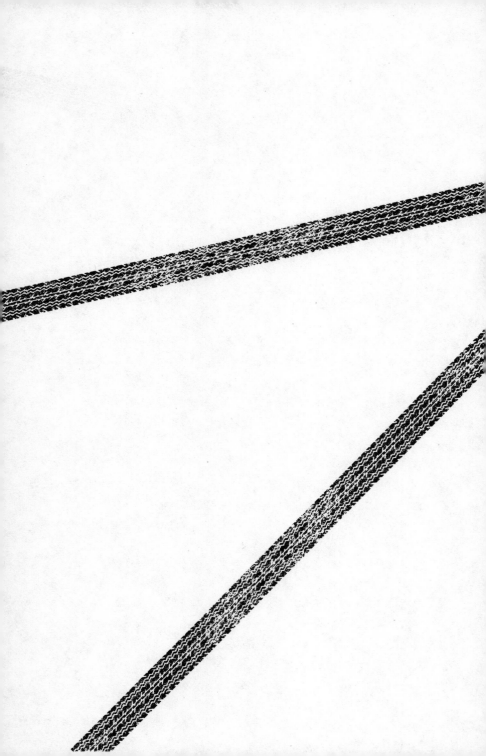

DAY TWO: SATURDAY, MARCH 23

CHAPTER 4

AUDREY
7:03 A.M.

WHEN I STUMBLE BLEARILY OUT OF MY NARROW, cramped bedroom the next morning, everything has been meticulously cleaned, even the stack of dishes that always seem to linger in our small sink. My shoes, so packed with mud the night before, are immaculate.

I text Mom, because this scares me. This fucking scares me. The way Mom looked at me last night when I got home, the mud on her own shoes, the sound of the hose trickling in the backyard. What I saw at the amusement park. And that *girl*, the one with the sundress and the eardrum-shattering scream, who looked me dead in the eye and saw me at the place where Pierce Anselm died.

Your shift almost done?

The bubbles pop up immediately as Mom types, and it takes a long time, because Mom is the slowest damn texter on the planet.

Coming home.

The shoes are clean. They're so clean. *Too* clean.

So I put them on, adjust my knife so it's hidden against my ankle, and pace outside in the dusty gravel as I wait for Mom.

She pulls up a few minutes later in the old red Honda Civic that she's had for as long as I can remember. She's wearing her scrubs, and there's a speck of blood on one of the sleeves, but she gets out and wraps her arms around me tightly.

"Mom?" I whisper against her shoulder.

"It's gonna be okay," she says sharply. "I promise, baby, it's gonna be okay."

I don't have time to ask what she means, or what's going on, or about her shift and the reason she was called in, the body, Pierce Anselm's body, because the sound of sirens cuts the still morning air.

Mom nearly jumps back from me, and then her face hardens. That look in her eyes goes still and calm, the way she was when they told her that Dad was dead, that they couldn't bring him back. Still and calm because Mom knows how to handle the worst shit. She always has.

"Mom." My voice cracks on the word. "Mom, what's going on? Why is Cliff here?"

"Don't tell them anything," Mom says softly, and then she's pushing something into my hands.

It's her phone, the *Friends* phone case and cracked screen, and I shove it into my pocket, staring up at her. "Mom?"

"Promise me. No matter what happens. No. Matter. What." She cups my face gently with one hand as the sheriff's car pulls up in front of our trailer.

But then it's too late for any more questions, because Cliff gets out of his car.

I've known Cliff my whole life. He was the one who picked me up when I was drunk that first time, spray-painting shit on the Anselms' gate, and later that weekend, smashing the windows of the bank because they had fucked us just like the Anselms had. I know he remembers it every time he looks at me, remembers that I'm the delinquent. That I'm the loud kid, the kid from this side of town who will never amount to more than the drinking and the spray paint and the uncaged anger.

Today, though, today he looks sad. Almost regretful.

"Morning, Langley," he says. "Audrey."

My mom nods stiffly at him.

"What do you want?" I take a step forward, my fingers drifting toward my knife.

Mom's hand digs into my shoulder, pulling me back. "Audrey."

My name is a warning.

Cliff shoves his hands into his pockets, his eyes looking past us both for a minute. "Langley," he says finally. "Langley, you gotta know why I'm here."

"*I* don't," I snap. "And I'd fucking like to. The sirens, Clifford? All the lights? What do you think happened out here?"

"Still not Clifford," he corrects me wearily. "Langley, we gotta just ask you some questions, okay? It's gonna be easier if you come, yeah? It's gonna be easier on all of us."

Definitely easier on Cliff, but Mom's face has gone bone white, so I don't say that.

"Yeah," she says. "Yeah. Okay."

"Ask questions about what?"

Cliff sighs and looks down at me. "Pierce Anselm is dead," he says. "Someone killed him."

A choked sound escapes my mouth, something strange and feral. I look down, away from Cliff, because if I'm looking at him, he'll see, and he'll know. That I'm not sorry Pierce is dead. I'm not sorry at all.

"They called me in this morning," Mom explains quietly. "The medical examiner—she ruled it a homicide, baby."

"What does that mean? Mom, what does that *mean*?"

Mom laughs, but the sound isn't humor. It's a harsh, short thing that sounds painful. "It means they think I did it," she says.

They would always have come looking for us first. Because we're shit from the south side of Haeter Lake. Because we live in the trailer and we lost too much and we were too loud in our grief.

"Did you bring Veronica in?" I ask Cliff. "Show up at her house with all the fucking sirens? Drag her down to the station? Arrest her, too? Because if you're looking for—"

"No one is being arrested," Cliff interrupts me. "Just questioned. Audrey, you gonna be okay out here on your own? Langley, she can come, too, if you'd feel that's safer. We—"

"She stays here." Mom is looking past me, eyes hard as steel when she meets Cliff's gaze. Her hand settles on my shoulder, the touch gentle but insistent. "Do you understand me, Cliff? She stays here, or I don't go with you until you have an arrest warrant."

He does understand, I can see it in the way his gaze flashes between us, and then he nods once and opens the back door for Mom.

She looks at me, emotion crackling in her eyes, and then she lets me go.

And the sheriff takes her away, still in her scrubs, with her too-clean shoes and that look in her eyes that says she knows it's already too late for her.

I stand there for a long time, my thumb rubbing the bracelet Dad left me, staring down the narrow road long after the sheriff's car is gone.

Mom told me not to say anything to the cops or the Anselms or anyone else. But she *didn't* tell me not to find the girl at the park, the one who saw me. And if she saw *me*, she might have seen more. Maybe enough to clear my mom.

And maybe enough to add me to the suspect list, but that's a problem for future Audrey.

CHAPTER 5

LUCY
7:34 A.M.

A HOUSE LIKE THIS ONE SPEAKS AT NIGHT.

Katy would say I'm being dramatic, but. Well. *Someone* in this family has to be.

But I spent the night tossing and turning, seeing the slumped body every time I close my eyes. And somehow more unsettling, my mom's eyes, wide and scared in a way I've never seen.

I'm not usually much of a morning person, but by the time Katy knocks on my door, I'm more than ready to be up.

Katy is at the door early. Well, okay, so maybe 7:30 isn't that early? But it's early when you've been up all night in a creepy old house where your mom apparently lived but never once told you about.

Yeah, way too early when you take all of that into consideration.

I stumble out into the hallway, and Katy puts a finger to her lips.

"Let's go," she says. "Get your bag. You didn't unpack, did you?"

"I didn't lose my mind, *Mother*," I tell her, stepping back into the room to grab my duffel and charger. "My bag is still packed. Because we're not supposed to be staying, remember? I had spring break plans."

A smile ghosts across her face. "Glad to see you're your usual self this

35

morning." She grabs my duffel bag from me. "Phone, charger, all of that? My stuff is already in the car."

I nod, hold them up with each hand. "Present and accounted for."

"We're going to the motel," she says. "Move your ass. They'll all be up any minute."

"Why are we sneaking out of the rich people's creepy house?" I whisper as I trail behind Katy. "Are they gonna kidnap us if they catch us? Are they in a cult? Are *we* in a cult now?"

"No one's in a cult, Lucille." Katy sounds exasperated.

Which is a definite improvement over scared out of her mind and emerging from my walls in the night.

Below, a door shuts gently, and Katy nearly jumps out of her skin.

So maybe not that improved after all.

"Must be Blake," Katy says, as if I should have any idea who that is. "She's the only one who gets up this early." She grabs my arm and drags me around a corner into a bedroom that is furnished both elegantly and impersonally. "This way. Come on."

I follow her, shoving my phone in my pocket as Katy shuts the door gently behind us.

A moment later, footsteps sound in the hallway.

Katy freezes, her body perfectly still until the footsteps pass. "Definitely Blake," she says. "Come on. We can take this—" She leans against the wall at the foot of the bed, and I bite back another scream when this wall moves, too.

"Are there secret passageways *everywhere*?" I whisper-hiss at Katy. "This house is so freaking creepy."

"Not everywhere," Katy answers, ducking into the passage. "Just to a few of these rooms. Come on, Lucy."

I do *not* want to go in there.

It is old and dusty and dark. Plus, there are probably spiders as big as my hand. Maybe more dead bodies, too.

"Lucy," Katy says impatiently. "Let's move."

I breathe deep and then force my feet forward, my bag clunking against the narrow passageway. I'm sweating heavily, a sign that I'm about one step away from an anxiety attack, but Katy doesn't need to know that.

I try to keep those out of Katy's sight most of the time, anyway. She has enough on her plate. She has enough of my bullshit.

The secret corridor stands out in sharp contrast to all the sleek, modern decor throughout the rest of the house. Here it's just old wooden beams and bits of insulation covering the floor in some places.

"Don't breathe too deeply," Katy warns. "Dust. Old insulation."

"Asbestos," I continue for her. "Cancer-causing lead paint. Ghosts."

"Don't be dramatic." She sounds more like herself, hidden away back here, fierce—the way I've always known her to be. "I'm sure the family made sure there was no asbestos or lead paint in the house."

I gulp. "But there could be ghosts?"

I don't have to see her face to know she's rolling her eyes.

"Before you say that ghosts aren't real," I say, my voice rising before I mean it to, "may I remind you that last year Jules and I saw—"

"Lucy." Katy cuts me off. "You have to be *quiet*. We're about to go past Blake's bedroom. She might be in there."

I am silent the rest of the way, down the long, narrow corridor that turns at what I imagine must be the corner of the house. A rickety old staircase lies at the corner, leading down into the dark.

I gasp, suck in a breath of air.

Okay, so maybe I'm a little closer to that anxiety attack.

"Katy," I whisper.

Without looking back, she stretches out her hand and takes my hand in hers, her grip warm and firm.

I hold on for dear life.

At the bottom of the stairs, Katy pauses and then pushes on the wall with the flat of her hand. It groans but opens for her, and we step into another hallway, one I haven't seen before.

"We're at the back," Katy tells me. "Keep moving."

She shoves open a door along the hallway and we step out into the morning light. I shiver, and Katy doesn't have to turn and look at me to know. She just hands me the sweatshirt she had tied around her waist, a total mismatch with the dark-green jumpsuit and heels she's wearing for herself.

"Katy?" a smooth, almost silky voice interrupts. "Is that you?"

Katy freezes, but she masks the motion so quickly I wouldn't have noticed if I wasn't standing next to her. She turns around, a serene smile frozen woodenly on her face as her hand closes roughly over my arm.

A tall, slender blond woman is standing at the front door, looking elegant in a matching silk T-shirt and short pajama combo. "Wherever are you going this early in the morning?"

Katy's face is a smooth, calm mask.

I shift, scuffing the toe of my boot against the ground.

"Heading out for breakfast," Katy says easily, though her free hand is balled into a fist at her side. "Lots to do today, and I wanted to give your family the time that they need, Blake. It must be devastating."

Blake looks more complacent than devastated, and her eyes narrow a bit at Katy's explanation. "This must be your child," she says a moment later. Her voice softens, but it's not a gentle sort of softness. It's something silky and dangerous, a snake coiled to strike.

Or maybe that's just in my head because Katy's freak-out is making *me* freak out.

"This is Lucille," Katy says woodenly. "Lucy, this is Blake. Pierce's daughter."

Blake smiles, holding out one well-manicured hand. The nails are painted a sharp red, though the index finger on her right hand is chipped and scraped. It is jarringly out of place for someone who looks so put-together, even in pajamas. "Why is your mother stealing you away so early?" she asks. "Stay and have breakfast with us. I promise we'll have a better display than whatever that diner serves."

I shake her hand, and she holds on, her grip as tight on my hand as Katy's is on my shoulder. I feel for a moment as if they're going to start pulling, their grips impossible and cruel, and I'll just be caught here, stuck in the middle. "You're Gus's mom," I blurt.

Something flashes in her face, and then the strange look on her face clears as she steps back. "His aunt, technically," she says easily. "He's my brother's son. But I've been raising him, yes." Her gaze falls on my mom again. "I heard my brother returned to Haeter Lake last night, though." She watches Katy carefully as if waiting for a reaction.

Katy does not react, just tilts her head slightly. "I look forward to saying hello," she says. "Lucille? Let's go."

"Breakfast first," Blake says. "I insist." She shivers a little, the gesture looking as practiced as Veronica's display of emotion last night.

My stomach grumbles traitorously.

Blake gives me the smallest of grins, the first truly human look I've seen on her face so far.

Which is maybe unforgivably bitchy of me because this woman just lost her dad last night.

If I wasn't so unsettled by my mom's reaction to these people—and by what I saw last night—maybe I'd be able to access more sympathy. As it is, it's all I can do to keep the anxiety attack from spilling over.

"Eggs and bacon and a fruit platter, I think," Blake says, waving her hand again.

Katy falls into line, following her inside, and I trail after her.

Veronica isn't up yet, and neither is the wide-eyed boy, Gus, from last night. It's just Blake at one end of a long dining table, all the places set, and Katy at the other end, and me in a chair at the middle.

Even the way Blake spreads jam onto her toast is measured and methodical, the knife steady in her hands. She looks up at me with a smile. "These are horrible circumstances to meet under," she says, leaning over to pass the platter of fruit my way. "But I am so glad to know Katy's daughter. Did you know she's a secretive one? We didn't know you even existed until recently."

I catch my breath, avoiding Katy's look. There are so many layers of secrets here—*I* was a secret to these people, like they were a secret to me, and the only common denominator here is my mom, unwilling to share a single thing with the people who care about her.

The anger hits me a moment after the anxiety.

"She sure is," I say, spearing a pile of scrambled eggs with my fork. "I'm sorry for your loss," I add automatically.

Blake sighs softly. "I am, too," she says. She is talking to *me*, her eyes on me, but somehow I still feel as if the words are directed at Katy. "Of course I am. He was a good father, despite his flaws."

"He was," Katy says.

I turn to look at her.

Her eyes are focused on her plate, her knife trembling in her hand.

"Lucille, finish your breakfast," Katy says coolly.

When she looks up, her gaze is blank, giving me nothing.

I look back at Blake, who is taking small, delicate bites of toast. She smiles slightly. "You haven't changed a bit, Katy," she says.

"Does Curtis know yet?" I blurt.

Everything in the room pauses, the air around me thickening.

Katy sighs, but Blake sets down her knife and pats her hands gently on the navy blue cloth napkin next to her plate.

"My brother," she says icily, "will find out if he ever resurfaces."

"I'm sorry," I manage, because Katy is now glaring daggers at me. "It was rude to ask."

Blake gives me something that could be called a smile, theoretically, though it has no warmth behind it. Not that I deserve any, after impulsively blurting out an awkward question nobody wants me to ask. "It's all right," she says. "I'm sure Katy hasn't told you as much about our family as you want to know."

She hasn't told me shit, but it seems wise to keep my mouth firmly shut at this point.

I fight the urge to make conversation to fill the gaps after that; the awkward pauses stretching on and on, Blake's gaze finding Katy's, and Katy's gaze avoiding hers as much as possible. The breakfast is a good one—of course it is—but the anxiety has made everything taste like gravel.

Mom doesn't relax until we're finally in the car, goodbyes said, and the gate at the end of the drive opens automatically for us when our car approaches.

"Katy," I venture when the mansion disappears in the trees behind us, "what just happened? Why haven't you ever told me about these people?"

I don't ask the rest of it: *Why didn't you tell them about me?*

Which of us was my mom ashamed of?

"Lucy," Katy says wearily, "I lived with them, okay? They raised me. I left when I was a teenager to make my own way in the world. And I came back because Pierce asked me to. That's all I can tell you right now."

She puts one hand over her chest as if it aches.

I know mine does, feels a little hollow at the thought of all the family, all the story, all the connections I'm missing.

"Why didn't I know we were filthy rich?" I manage, forcing a smile onto my face. "You're saying we could have had that?"

"*We* are not filthy rich," Katy corrects as she turns the car down a gravel road outside of the town. "Their money is not our money. It was a place to stay when I needed one, Luce. That's all there is to it."

"Katy." I stare around us as we drive farther into the woods and clouds begin to obscure the morning sun. "Are we filming a slasher up here? What the hell?"

The road is so narrow, trees growing so close over the road that twigs caress our car on either side, a gentle *tick-tick-tick* pairing with the crunch of gravel beneath our tires.

Katy snorts. "This is hardly scary enough for that," she answers. "The most you'd have jumping out at you here is a stray rabbit or raccoon. Maybe a bear if you're unlucky enough."

I sit up straighter, peering into the pitch-black forest. "That is the least comforting thing you've ever said," I tell her. "And you're not exactly known for saying comforting things."

Katy sighs. "What's that supposed to mean? I'm comforting." Her voice is still playful, but there's an edge to it that wasn't there a moment ago.

She slows, and there it is.

I thought my bar had been sufficiently low when Mom had said the words *small town motel*, but I still manage to feel a unique mix of horror and disappointment I haven't felt since we visited LA for a case and Katy managed to embarrass me in front of my favorite actress.

Long story.

It is a lengthy, low building, small for a motel. Trees hang low over the building, branches whispering against the roof, and one yellow light flickers at the far end. In the middle, in front of one of the rooms, a lone rocking chair rocks gently in the wind. Despite the fact that it's day, the darkness of the surrounding forest and the uneasy night we spent in the mansion are making my chest tighten dangerously.

No panicking in front of Katy.

That's my rule.

"Katy," I say cheerfully. "If you wanted to scare me, you didn't have to drive all the way up here. You could have just done the usual jump scares, like going to a parent-teacher conference or signing me up for band again."

She doesn't even grace my comment with a response, just gets out and retrieves the key from a lockbox. They don't even have a front desk person. Or a front desk.

And somehow, perhaps because my mother has an unhealthy lack of fear, she's just comfortable with that whole arrangement. Or at least way more comfortable than she was in the creepy Anselm mansion.

She holds the key up, and I roll my eyes at her.

I take one more look around us, at the forest, which seems to have grown closer in the last five minutes, and the rocking chair, which is rocking slightly faster than before.

Great.

I've been transported into a spring break slasher film.

I haul my backpack and suitcase with me into the motel, one last backward glance at the forest around us. At the edge of the circle of yellow light the lone streetlight provides, just beneath the long shadows of the trees, I see the flash of two yellow eyes. Watching us.

I let out a little shriek, and Katy jumps, bumping her head against the low-hanging doorframe.

"Jesus Christ," she snaps. "Why are you screaming?"

I glance again at the forest, but the eyes are gone, vanished into the deep, dark woods. "Something is out there," I tell Mom.

She tenses, but then she sighs. "Luce, I know the wilderness scares you a bit," she says. "And that's okay. But we're safe here, and there's nothing truly deadly in that forest. I'm sure it was an animal. A deer, a raccoon, a fox. There's all sorts out here."

All sorts.

Was that supposed to be reassuring?

This is what happens when Katy tries to make me feel better. Maybe fear skips a generation, because I seem to have gotten enough of it for the both of us.

I never met my grandma, but maybe she was like me, a girl who was scared of the dark. All I have of her is guesses, because Katy isn't much for talking about her past.

Shocking, from the woman who never mentioned the people who raised her or the town she grew up in.

I've always made up stories, since I was little, every time I asked Katy and got no answer. Now it's clear that my grandparents are long gone, long out of Katy's life, if she spent her childhood in someone else's home. But before that . . .

Before that, maybe my grandma was an astronaut, on a top-secret mission for NASA that took her to Mars. Maybe she was a spy. A marine biologist who lived on a research base underwater. A time traveler. A freedom fighter. Something, something badass and heroic, something that had forced her to leave us behind, because no way would she have just chosen to leave me and Katy on our own.

The wind whistles around the motel, and I shrug off the thought.

Those are kids' stories, things I invented for myself before I knew better.

"It was probably a serial killer out there," I tell Katy as I toss my bag onto the narrow bed. "Lying in wait. Sleeping in the room next door. Just waiting for the right moment—"

"Lucille," Katy cuts me off. "I think you've seen too many movies. Maybe I should cancel HBO when we get home. Netflix, too."

"Katyyyyy." I stretch the word out into several syllables. "*Or* you could take us on an actual spring break vacation, somewhere nice and safe. Preferably with Wi-Fi. And a beach."

Katy rolls her eyes. "Get some more sleep," she tells me. "I know I woke you early."

"Where are *you* going?" I drop onto the bed, hugging my bag to myself.

"I have to get down to the station," Katy answers. "I want to be in before Cliff comes to get me. I'm giving him my alibi, because he'll need it, and then I'll see if I can assist with any of the interviews once I'm cleared of involvement. And *you* are staying here because it's safer."

"If I'm safer in the murder motel," I say, flopping backward on the bed, "then we really are in deep shit."

Katy raises an eyebrow at me. "Lucille," she says firmly. "The motel is very safe. You can get some homework done. I'll be back in a few hours. Stay here, you understand me?"

She's gone before I can remind her that I don't have any homework, that I'm not supposed to be stuck in a shitty motel in a nowhere town, that I'm supposed to be on *spring break*. She's gone before I can ask her to tell me who these people are to her, who they are to me. Who I am to them.

Finally, I pull out my laptop, connect to the spotty motel Wi-Fi, and open up a browser to google them—Anselms, theme parks, my mom's name.

The roar of a motor interrupts me, and—and perhaps I am not my mother's daughter in any way that counts, because I inherited none of her fearlessness. The sound sends me diving down beside the bed, chucking my bag to the side as I do.

The motor noise stops just outside my window, and I peer out from the bottom of the window, nervously fisting my hands in the fabric of my green dress.

There's a girl around my age straddling a motorcycle, her abruptly short brown hair curling over her face, her brow creased with worry. She glances around furtively, over her shoulder first, eyes on the forest as if she expects it to be watching her back.

I drop my phone with a thud, and the girl's dark eyes snap to mine.

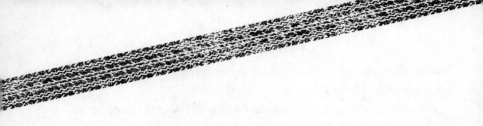

CHAPTER 6

AUDREY
9:14 A.M.

GUS HAD ARRIVED TO HIS SHIFT AT THE DINER despite what happened yesterday—trust an Anselm to still be chasing money even when someone has just fucking died—so I spent the morning searching for the newcomers.

Katy is back, people were saying. At the diner. At the gas station. At the library down the street.

And I came looking for her, because if anyone can help clear my mom's name, it's the world-famous private detective. Unless, of course, she decides to help the Anselms.

Either way, all I find is someone staring at me from a motel window as I swing my leg off my bike.

Shit.

Shit.

It's her.

The girl from the park, the girl who screamed in the dark, the only person in that fucking park reacting normally to the sight of a dead body. The girl who saw me in the forest.

As soon as my eyes meet hers, she dives down out of sight, as if somehow that will make me un-see her.

"You can come out," I yell, booting my kickstand in place and then leaning against my bike, arms crossed. "And you can stop panicking."

A moment later, the door creaks open.

She is about my age, like I thought last night. She has curly red hair that sits in messy waves just past her shoulders, and she's wearing a short green dress that hugs her curves. She's stunning, even framed by the sagging motel door. "Um," she says. "Hi? Why are you here?"

Sundress says everything like a question.

"Why are *you* here?" I glare at her because that's my default these days. My friend Chris says that's a coping mechanism, but Chris is spending spring break far away from here, so I'll cope how I damn well please.

"I live here," she says, and then blushes. "I mean? I don't live *here*. Obviously."

"Thanks for clearing that up, Sundress."

"Sundress?" She wrinkles her nose at me and then looks down at her dress. "This isn't exactly a sundress. The one I wore yesterday was, though. Plus, it had pockets. This one has those annoying fake pockets—look."

"Great talk," I say. "I got shit to do, okay? I just need to know you aren't going to be lurking in the window and staring at me while I do it."

Ask her.

It pulses against my temples. I should. I should shove her back against the wall and say, *What do you know, what did you see?*

Did you see my mom?

But if I ask—and if she did—

"Oh," the girl says. "Oh. Yeah? Sorry. I panicked." She hesitates, and then holds out her hand. "I'm Lucy."

"Lucy." I shake her hand. "I'm Audrey."

"Why are you all the way out here?" She tilts her head.

"Shit to do," I repeat. "See you around, Sundress."

I make it all the way to the end of the building, though I can feel her eyes on me, singeing where they touch my skin.

"Wait," she calls.

Her bare feet smack the pavement as she runs to catch up. She's out of breath by the time she reaches me, and she leans on the wall for support.

"Wait," she says again. "Wait, this is going to sound weird, but I—I *know* you." She blushes violently as I raise an eyebrow at her. "I mean—"

And then she stops cold.

I see the moment she realizes.

I brace for impact. Or to do what I have to, again.

"You were there," she whispers.

I don't think. I just grab her by the shoulders, shove her back against the wall of the motel, and lean close, my face inches from hers, my breath caught in my throat. "You didn't see anything," I say. "You didn't."

Her chest is heaving, her eyes wide, and she looks scared but— something else, too. Determined. "You were scared," she says, and all the fight goes straight back out of me.

Dad used to do that, too; I could be raging and yelling and arguing, and he'd just disarm me completely by being kind.

I let her go, and she steps back, watching me carefully.

"I wasn't—" I begin, and then shake my head.

When does anyone ever believe my side of the story in this town?

"You didn't do anything," Lucy says firmly. "Well, maybe you did something. But not *the* thing. Right?"

She's staring at me as if she desperately *wants* me to reassure her that yes, I'm a normal kid. That no, I didn't murder anyone.

"I didn't do anything," I say finally.

"You had a—" Lucy takes another step back from me. "You had a knife. I saw it."

"He wasn't murdered with a knife," I say, because that seems like the first and most important thing. "Besides, don't you carry one? I always have it on me."

"My mom's like that," Lucy says, sounding utterly unimpressed with both me and her mom. "Okay. So you didn't do anything. But you were *there*, and you don't want anybody to know. That's why I think we can help each other."

"Why do you think I need your help?" I snap, because I am who I am. Sharp and vicious, even when someone is trying to help me.

"I don't think you would be out here all alone at the murder motel if things were going great," Lucy says with a shrug of one shoulder, her dress slipping down over pale skin as she does. "So I'll help you with your"—she waves her hand—"your 'shit to do' or whatever you're off to go do on your own. And you can give me a ride into town."

"The . . . the murder motel?" I feel a laugh bubbling in my chest, despite everything. Despite Pierce Anselm and Cliff and Mom and everything else that's gone wrong in the last twenty-four hours. "Listen. I don't think there's much you can do. My mom's in trouble, and I gotta help her."

Ask her.

But I can't.

Not because she wouldn't tell me. But because I think she would. And if she saw me, what else did she see?

"Oh," Lucy says. "Yeah, I can definitely help. My mom's a detective— not like the cop kind, because ew, but like the private investigator kind? If your mom's in trouble, she can help. Her name's Katy. Katy Preston."

And I've got her.

Of course it was Katy at the park last night, and of course the scream- ing sundress girl is Katy Preston's daughter. I didn't recognize Katy last night—she left Haeter Lake before I was born—but of course it's her. Of course they're here. Of course they're involved, because Katy Preston and the Anselms have always been bound up tightly in this town.

"You're her daughter," I repeat flatly. I don't say the rest of it—the *I've been looking for you* or *I think you can help*. I don't show my hand, because she's a Preston, and Prestons are as good as Anselms in Haeter Lake.

Well. Just about, anyway.

"You've heard of her?" Lucy's eyes light up with pride.

"Everyone in Haeter Lake has heard of her," I answer.

Lucy's eyes brighten, and then her expression falls. "I— She doesn't talk much about her past," she says carefully. "I'd like to know more."

I arch an eyebrow at her. "You don't know much about your own mom?" I say, and regret the harshness of my words a moment later, because Lucy's mouth snaps shut and for a moment her eyes look teary.

"Of course I know about my own mom," she says. "Anyway. *Your* mom. What's up with her?"

"Mom got arrested this morning," I say bluntly.

I'm not sure why I'm being so honest with a girl I just met, but maybe it's that thing I do, where I throw out a harsh, uncomfortable truth about myself to see if people back away. Because they usually do.

I would do it in the years after Dad died, announce it loudly and angrily to someone who didn't know, just so I could skip past the pitying glances and the *oh I'm so sorry, honey*s that would inevitably follow.

Lucy doesn't look bothered, though. Or even surprised. Just curious. "Is she one of the suspects?" she asks. "My mom said they hadn't arrested anyone yet. Detained a few people, though."

"Yeah," I mutter. "Is your mom helping the cops?"

"My mom investigates on her own," Lucy says proudly. "Okay. So you want to clear your mom's name. I can help. I've tagged along on a bunch of my mom's investigations, and I know how we could help. Especially if they only have circumstantial evidence against your mom."

"And *why* are you interested? What do you get out of this? It seems like a lot to trade for a ride into town."

Lucy looks down at the ground. "I— It's complicated," she answers finally, the wind lifting her hair gently. She looks like she wants to say more—and maybe she would have, if I hadn't given her shit about not knowing much about her past. "Listen. I'll give you my number, you drive me to town, and later this morning after I talk to my mom, I can tell you what they have on your mom. Where were you headed? Before this?"

"Park."

It's not quite true, because I'm not actually sure I could go back there yet, but she doesn't need to know this.

Her eyes widen. "The creepy amusement park? Holy shit. Holy *shit*, Audrey. What were you gonna do? And you can get there from here?" She looks past me, into the shadows of the forest, and shudders.

I lift my hands, palms out, but I don't explain myself further. Truly, I didn't have much of a plan. Just show up at the crime scene. See if there was any evidence that Cliff hadn't found yet. See if any of it pointed to Mom. And if it did? Get the hell rid of it.

Or have a panic attack in the forest again before I even get close to the park.

Either way.

Mom had been smart last night, cleaning the mud from our shoes, which means she either knew that I was there and was protecting me—or because she was there with Pierce before he fell. And she had been smart this morning, shoving her phone into my hand so the cops wouldn't be able to take it from her.

"Come on, Sundress." I pick up my sunglasses, wipe them off, and then brush past her before she can ask any more too-pointed questions about plans I don't have. "Let's get you to town."

"It's Lucy," she huffs, hurrying to catch up with me. "And I need to grab shoes. But we have a deal, yeah? I help with your mom, and you get me to town so I can learn about mine."

There's some sadness behind the brightly spoken words, and it tugs at my own chest.

My gaze snaps to her. "You're doing recon on your own mom?"

Lucy claps a hand over her mouth as if she hadn't meant to let that last bit slip. "Just a little," she says, and that grin is back on her face, bright and endless. "Some mild snooping."

A grin tugs at my mouth. "Okay," I say. "Yeah. We have a deal."

CHAPTER 7

LUCY

10:14 A.M.

AUDREY IS—AUDREY IS STUNNING, AND THAT DOES *not* help my natural tendency to nervously chatter at people I've just met.

She follows me back to the motel room, her movements smooth and easy and controlled, the opposite of my own clumsiness. Her gaze makes my body feel warm and even more unwieldy as I shove my phone into my pocket and grab my water bottle and shoes. I follow her out the door, more mesmerized than I would like. This girl with the leather jacket and the motorcycle and the raw anger in her eyes. This *girl*.

The girl in the dark, with her wide, terrified eyes and the glint of something sharp. Perhaps it was her fear I trusted because it was so similar to mine.

Either way, I'm going to let that slide for now because 1) I have too much of my own investigating to do and 2) I have no other way out of the murder motel.

And I could ask her. I could ask this girl about my mom, fill in the gaps about her, the holes in her history so wide that they're a missing piece of me, too.

You don't know much about your own mom?

The scorn in her face had shut down my questions, but still. *Still.*

Dad's parents are distant, a FaceTime once a year because they'd never move back from São Paulo. A check on my birthday.

But Mom's family is nonexistent, as if she sprang into the world fully formed, already dressed in a pantsuit, interrogating suspects from the beginning.

All the stories I invented—my grandparents the astronauts, the spies, the pirates, the freedom fighters—tangle in my head, trying to fit themselves into the piece I've just found here.

"So where are we off to first?" Audrey asks me, swinging a leg over her bike.

"Um," I say. "So. I know I asked for a ride and all. But I really have to get on that thing?"

She laughs, something that was supposed to be a snort but comes out almost a giggle. "Yeah, I was serious. Come on, I'll keep you safe."

"You don't have a helmet?"

"Nope," she says. "We'll go slow. We can stop at my place and grab a helmet if you're really that scared, but we'll be okay. Besides, if we get hit by a truck or something, it's not like a helmet would save us anyway."

That seems both horrifying and vaguely inaccurate, but this girl is my only ride.

"Comforting," I say. I try to swing my leg over the seat as smoothly as she did, but I trip before I even reach her and fall hard against her shoulder, my fingers digging into her arm.

She doesn't so much as waver, just plants both legs firmly on either side of her death-machine motorcycle and catches me, biting back a smile. "You've really never ridden one of these before, have you, city girl?" she says.

"I don't know what being a *city girl* has to do with motorcycles," I say irritably, still clinging onto her arm as I try again to hop on the back of the motorcycle. I liked it better when she called me Sundress.

"Plenty of people in the city have—damn it—motor—*oof*." I succeed in getting my leg over the motorcycle and then slip and fall forward, face-planting against Audrey's back. Her back is muscular, so firm it's like falling face-first into a brick wall, so I clutch my aching nose with one hand and wrap the other arm around her waist.

Who *am* I, getting onto a motorcycle with a girl I've just met, in a town I've just arrived in?

Maybe it's the news that Mom is from here, the shock to my system that's making me more daring, more reckless, a thread of anger running through me and shouting down my fear just enough that I'm taking a leap like this.

Audrey laughs again, but it's a softer sound than her snort-giggle, and the sound reverberates through her body into mine.

I'm suddenly warmer than before, and I lean back a little, creating space between our bodies. We are strangers, after all.

And then she revs the engine, and we're off, and I'm clinging to her so tightly I don't know how she's still breathing. Okay, so we are definitely *not* strangers anymore, because I have my head tucked in against her shoulder so I don't have to see the world speeding by all around us.

Shit.

Holy shit.

My green dress, a reasonably modest thing that usually goes to my knees, flaps in the wind around my thighs, and my long red hair streams behind us like a banner.

"Where to?" she shouts over the roar of the engine.

And if she has asked me to be brave, then I will ask her the same.

"To the Anselm house," I say. "To investigate the murder ourselves."

AUDREY. 10:17 A.M.

Well, this girl is a dumbass.

When she tells me she wants to do the one thing that puts her in the most danger in this town—literally, the *one single thing*—I nearly fall off my bike. We tilt dangerously to the left, and Lucy screams. I come back to myself and right us just in time, and then I pull over and knock the kickstand into place with more violence than my bike deserves.

"What the hell did you just suggest?" I snap.

"Investigation," Lucy answers breathlessly, her eyes still round with panic. She's still clinging to me as I twist to look her in the eye.

She doesn't let go, even though we're basically facing each other at this point.

"Jesus," I say. "We're not moving. You're not going to fall off. You can let me breathe."

She lets go and promptly proves me wrong by tumbling off my bike and falling on her ass with a little shriek. "You *said*," she huffs.

"Well, it takes skill to fall off a bike when it's parked," I retort, and then bite my lip as she picks herself off the road. "And you just said you wanted a ride to town. That we would investigate after you have more info from your mom. Besides, isn't that your mom's job? And the cops? Do you think anyone is even gonna let us get close to that mansion?"

The mansion is north of town, adjacent to the abandoned amusement park, and just the thought of the park brings bile to my throat. Despite what I told Lucy this morning, I can't go back there. I can't.

Not after seeing Pierce's body broken on the concrete.

Beside me, Lucy shivers, as if she can feel the chill of what I've seen.

But the mansion?

Maybe I could do the mansion.

It actually isn't even just one mansion, not anymore, though everyone in Haeter Lake calls the whole property that. The Mansion. There's the main mansion, where Pierce lives—*lived*—with his wife, Veronica, and then two more houses adjacent, one for each of his children.

Not that Curtis Anselm is welcome in his anymore. Not since he threatened to blow his father's head off fifteen years ago.

Either way: Haeter Lake royalty, that's the Anselms.

Even back when Dad was alive, I'd say shit like that. Mom would agree with me privately, but Dad was always kinder than me. Kinder than both of us.

He'd take my face, cup it in his calloused hand gently so that I had to look him in the eye. *You can't know the private pain*, he'd say. *Everyone has some, privileged or not.*

And then he'd take my hand and spin me around in the living room until I laughed, until the anger I've always had dissipated like fog before sunshine.

But Dad is gone, and he took the gentlest part of me with him. The part that danced with him, that listened when he asked me to think about the pain others hide away.

I wish I had asked him how he knew, what pain he carried secretly that made him react with such empathy, even to the Anselms.

So I lost the gentleness, every last bit of it.

I got to keep the anger, though. That stuck around.

And the Anselms? Well, they're the kind who can get away with anything, at least for a while.

It catches up eventually.

At least it did for Pierce Anselm.

"Are you okay?" Lucy asks me, and it's only then I realize my hands are clenched over my bike's handles.

"Not really," I answer sharply. "Why do you want to butt into your mom's investigation? I'm doing this because I have to. Because someone—probably one of the rich assholes in the house you want to visit—is trying to pin a murder on my mom. And I won't let that happen."

She raises an eyebrow at me. Her soft auburn hair is ruffled and wild, and it looks right on her, to be wind-messed and breathless like this. She looks as if she is weighing her words very, very carefully.

"Because I think we can help," she says finally.

I can't help but feel that it's not the whole truth, but I have given her nothing but half-truths and vague answers at best.

"Besides, don't *you* want to do this?" She watches me carefully, as if the answer I give her will determine more than just this one question.

"Obviously," I admit as I try to push thoughts of Friday night out of my head.

It all haunts me. The texts from him—two in a row—and then the drive to the park, the first time I had returned in years.

The darkness of the night, the panic in my throat.

And then Pierce Anselm's body, falling.

Falling.

Falling. It hits me that they'll find out. Lucy's mom, Katy, who looks like she doesn't let go of an idea once it's taken hold.

"It can't be just curiosity," I say finally, folding my arms over my chest. "That's enough for you, really? Boredom and curiosity? You're scared of my bike. How are you so willing to join a murder investigation?"

She stares back at me for a long moment, the softness in her eyes hardening into determination. "First, calling this death trap a bike is misleading. And sure, okay," she says. "It's more than that." She shivers, and I resist the urge to wrap an arm around her.

"Yeah?" I ask softly.

Is Lucy haunted by this place the way I am? She must be, after what happened to her family here, even if it was before she was born.

She shifts, scuffing at the ground with the toe of her sneaker. "Usually I stay out of Mom's investigations," she says.

I snort.

"I'm serious," Lucy insists, her hazel eyes meeting mine. "But... Mom's life and your life and my life are all wrapped up in this case, aren't they?" She looks suddenly hesitant.

"Yeah," I say finally. "We are, aren't we? All right, fine, we'll go to the mansion. But I don't want to go to... to the crime scene with you," I say. "I was gonna do that on my own. And I think I still have to do that on my own."

"Okay," she agrees. "Deal."

"All right. Let's go." I nod. "If you can manage to get back on my bike. And after we grab muffins from the diner."

Lucy flips me off, but her grip is just as tight as she climbs back on behind me.

"Ready?" I ask her.

"Ready," she says, and this time she manages to disguise the shake in her voice.

We stop by the diner, and I leave Lucy balancing dangerously on my bike as I run in to grab two blueberry muffins before Mickey can stop me.

A few minutes later, we speed away, because neither the sheriff nor my mother are actually going to know if I'm speeding, despite what they may say. Despite the fact that my mother may really have eyes in the back of her head, like she used to claim when I was little. Not much escapes her.

Maybe that's why my mom, who I have never known to keep a secret from me, was cleaning mud off our shoes in the dead of night and hiding her phone from the cops.

Maybe, like me, she thinks that Pierce Anselm is not the only one who needs to pay.

There's still a whole family of them up on that hill, safe behind the gate and new security system.

I clench my fingers tighter around the handlebars, and I hear Lucy's terrified little squeak as we accelerate again up the winding road into the green mountains north of town. On a road I thought I would never drive again.

ANSELM AMUSEMENT PARK, 3.4 MILES, a brown sign reads, the paint chipped with age. The sign has faint indents from bullet holes. Probably some bored high school seniors with their shotguns. It happens to all the stop signs around here.

One of my last good memories of this road was three years ago, driving with my parents on Mom's first Saturday off all summer. All together, Dad belting out 2000s songs off-key, Mom laughing at him.

Lucy and I are silent as we drive, and a shiver snakes down my spine as we pass the sign.

Lucy's right. Both of our lives are so wrapped up in this—her family, the Anselm family, this park. All of them here, haunting me, like I've never actually left any of this grief behind.

Like the park has just been waiting all this time. Waiting for me to return.

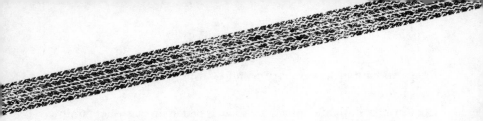

CHAPTER 8

LUCY

10:29 A.M.

WHEN AUDREY SLOWS THE BIKE TO A STOP AT THE gate in front of the mansion, it feels like a miracle, despite what she has claimed about the safety of motorcycle rides. And her theory about helmets not really mattering.

Helmets *do* matter.

"What?" Audrey asks as she pulls over in the grass.

It's only then that I realize I've said it out loud.

I square my shoulders. "I said helmets do matter," I tell her primly, trying and failing to smooth my hair back to its usual state. "There's research about it and everything."

"Okay, Lucille," Audrey says.

She says it like you might say *Okay, boomer*, and I elbow her.

She moves out of the way deftly, hopping off the bike, and I trip and tumble to the ground for the second time.

Audrey smirks down at me but offers her hand to help me up.

If I had more self-respect, I would ignore her proffered hand. But I do not, and my butt hurts from falling off this stupid motorcycle multiple times, so I let her haul me to my feet.

She wheels the bike farther off the road until it's barely visible beneath the trees, raising an eyebrow when she catches me staring. "You didn't think we'd actually just walk through the gate, did you? In Haeter Lake, you're as likely to get shot for trespassing as you are to be welcomed inside."

My phone buzzes, a single patch of service out here at the edge of the Anselm mansion.

It's Mom.

Alibi cleared. Cliff and I headed to Mansion. See you at lunch?

Shit.

Mom is in the house we're about to sneak into.

The house she was so insistent I get out of.

See you at lunch, I text her.

Audrey is watching me carefully, so I point at the motorcycle's hiding place.

"You seem practiced at hiding this," I blurt, and then the rest of her words sink in. "Wait. Did you say we could get *shot*?" My voice is about three octaves higher, pinched and strange. "Audrey."

She smirks. "Not if they don't see us," she says. "We'll be fine."

This is from the girl who called her motorcycle safe. I'm not sure I trust her definition of fine.

By now, the motorcycle is so well-covered it's practically invisible.

"Do you sneak out a lot?" I ask her. "Because you're good at this." I wave my hand at her quick work disguising the motorcycle.

"Sneak out and go where?" Audrey laughs. "Do you want to know what this town has? A grocery store. Two meat markets, because Haeter Lake scorns vegetarians. A bowling alley that went out of business, but we can get into if we sneak. Four churches. And three shooting ranges."

"That's an interesting church-to-gun ratio," I say, reaching for that real smile she treated me to earlier.

"That's Haeter Lake for you," she says.

Audrey says it the way Mom does—not like *hate*, the way I'd originally tried to pronounce it, or even like *hotter*, which is the best I can manage now. Mom says it like it's a word she grew up with, the vowels, the *a* and the *ah* mashing together in her mouth in a way I can't quite catch.

Did Mom grow up going to one of these churches, bowling at the alley, exploring the amusement park? Shooting at one of these gun ranges?

Why did she never tell me about any of it?

And why can't I bring myself to just ask this girl with the cuff bracelet and combat boots, this girl who seems as dangerous and fearsome to me as motorcycle rides and murderous forests and people who would shoot you just for trespassing?

Audrey takes my hand and tugs me forward, and I forget the rest of my questions. My hand tingles where she touches it, and I suck in a deep, sharp breath of air before I can stop myself.

Am I flustered because she's cute or because she's dangerous?

A blush creeps up my cheeks, and she drops my hand immediately, her eyebrow quirking. "Sorry," she says quickly. "But come on. I'll show you how to sneak in."

I didn't gasp because I didn't *like* her holding my hand. "I wasn't—" I say. "I only— Okay. Yeah. Wait, have you snuck in here before? How do you know so much?"

"Come on, Sundress." Audrey leads the way into the thicket of trees.

The foliage is dense even without leaves, and I have to duck every other step to avoid low-hanging branches.

Audrey makes it look effortless, slipping between trees and across the moss and damp leaves as soundlessly as if she was a part of this forest.

I thunder behind her, managing to crunch every single stick, so loud we'll probably scare off any wildlife in the state of Tennessee.

Which is a good thing, as far as I'm concerned.

She glances back over her shoulder at me, her brown eyes glinting. "You have as much stealth as a wild boar," she tells me. "I hope you're quieter once we're in the house."

We've only just entered the forest, but the trees are so thick that it's already impossible to see the road, and my heart beats a little faster at the realization.

This girl could take me anywhere she wanted—leave me, too. The woods are vast, and I'm a dumbass from the city who wouldn't know if they were ten feet from the road.

"You okay?" she asks me, and I feel guilty for even letting myself think that.

Audrey looks concerned, her eyebrows furrowed.

"Yeah," I say a little breathlessly. "I just . . ." My voice trails off because I realize I don't want to verbalize my fear, not to her, ever. But especially not when we're out here alone. "How far to the house?"

She looks at me strangely. "Just up ahead," she says. "We're following parallel to the drive. Can't you see it?" She gestures to the left, and I realize she's right.

If I squint, I can see pavement, the fading yellow line down the middle.

"You got turned around that fast?" Audrey asks, but she's not mocking me this time. "It's okay. It happens to a lot of people in these woods. You could just walk in and never walk out. Not that we're in any danger of that," she adds at the look on my face. "We can see the road, remember? Really. We'll be okay. Besides, it's good cover. We don't want to be seen."

"Right," I squeak. "Because we'll get shot."

A grin flits across her face. "I was mostly messing with you," she says. Mostly.

I nod, letting my breath out slowly. I think of the eyes I saw in the dark outside the motel, yellow and round and too close together. Of that half-feral look on my mom's face when Veronica Anselm was speaking to me. "What kind of animals are in these woods?" I ask Audrey, wiping my sweaty palms over my thighs in an effort to dry them.

"Nothing that wants to eat you, Sundress," Audrey tells me. "If I grab your hand again, are you gonna have a heart attack?"

A laugh escapes me, part anxious huff and part giggle, so though that answer wasn't quite an answer, I reach for her hand as the wind carries the smell of half-composted leaves and rotting logs to us. "Let's investigate," I say. "Do you know how to get us into the house?"

"You have to do at least some of the work today, Sundress," Audrey retorts.

"I'm the brains," I tell her, hoping she doesn't notice that my hand is slick with sweat. I was not made to sneak around in the woods. "You're the muscle."

When she laughs, it's already a familiar sound, like something I've known my whole life and just been waiting to hear again. "The muscle, huh?" she asks. "So did you want me to kick in the door for us?"

"That doesn't seem subtle," I tell her.

"No one ever accused me of subtlety." Audrey shrugs one muscular shoulder.

"Well, I *am* a very accomplished picklock," I tell her, grinning. "Though if the locks are fob locks, I can't help us."

Audrey stops walking so abruptly I crash into her, and both of us stumble.

Of course, she regains her balance first, because the world isn't fair, and steadies me with an amused expression on her face. "Shh," she says when I open my mouth. "Do you hear that?"

The crunch of sticks. Footsteps.

Loud, like mine. Someone who isn't used to walking through the woods, or perhaps someone who doesn't care what they crush as they walk. "Look," Audrey whispers.

Just up ahead, a narrow footpath cuts through the thick grove of trees. There are footprints in the early spring mud, and her face pales a little. Then she pulls me back into the shadow of a large oak, nearly lifting me off my feet.

I let out a little shriek of surprise, and she claps a hand over my mouth, holding me close to her as she presses both of us against the tree.

I am suddenly very aware of the steady *thump-thump-thump* of her heartbeat, of her breath hot on the back of my neck, of every ridge of tree bark against my back. Of her hands holding me up. "Audrey," I whisper.

"Shh," she hisses, and then she raises a hand and points.

Through the foliage, I can make out two figures walking slowly along the footpath. As they draw closer, I catch a few words.

"Police said it wasn't—"

"Wouldn't trust..."

And then the two figures round a bend, and Audrey claps a hand over my mouth again, this time preemptively, stifling my gasp.

Veronica and Blake are walking slowly down the footpath, examining the footprints. Sunlight filters through the trees and glints cruelly off Veronica's gold earrings.

It was her footsteps I heard, crushing everything beneath her feet.

I turn my head just enough to see Audrey.

She's white as a sheet, and the hand covering my mouth has gotten suddenly slick with sweat.

I push her hand off me and mouth, *Ew*, at her, but she doesn't even crack a smile.

We hide in the thick underbrush, crouching low beneath the shadow of the oak, but that almost seems worse if they do find us, so obviously hiding out here.

"Did you hear that?" Blake's hand falls to her hip the way Mom's does when she's carrying her handgun.

Audrey looks half-sick with terror, an expression that seems strange on someone usually so fearless, so I summon every brave, reckless piece of me and shove Audrey's hands off me.

I back up slowly, skirting the oak tree so that when I emerge onto the trail it will only be me they see.

"Just me," I shout, tromping out of the underbrush and leaving Audrey behind the oak. "Sorry. Mrs. Anselm? It's just me. Lucy. Katy's kid?"

Blake is still glaring at me, but Veronica's face eases into a smile.

"Oh, there you are, darling," she says, putting a cool hand on my shoulder when I reach them. "I thought you left with your mother this morning. She ran out so early. All that investigating, I'm sure."

"Yeah," I say pleasantly. "Yeah, lots of work for her. I went for a walk and I got a little lost. I'm so glad you found me."

Veronica pats my shoulder gently. "It's so easy to get turned around out here, isn't it? I'm lucky I have Blake with me. Blake, have you met Katy's girl yet? This is Lucy. Lucy? This is my daughter, Blake."

"We met this morning at breakfast," she says coldly, but her hand eases away from her hip. She's wearing a suit now, though her long blond hair is loose down her back and her impeccable Louis Vuittons have a hint of mud from the path on them. There still could be a gun tucked beneath the coat, but she looks at ease now. She holds out her hand to shake mine again.

Her grip is firm.

This is what Mom means when she talks about fearsome women.

"Can we help you, Lucy?"

"Oh. Yes. Yes, of course. I'm so sorry. Do you think you could show me back up to the house?" I ask, willing Audrey to be listening, to be understanding my plan. "After breakfast, Mom dropped me off, but I got a bit lost—" I ramble for a moment, before I realize that my saving grace is that neither woman is really listening to me.

We walk up to the house, Veronica and Blake on either side of me. It's like being flanked by a pair of lions—and it means, of course, that I have to walk in the center of the path at its muddiest, mud kicking up the back of my calves as I do.

Audrey is quiet as she moves through the forest, tailing us, but I can feel her. Feel her dark, furious eyes on me.

Because I didn't tell her that I'd stayed at the Anselms the night before, or that I had a way in, or that I had met them. I didn't tell her any of that, and now we're all walking toward the Anselm mansion, the one place my mom wanted me to stay away from.

And I can't tell if having Audrey trailing behind me in the forest makes me feel safer than being left alone to the mercies of the Anselm women—or if it makes me feel like I'm being hunted.

AUDREY. 10:43 A.M.

I keep my footfall silent, treading softly on moss and deadened leaves, avoiding underbrush and sticks that will crack like a gunshot out here. Haeter Lake has always thought Curtis was the worst of the lot, the black sheep of the family, getting busted for drugs at sixteen and narrowly ducking aggravated assault charges at seventeen.

But Blake has always felt more dangerous to me, and it doesn't sit right to let Lucy go off with her without any backup at all.

I trail behind them all the way up to the big house, to the edge of the woods where forest meets manicured lawn.

They're nearing the edge when someone else stumbles out of the forest from the other side of the path.

Gus.

Who was *supposed* to be at his shift at the diner.

"Oh," he says. "Lucy, I was looking for you."

I creep a little closer, still hidden by the underbrush, but close enough I can see the surprise and confusion flicker on Lucy's face before she masks it.

And then he looks directly at me, his blue eyes sharp and knowing. For one endless moment, I think he's going to point at me, tell Blake and Veronica I'm here, lurking. But instead, he angles his body between me and them and says, "Grandma, it's okay. Lucy and I were just going for a walk. She was trying to cover for me."

Lucy opens her mouth and shuts it again, and then nods. "Sorry," she says in that charming, half-apologetic tone that puts people at their ease. "I didn't want to get Gus in trouble."

The two women don't look mollified, exactly, but Veronica does ruffle Gus's hair before they move on without us.

As soon as they've disappeared up the hill, Gus looks back at me.

"You can come out, Nelson," he says a little roughly.

My stomach twists.

We haven't been friends, haven't talked in years. But hearing that familiar voice—and knowing he just covered for me—makes my breath hitch strangely in my throat.

I step out, staring at him and then up at the house.

The mansion looms through the twisted branches, distant and imposing at the top of the hill. The lawn that slopes toward the house is well groomed, the grass close-cropped, vicious in its perfection.

A pool, still covered for the winter, stretches out behind the house, and then wooden steps lead up to a deck high above the ground with covered lawn chairs and a grill. Beyond all of that is a greenhouse, and then past that a mosaic path winds its way toward a gazebo. The path leads on past the gazebo into the forest.

Even when I was friends with Gus, I was never invited into the big house. The pool, though—he snuck me in there a few times before we were enemies.

This house has seen some shit, Gus used to say.

And it may be nice and shiny and well kept, but it's *old* and I think Gus might be right, about just this one thing. He was wrong about literally everything else, but he was right about this.

Lucy is flushed and wide-eyed, her red hair even more tousled than it was when she fell off my bike. "Hi," she says.

"What the hell is going on?" I glare at her.

"Yeah," she says. "Yeah, okay, but when was I supposed to tell you?"

"Right away?" I snap.

"Does anyone want to tell *me* what's going on?" Gus snaps. "Why are you both lurking around the woods?"

"You didn't have to cover for me," I mutter, knowing I'm being an ass about this and not caring.

My fingers find the cuff bracelet Dad gave me. It was both something to fidget with when I got overwhelmed and a tangible reminder he was with me and I'd be okay; something that sometimes helped when I was ready to snap at someone I shouldn't.

"Yeah, I did," Gus says irritably.

As I get closer, I realize his eyes are red and a little puffy.

"Gus," I say hesitantly.

"Don't," he says. "*I* was out here because my house is a fucking prison, and if I have to look at any of them for a single second longer, I'll lose it. What are you doing out here?"

I exchange a glance with Lucy.

"Well, my mom told me not to come back here," Lucy says, sliding a bit so she's standing closer to me than to Gus. "So I wasn't planning on just walking in the front door. She's also on her way here with the sheriff, because she's helping with the investigation, so we have to look around quick or we are—"

"Fucked," I finish for her.

She blushes.

"I . . . You're *investigating*?" Gus narrows his eyes at both of us. "Who are you, Sherlock Fucking Holmes?"

"My mom's a private investigator," Lucy says hotly, and then reddens again. "I mean, I know you know that. But I'm actually just trying to . . . to learn a little more about her. She and I aren't super close." She shoots me a hesitant look, as if expecting me to give her more shit for not knowing where her mom is from.

"You know why I'm here," I tell Gus tightly.

He ducks his head. "I'm sorry they questioned your mom," he says in a small voice. "I didn't— I'll help you, okay? Something bad happened to—to my grandpa and me—"

He chokes on the rest of the words, and because Lucy is a better person than I am, she reaches out and places a hand on his shoulder, squeezing gently.

"Of course you can help," she says kindly. "I'm so sorry. I can't even imagine what this is like for you."

If Dad was here, he'd be kind, too, maybe even pull Gus into a big hug. He'd give me that look, the one that says *play nice*, but he's not here, he's not, and even if it's not Gus's fault specifically, it was his family that did it.

So I stay where I am, and I keep hold of my anger because it's the only thing that's been keeping me on my feet all these years.

"Okay," I say finally. "Fine. We can work together. But if you—"

"Audrey." Lucy puts her hand on my arm, too, her touch warm, cutting off the stream of sharp, unkind words I had ready for Gus.

"Yeah," Gus says. "Sure, Nelson, I know. Do you want inside the house, then? We can look in my aunt's office. Oh, also, you should know. My dad is back in town. Got back the night G— my grandpa died."

Lucy nods slowly, but I feel the jolt of it in my stomach.

Curtis Anselm was the black sheep of the family, leaving his son behind when he went off to go his own way, playing in a shitty band that toured on Pierce Anselm's money until Pierce got sick of his shit and threatened to disinherit him, and then toured on money Curtis found—well, the stories change every time they're told. Some say the money was from selling drugs, some say it was stolen from Pierce, but he was too prideful to send the cops after his own kid. Some, of course, say it was just the child support money he got from his ex-wife before he gave up custody of his son completely.

Either way: Now he's back.

"Yes," I say. "Let's go inside."

Gus gets us in the back door, punching in a code, but leaning his shoulder over it so that I can't see. He doesn't take any such precautions with Lucy, who he allows to stand next to him as he enters the numbers.

He leads us down a long hallway. "Offices first?" he asks. "We'll have to be quiet. Blake can hear just about anything, and she won't want anyone snooping in here."

I don't know what we're looking for, or what we'll find, but it's a place to start. It's something, and without Mom I don't have anything at all, so I have to try.

"Third floor," Lucy answers too loudly, chewing her lip a little.

"You're *loud*," I hiss at her as we tiptoe down the wide hallway. "I hope you know how to interrogate people, or find clues, because you are shit at the stealth part of detective work."

The proud smile on her face does not falter for a moment. There's a warmth to her, and I draw closer to her as if she is the sun, as if being pulled into her orbit will somehow make the cold in my chest disappear.

It can't, of course.

Not after Friday night.

But she makes me forget, at least.

And I like that.

"We could also check in Blake's room?" Lucy asks as we trail behind Gus. I marvel at her daring.

How can someone be afraid of so many things—even my damn bike—but break into the Anselm mansion as if she has never heard of fear?

But maybe it's just that she doesn't *know* to fear these people. Maybe her mom didn't warn her, or maybe she's safe because of her connection to the Anselms. Maybe she's not the kind of girl they'd level a gun at if they saw her in the woods outside their house.

Maybe she's not a girl like me.

When my eyes adjust to the dim light, I realize we've found ourselves in a long room with stadium seating. A massive screen is mounted on the wall, and speakers tower on either side of the room.

I let out a low whistle. "You have your own movie theater?"

Lucy glances back at me. She seems less overwhelmed by the riches than I am.

Maybe her fancy detective mom can afford this kind of thing. Maybe this opulence doesn't shock them.

But this room is bigger than my entire home.

Gus doesn't look back at all, just pauses at the door to check that we don't have any company.

I keep moving, tiptoeing toward the door at the opposite end, though I think my feet would be soundless on the soft carpet regardless.

How much would it cost, to build and furnish just this one room? A year of my mom's salary? Two?

Anger tightens my shoulders, and I hurry to catch up with Lucy and Gus.

It isn't just.

Nothing about this is just.

The only justice we got was Pierce Anselm's death.

But the rest of the Anselm family, they get to keep living in this splendor while the rest of us suffer. While our dads die. While we struggle through, choosing between peanut butter and corn flakes at the grocery store, picking up extra hours at work while bills pile up.

And the Anselms could help, they could help this whole town, and they choose not to. They choose to stay up on this well-groomed hill, inside their fancy security gates, and none of it ever, ever trickles down to us.

And that won't change.

Not unless we do something about them ourselves.

"Come on," Lucy whispers, pulling me back to the moment. She and Gus are both looking at me strangely.

And she might be here to solve a murder, like she said, because Lucy Preston's life has been entangled with the Anselms since before she was born. Because she needs to *understand* them to understand what happened.

But me?

Maybe I'm here to prove to the world that Pierce Anselm and the rest of his family deserved exactly what they got.

We tiptoe to the end of the hallway, Gus at the lead. At the end is a balcony opening over the lower floor—the main floor, which I can see from here is a wide, empty space with tall, arched bay windows. Beside the little alcove where we crouch is a spiral staircase leading down to the living room.

Lucy and I creep forward, our bodies pressed against the wall, until we're as close to the edge as we dare.

"This is a bad idea," Lucy whispers to me.

"We should use the back stairs," Gus whispers back.

I shoot her an exasperated look, but my heart is thundering in my chest. "Come on, Sundress." I jerk my head to the left, ignoring Gus completely. "Let's take these stairs."

Lucy follows, her body pressed close to mine. It's an instinctive thing for her, I think, like she's scared and if she stands closer to me, so close we're almost touching, she feels a little less scared.

So I let her.

Once we're safely out of the hallway and on the stairs to the third floor, Lucy lets out her breath in a *whoosh* of air. "Do you know Blake?" she asks me.

"Everyone knows Blake."

"She's scary." Lucy shivers a little. "I think—I think she had a gun. When they were in the woods. She reached for her hip. My mom does that when she's scared."

"She does," Gus says softly.

"You thought she had a gun and you decided to stomp on out there and say hello?" I whirl around, so sharply that Lucy trips on her own feet and falls against me hard. I hold her up by her forearm, my fingers digging into her skin. "Jesus Christ."

"Well," Lucy says, flushing again. "It seemed like a good idea at the time? I thought she probably wouldn't shoot me?"

"Probably?" I let her go, and she nearly falls again, though this time she rights herself on the banister. "Come on. We have offices to search." I shoot a look at Gus, who is looking at us both strangely.

When we reach the third floor, a long hallway stretches out in front of us. To our right is a bathroom, ornate and wide. There is a bathtub *and* a shower, and this isn't even the primary bathroom. The next room is a sunlit space facing south, with plants hanging. There is another sofa and more bookshelves and a grand piano.

There's another grand piano in their living room on the main floor, of course.

Because who doesn't need one grand piano for their living room and one for their private parlor?

The next two rooms are clearly offices, opposite each other. On each mahogany door is a tasteful little sign, one that says HIS, one that says HERS.

"We can split up?" Lucy suggests.

"That's exactly what they say in horror movies," I tell her. "Then they die."

She shudders. "I thought *I* was morbid."

"You're both morbid," Gus mutters. "I can get us into my aunt's office. She's the only one with a passcode on her door." He turns away from us, stopping at a door at the end of the hall and hunching over the keypad.

"What are we looking for?" Lucy asks in a hushed voice.

"Blood," I tell her.

She lets out a small sound that is half whimper, half hysterical giggle, and then immediately shoots a guilty look at Gus.

I don't wait for Blake's office. Instead, I shove open Pierce's door. His office is bigger than our whole trailer. His desk is large, made out of dark wood, and there's an empty leather swivel chair behind it. A cup of fancy pens with his name on it. A laptop, which is—

Open.

"Check the laptop," I tell Lucy.

There are long floor-to-ceiling bookshelves in here, all filled with books. There are mostly law books, and a few of the insufferable businessman self-help books about how you, too, can become a millionaire if you just work hard and already have rich parents and a million dollars. But there is one set of shelves with thriller novels from top to bottom.

Mom would love a space like this. Dad, too.

But instead, Mom and I got the trailer and Dad got the cemetery.

I slam my fist down onto his stupid desk. The mahogany—or what the fuck ever it's made of—hurts my hand.

"What happened to *quiet*?" Lucy snaps. "You're gonna get us caught."

Gus enters the room then, eyes wide. "I thought we were going into

Blake's office," he says snappishly. "My grandpa didn't even do any work in here. It was mostly Blake and Grandma running all the business stuff."

I ignore him and sweep the room from one end to the other, my steps slow, my eyes on the carpet. The room is immaculate from the neatly dusted bookshelves to the tidy desk to the smooth hardwood floors. Beneath his swivel chair is a tastefully simple rug.

"Anything on the laptop?" I ask her.

Lucy shakes her head, avoiding Gus's look of annoyance. "I could get in if I had an install disk to bypass the password," she says. "But I don't think we have the time for that. What would we be looking for on his computer, anyway?"

I take a deep breath. I don't know her well enough to tell her about the Post-it note summoning me to the theme park, about the texts that said, *I didn't know, I swear I didn't know.* I don't know her nearly well enough for that, and I'm definitely not about to tell Gus that.

But I think Pierce might have been about to tell me the truth about what happened to my dad.

"I don't know," I lie.

She steps away from the computer, and I flatten the rug for her so she doesn't trip.

Lucy looks up at me, a hint of a smile tugging at her lips. "Thanks," she says. "Me and rugs, we don't always get along."

"Veronica's office next?" I ask. My eyes drop to the rug again.

"Hang on," Lucy says. "The rug."

There's a tag on the edge of it, like it's brand-new. "Probably to protect the hardwood?"

"I don't know," Gus says uncertainly. "Can there be a clue in a *rug*?" He looks skeptical. "We could—"

But Lucy has a light in her eyes, and she moves the office chair back and flips the rug up.

Beneath it is a dark red stain, darker than the wood.

"Oh no," Lucy says. "Oh no, no, no—"

I lunge forward, press my hand over her mouth. "Shh, shh," I whisper. "I got you. Shh." I move her gently backward, my hand firm on her shoulder. "I'm gonna take a picture, okay? For evidence? Don't look. Don't look if you don't want to."

"Oh *god*." Gus, too, looks as if he's about to throw up. "No. *No*."

He turns and nearly runs from the room, his feet thumping on the hardwood floor as he leaves us behind. I do feel for him now, despite myself. Anselm or not, it was pain I saw in his face, and horror so deep he couldn't stay here a moment longer.

And Lucy hasn't seen death before, like I have. She didn't see Pierce fall from the ride. Didn't see him break when he hit the ground.

She didn't watch her dad die in front of her.

So I take the picture of the bloodstained floor and then kick the rug back into place. Shove the phone into my pocket, just as Lucy says in a high, shaky voice—

"Oh. Hi, Mom."

CHAPTER 9

LUCY

11:47 A.M.

"LUCY?" KATY IS STANDING IN THE DOORWAY, HER eyes flashing. "What the hell are you doing here? Who is— Oh. You're Langley's kid."

Audrey's eyes snap to Mom's. "You must be Katy Preston."

"Yes," she says icily. "Both of you are coming with me *now*."

Audrey laughs recklessly, harsh and loud. The sound chills me. And also excites me, just a little bit. Like if Audrey looked at me and said something wild like, *Let's run*, I'd take her hand and do it, consequences be damned.

"Why would I do that?" Audrey demands.

Katy levels a glare at both of us. "Because I won't tell the Anselm women you're here," she says. "And because I can bring you to your mom."

"Katy," I say hesitantly. "Katy, this is Audrey? I... made a friend. And also, the Anselms might know anyway? Because Gus was here?"

"I talked to Gus," she says. "He was panicking just now, ran out of here and down the stairs and came to get me. He said I needed to get both of you out of here right away, and I agree. With me, both of you. *Now*."

Katy stalks down the hallway, and I grab Audrey's hand, tug her after me.

"We'll come back," I whisper in her ear. "I promise."

"Where's my mom?" Audrey snaps.

It's not that Audrey has been the most approachable or gentle today with me, not by any means, but the way she changes when there's an adult in the room is truly incredible. She is all hard edges, demanding answers and shooting daggers with her eyes.

"Out of custody," Katy says shortly. "I'll answer your questions on the way, okay? Blake and Veronica cannot find you here. *Especially* here. For fuck's sake."

"Why?" I ask. "Maybe if you would *answer* that, I wouldn't have to sneak back in here for answers."

"And maybe if I didn't have to rescue your asses from this place," Katy snaps, "I would have *time* to answer."

This time, Katy doesn't lead us into the passageways. Maybe it's because she doesn't trust Audrey, or maybe it's because she's in too much of a hurry. Either way, she rushes us down the stairs, back past the in-home movie theater, and out the back door toward her Jeep.

"How did you get back in?" I ask as Katy slams the Jeep door and starts the engine.

"I told you," Katy says. "I'm helping Cliff with the investigation now." Her voice softens, goes distant. "Apparently—apparently Pierce put it in his will. Asked me to come home if he died. Asked me to be part of the *investigation*. As if he knew there would be one."

Her voice is strange and stilted.

I'm not sure actually if I've ever heard her say the word *home* before.

"What's your excuse for leaving now?" Audrey pipes up from the back seat. "What did you tell them?"

"They're in the living room with Cliff," Mom answers when we pass the gates. She accelerates fast, so fast my head thumps back against the headrest. "I said I had to check on you. I was pretty vague."

"And Blake and Veronica didn't mention that they had *seen* me?"

"Blake and Veronica *saw you?*"

"Um," I say. "Yeah? They... They found me in the woods while we were trying to sneak in?"

"You." Katy's voice ices over. "Are grounded until you're at least thirty."

It's usually an empty promise—Katy has a tendency to ground me and then immediately forget—but this time she sounds so deadly certain I *do* go quiet.

"It *is* weird that they didn't mention it," Audrey says, as if Katy's anger doesn't frighten her at all. "Did Gus tell you anything when he came to get you?"

Katy's knuckles are white where her hands are clenching the steering wheel, her jaw set as she shakes her head. "Maybe they thought I already knew you were walking around the woods unsupervised," she says finally.

"Or maybe they're just a weird, creepy fucking family," Audrey says, leaning back in her seat as if that settles the matter. "So you're helping the cops, huh? Helping Cliff?"

Katy is silent.

"You know what the cops here are like," Audrey continues. She slides her sunglasses on. "Hey, you can drop me off. My bike is here."

"I'll drop you off with your mom," Katy says. "And not before. You can let Langley decide if you get that bike back."

Audrey kicks the back of the seat. "You're kidnapping me?"

"Your mom specifically said to bring you to her." She takes one hand off the wheel and unlocks her phone, holding it up for us both to see.

The contact is just named *L*, and it's one text message that reads, *This yours?* And a picture of Audrey glaring at Katy across Pierce Anselm's office.

There's a text from Audrey's mom beneath it. *Yeah. Meet in 15?*

That makes less sense. Were they friends once? Are they friends now? Is Katy investigating her or working with her?

Katy drives the long, winding road from the mansion to downtown Haeter Lake, where the houses are close enough together that trees don't block them from seeing each other, though there seem to be more potholes on this road than open businesses.

"Why did they put the murder motel out in the forest instead of the middle of town?" I ask Katy curiously when the silence stretches out for a few minutes too long.

"Can you please stop calling it the murder motel?" Katy asks wearily as she pulls up in front of a small, low building a few blocks down from the diner. "It's a lovely establishment that was built there by one of the oldest families in Haeter Lake. And it's absolutely safe."

"A lovely establishment?" I interrupt. "You can't possibly be talking about anything in Haeter Lake."

She sighs deeply as she parks in front of an old building that resembles a schoolhouse.

I push open the door to the Jeep and hop down. "Besides. It's a motel in a small Appalachian town. In the middle of the very creepy forest. Of *course* it's a murder motel. I can't believe you don't see that. And does that 'oldest family' happen to be our very own Anselm family?"

Katy exits the Jeep, raising a perfectly threaded eyebrow at me. "No. The Anselms do not own the motel. You only think it's a creepy forest because you don't go outside enough," she tells me. "And because you watch too many horror movies."

"Maybe *you* don't watch *enough* horror movies," I retort as she hesitates on the curb beside me.

Katy says, "Say goodbye to your new friend, and then I'm dropping you off here, Lucille."

Audrey's eyes spark with humor, and she mouths *Lucille* at me.

That might be worse than Sundress.

Not that a nickname coming from Audrey is the worst thing, after all.

Anyway.

"Here? Not back at the motel?" I ask with a sigh.

"No, you have questions, and the library will—" Her face twists suddenly, pain flashing in her eyes. "The library will have some answers for you. Okay? And I'm sure Audrey's mom will want to keep her home after all this anyway."

And for the first time, I realize that maybe Katy hasn't been trying to keep me out, keep me away from her, keep me at arm's length. Maybe whatever it is that ties Katy to this town is so painful that she's never quite known how to say it.

Maybe whatever brought her back here hurts so deep she can't say it out loud.

"Okay," I say, shooting a glance at Audrey. "Audrey? See you soon?"

Audrey nods, and then Katy pulls me away from the car. "You," she hisses into my ear, "need to be *much* more careful. That Anselm boy didn't sell you out today, but that doesn't mean he won't. Do you understand me? And Langley Nelson's kid has no loyalty to you either. Don't let them fool you. Either of them."

My head snaps up in shock. "Katy?"

"I know this family better than you do," she says carefully. "And I know Audrey's mom, and I know what happened to her dad. So just—believe me. Stay away from the Anselms, those two women, their kid, and god forbid you run into *Curtis*."

I tilt my head and look up at her. "Katy? What's wrong with Curtis?"

Katy barks out a laugh, her eyes distant. "What *isn't* wrong with the golden boy?" she says, shaking her head. "He's kind and charismatic and funny until he's not. He's smart and pretty and good until he's not. Pierce bailed him out for *years*, and when he finally set a boundary with Curtis, that man said Pierce owed him his inheritance and more."

"Was he—violent?" I ask it in a small voice because I want her to reassure me like I'm a little kid. I want to hear that it's fine, that what happened to Pierce was all a sad accident.

"Yes," Katy says without missing a beat. "But I suppose they all are, in their own way. Violent and charming and rich, and you need to stay *away.*"

"Is he a suspect?" I blurt with all the subtlety of a freight train. "Because it sounds like nobody in his family trusts him."

"*No,*" Katy says sharply. "I *told* you. You're not investigating. You're not hunting suspects. You can learn more about our family—Arthur can help you with that—but stay away from the Anselms. Trust me on this."

How can I trust you? I want to yell. *How can I trust you when I don't even know you?*

But as ever, Katy does not wait to see if I need anything, or if I have questions, or if I'm okay. She turns on her heel and stalks back to the car, looking over her shoulder at me before she gets in. "And stay *here,*" she says sharply. "Until I come get you."

And then she is gone, leaving me alone once again.

CHAPTER 10

AUDREY

12:03 P.M.

AFTER LUCY'S MOM DROPS HER OFF AT THE LIBRARY, she drives back out of town, taking the dirt road toward the motel.

"Where are you taking me?" I grab for the door handle, opening it even though we're on the road going out of town.

"Jesus," Katy says. "Jesus, don't jump out. Your mom asked me to take the long way home."

I text Mom, because no way am I trusting anyone who works for the *cops*, for fuck's sake.

Where are you?

At home, Mom texts back a moment later. *You still with Katy?*

Yeah. Coming now.

I sit back in my seat, forcing my breath to even as I shut the door again.

Katy shakes her head in annoyance. "Forgot for a moment that you were Langley Nelson's kid, I guess," she says. "Of course you were about to jump out of a moving car. That tracks."

"You don't know me."

"No," she says. "But I know where you come from."

Lots of people have said that with a sneer, and they're usually referring to the trailer, to the WIC cards and the food stamps and the beater cars.

But Katy says it with something like respect in her voice. Says it like she's talking about my mom.

"Were you two friends?" I ask her, as if I haven't heard every detail Mom ever had to tell about their days growing up together, the good and the bad.

Katy shoots a look at me. "She never mentioned me?"

"No," I lie.

"I guess not, then," Katy says.

We pull up in front of the trailer a few minutes later.

Mom is waiting in front of our place. She's still wearing her scrubs and those too-clean runners, her arms folded across her chest. The wind is tugging at her dark brown hair, pulling it from its loose ponytail.

She tugs me into a tight hug even as she lights into me, saying something about *damn reckless* and *didn't listen to a word I said* and *can't believe you went straight to the mansion* and *grounded until the day you die*, but she keeps on hugging me.

"Can we talk?" Lucy's mom asks her.

I can feel Mom glaring at her even if I can't see it. "Let me hold my baby, Preston," she says coolly. "I just got out of jail, in case you'd forgotten."

Katy snorts. "You weren't arrested," she says. "No one forced you to go."

"Why are we out here?" I look up at Mom. "What did Cliff say? Did you give him your alibi? You were home all night. They don't have anything on you. They *can't.*"

Mom strokes my hair back, one arm still tight around me. "They wanted to know my whereabouts last night," she says. "And Cliff had a few questions about some things I said to the Anselm family in the past. But we don't have anything to worry about, honey. We're gonna be okay."

She looks down at me, her eyes both fierce and affectionate.

This is the safest place I know, right here with Mom, because even when shit is bad, even when shit is *really* bad, dead-dad-and-I'm-falling-apart bad, Mom is here.

But when she says that we're gonna be okay, I don't know if I believe her.

Because she's looking at me like she's gonna make sure *I* am okay. But not her. Maybe not her.

"Mom," I rasp. "Mom, we didn't do anything to him."

"No, baby," she says. "Of course we didn't."

"You can't be the only suspect," I say, tucking my head against her shoulder. If anyone in Haeter Lake saw me like this now, cuddled up like a little kid, I'd probably have to get in a fight with them about it. But it's just me and Mom here now, so if I'm comfortable tucked against her shoulder, nobody needs to know.

"In Haeter Lake?" Bitterness threads Mom's voice. "There's a house full of Anselms with motives—and god knows Curtis swung at the old man enough times that the police *should* be talking to him first. But of course I'm the one they're looking at."

"It's not fair." My own voice echoes Mom's bitterness. "It never has been."

She nods. "Listen, I need to talk to Katy, okay? And I need you not to talk about this with anyone. Not even your new friend." She smiles slightly when she says *friend*, and my cheeks warm.

I push back, take a small step away from her. "Can you drive me back to my motorcycle?" I ask the gravel road, because if I look up at her, I'll see that stern look and disappointment and fierceness, and I can't handle any of that right now.

"We'll talk about that, young lady," she says. "Katy. Let's step over here."

She walks away with Katy, and I lean on Mom's Honda Civic and watch them.

They look like they're arguing, though their voices remain hushed whispers.

Finally, Katy steps back from my mom. "Just keep your kid away from it, okay?" she says, loud enough for me to hear.

Mom's eyes go dark. "You don't get to tell me how to parent, you hear me?" She jabs a finger against Katy's chest. "You don't get to tell me *anything.*"

"I got you out of jail," Katy snaps.

Mom is already stalking back toward me. "Get in the car," she says.

"Can we get—"

"Get *in.*"

Mom doesn't say anything about her meeting with Katy, about her time being questioned by the freaking *cops.* Doesn't say anything at all until she helps me haul my motorcycle out of the trees where I'd hidden it near the Anselms'.

She levels a gaze at me across the handlebars as I straddle it.

"Two things," Mom says, and then holds up one finger. "One, Katy Preston's daughter might be sweet and charming, but that family has always been too close to the Anselms to be worth trusting. Understood?"

I nod, and she holds up a second finger.

"And two, if you ever pull shit like this again," she continues softly, "I will haul this bike to the junkyard myself. Are we clear?"

I swallow hard. Nod once. "Yeah," I mutter. "Yeah, we're clear."

CHAPTER 11

LUCY

12:11 P.M.

WHEN MOM LEAVES ME IN FRONT OF THE LIBRARY, I hold the phone up above my head, begging the cell phone service gods that the one bar will be enough. *Meet tonight at the motel,* I text Audrey.

She leaves me on *read.*

I jot down ideas in my notepad: *library, local newspaper, diner.*

The three best sources of information, no matter what town you find yourself in. That's what my dad always says, but he might be biased because he's a journalist.

Back when we all used to travel with Katy for cases, Dad and I would always introduce ourselves at the local paper. He worked for CNN at the time, and when he introduced himself, reporters would recognize him and would fall over themselves trying to introduce themselves first.

Dad wasn't in it for the celebrity feeling, though. He just genuinely loved it, meeting other journalists, hearing the stories that were most important to them and their small towns.

The library Katy left me in front of is a small two-room building with a sign outside that reads, LISTED ON THE NATIONAL REGISTER OF HIS-TORIC PLACES. Well, lovely for them. I push open the door and enter. The room smells like old books, and I inhale deeply.

For once, Katy was right. This is exactly where I want to be.

An older man is seated behind the desk, nodding off over a book. He startles when the door shuts behind me and then smiles. "Katy," he says. "Is that you? I've got just the thing." He stands slowly, and I can almost hear joints creaking as he straightens. "The next Poirot finally shipped, just for you. It should be here—"

"Um," I interrupt him. "I'm actually Katy's daughter?"

He shakes his head, as if clearing cobwebs, and then his warm smile returns, his wrinkled face kind. "Of course, of course," he says. "My, I do get confused, especially after my afternoon nap. I didn't know Katy had a daughter! Spitting image of her, you are."

"Thank you?" I say. "I'm actually, uh, here to do some research."

"Of course you are," he says, clapping his weathered hands once as if the idea of research delights him. "About what, my dear?"

"The Anselm family," I tell him boldly. "And my mom's connection."

He tilts his head to the side, his eyebrows furrowing.

"I'm Lucy, by the way," I tack on. "My mom—Katy—is investigating the . . . the case."

"Ah," he says. "Well, are you looking for a book or would you like to look in our periodical section? We have copies of the *Daily* going all the way back to . . . well, before your mom, even." He grins at me, and I relax. Whoever this librarian is, he has been here since Mom was . . . well, a kid. Here. In this town where she left all her secrets. "I'm Arthur. Arthur Joyce. Been the librarian here in Haeter Lake for sixty years, and I don't plan on stopping," he says gently. "Are you looking for the articles on the accident, too?"

I return his smile hesitantly. "On Mr. Nelson's accident?" I ask.

"Well, sure," he says. "But I thought you might be interested in your granddad's, too."

My blood runs cold. "My—my granddad?"

Because this is it. Finally.

Finally.

Arthur shuffles out from behind the desk at the far end of the room. "We keep them all back here," he says. "It seems like such a difficult thing for someone so young to read about, but your mom was just like that. She'd spend every afternoon in high school poring over all of these. I used to ask her if she was writing a book on the case. Ah. Yes. Here it is."

He has flipped toward the back of some newspapers sheathed in plastic. He taps a gnarled finger on top of the page. "This is the first one after he passed," he says. "A good man, your granddad. Used to go fishing with him in Haeter Lake, back when it used to be a lake."

I stare at him, confused, but he just laughs.

I remember that flash of pain in Mom's face when she dropped me off here, the feeling that all those secrets she kept from me were just painful. I can feel the ache of it in my chest now, pain I've inherited even if I don't know how or why.

"They drained it, you know," Arthur continues. "The Anselm family. Rerouted the entire river that supplied it with a dam and drained the water from that little lake so they would have open space to build their park. We were so proud to have the park here in our town, we were. To have this beautiful park, bringing business to all of us. But I always did miss that lake. Ah." He shakes his head again. "Different days, they were."

He claps a hand on my shoulder, and it feels oddly comforting in this strange town. "You take your time, dear," he says, and then begins his slow shuffle back to the desk. "And let me know if you need any copies."

I stare down at the page, dated more than forty years ago.

June 17, 1979.

Haeter Lake Times.

"Tragic Death of Builder on New Park Site," the headline reads.

Beneath it is a black-and-white picture of a young family—a young man in overalls, with my mom's dark eyes, his arm around a woman with the same firm jaw as Mom. And between them, a child who looks about six years old. Wide brown eyes, round face, knobby knees.

Mom.

And those people standing beside her are my grandparents.

Were.

He died building the park. *He died building Pierce Anselm's park.*

So why does Mom love the Anselm family?

And why hasn't she ever spoken about my grandparents?

I scan the article. It doesn't say much, beyond claiming that the worker, Asa Preston, was careless atop some scaffolding. That he had a long fall.

Leaving behind his devastated young widow, Marie Emily Preston, and their seven-year-old daughter, Katherine.

Marie and Asa.

The grandparents I never knew, from *this* town. This town that Mom has never spoken of, that she won't answer questions about now when I *do* ask.

I am from this town.

I am *named* for this woman—Lucille Marie.

And they aren't anything like the people I imagined in all my childhood stories, aren't astronauts or spies or pirates or freedom fighters.

No, they were better than that.

They were *mine*, they were mine, and now they're gone.

I am from Haeter Lake. *I am from Haeter Lake.*

I have my grandma's name.

She's been with me this whole time because I have her name and his eyes. Because I am theirs and they are mine, and I'm suddenly so furious, so fucking *furious*, that I never got to know them.

It's my missing piece.

It's *all* my missing pieces.

I flip to the next week's paper.

"Tensions between Widow and Park Owners," the headline blares.

This time, there are two black-and-white pictures below: one of Marie Preston, my fierce grandmother, her hands resting on Mom's shoulders. The other, a younger version of Pierce and Veronica. I never saw Pierce alive, but this younger version of him looks determined, unstoppable. This younger version of Veronica looks the same: impeccably dressed, chin held high. Dangerous.

Like the kind of woman who would blame a man for his own death.

I flip to the next page, and then I nearly sink to the floor in shock.

"Widow Takes Her Own Life," the headline reads.

I grip the bookshelf beside me so tightly my knuckles turn white. Holy shit. Holy *shit*.

The article has few details, but it does say that my grandma died by suicide off the same scaffolding where her husband died. *Leaving behind a young daughter.*

I flip through more articles, more weeks of this town's misery. Of my family's pain.

The rest is not headline news, but I find it anyway. The Anselms, framed by the narrative as rich, benevolent benefactors, take my mom in and raise her as their own.

I force myself to breathe in, out.

This is the history Mom doesn't want to talk about. The loss of her parents. The Anselms adopting her as their own.

Is this why she loves them? Is this why she left?

Is this why she never mentioned it to me once?

I breathe in, out.

There are tears slipping down my face now, hot and silent, falling so fast I can't see.

It's relief and sadness all at once. Anger, too, flaming and burning brighter than I've ever felt. These are the people I've been missing my whole life. I finally know who I've been grieving.

I'm not sure how long I stay there, crying on the dusty sun-speckled floor of the old library, but when I finally return to myself, the shadows outside have grown longer.

Asa and Marie.

I turn their names over and over in my mind.

Finally, I check my phone. Still no new texts from Audrey, and I need someone to talk through this new information with because I'm reeling.

"Thank you, Mr. Joyce." I push myself to my feet. "I have to go."

He looks up at me over his reading glasses. "Are you all right, Katy?" he asks, and then shakes his head again. "Oh my. Lucy, of course."

"You said Mom came in here often?" I ask. "Did she have questions about her parents' deaths?"

He leans against the desk for a moment. "She wanted to know all about them," he answers finally. "Though in fairness, she had questions about just about everything. Inquisitive mind, that one. Very inquisitive."

"Was there some kind of cover-up?" I ask Arthur. "Do you think— Did my mom think—"

Arthur takes a step back. "Don't be asking me," he says, his voice suddenly hard. "I'm not supposed to talk. I'm not supposed to say any more, Katy. You know that. You know what they told you."

"I— Mr. Joyce—"

"I think you should go," he says firmly.

I stare at him for a long, long moment.

Is this what pushed Mom to become a detective all those years ago? All the unanswered questions about her own family?

I turn back, snap pictures of each of the articles.

My phone buzzes.

See you at the motel tonight, Audrey responds. *Are you okay?*

Not really, I text back.

All that longing—to know who I am, who Mom is, to know where I am from—has eased, but in its place, grief sits heavy in my stomach.

I feel slightly sick.

Did Veronica cover up what really happened to my granddad? And did my grandma really die by suicide, or is there more to this, too?

Or do I have this all wrong? Were the accidents only ever accidents—except for Pierce's death? And what does Audrey know about Pierce's murder?

There is no doubt in my mind that Veronica would do what she had to. *Anything for my family.* Maybe Pierce was that way, too.

I shiver, despite the warmth of the small library, and sit down cross-legged on the floor, the newspaper cradled in my lap.

There's a jingle of the bells at the door, and Arthur's slow, creaking voice as he greets someone—

"Pierce, is that you?"

My head snaps up, the surprise likely evident on my face.

It's a middle-aged man who looks a few years older than my parents. He has the same blond hair Gus does, except his falls to his shoulders, and the same soft blue eyes, though his, like his sister's and his mother's, show very little.

"Arthur, it's just me," the man says. "Curtis."

"Curtis?" I blurt before I can keep my stupid mouth shut. I unfold my legs and push myself to my feet, even as my stomach plummets. "Hi."

Curtis, the dangerous one. Curtis, the prodigal son.

Katy's words echo in my head.

He's kind and charismatic and funny until he's not. He's smart and pretty and good until he's not.

The man's eyes narrow and then widen, and then half a second later his gaze falls to the newspaper in my hand. He doesn't dress like the rest of the family—it's clear that he has, like Audrey told me, lived his life on the road in recent years—but he has the same set of his jaw. "You're Katy's kid," he says, wonder edging into his voice. "Damn, kid, I hoped we would get to meet you someday."

I wave my hand, shoving the newspaper behind me. "I heard you just got back to town."

Curtis smiles easily, the look much more disarming than Blake or Veronica has managed. "I'm not welcome at the big house these days," he says. "You've met my mother. I'm sure you understand."

"I don't," I say. "I don't really understand anything." Despite the friendliness of his expression, I take a small step back.

Good. Until he's not.

The rumors are harder to believe with him in front of me, the drug rumors and aggravated assault rumors, the brutality they say he's capable of harder to understand.

But not impossible.

Arthur looks up at me over his desk. "Don't be asking any more questions," he says irritably. "Come on, Katy, you know better."

"Poor man's confused," Curtis tells me softly. "It's all right, Arthur, no one will pester you with any more questions. Are you okay?" he asks me.

At that, the tears sting my eyes again. I nod my head determinedly. "I'm just . . . researching," I say finally.

He raises an eyebrow, and then he nods in understanding. "Your mom didn't tell you, did she?" he asks quietly. His eyes look a little bit sad. "You know, I thought she might have left us behind that thoroughly. Never even a mention, huh?"

I shake my head.

It's not that I trust him.

I don't.

But there isn't anyone in this town I can trust, not really.

Not even my own mom.

So if I have to be stuck in this library with the Anselm most known for violence—well, at least I'll get some answers.

Still, I eye the exits. And the back window.

Just in case.

Curtis shoves his hands into his pockets. He's wearing jeans that are ragged at the knees and an oversize band T-shirt that used to say THE GRATEFUL DEAD. "I don't blame her," he says finally. "I don't mention them much either."

I take in a shuddering breath and think of the grandma who gave me her name and the grandpa who gave me his dark eyes. I think of how young they were when they died, and how young my mom was when she went to live with someone else's family.

I hate him a little bit for it, even if it wasn't his choice. But he also looks *kind*, which is the most disorienting thing yet.

Kind. Until he's not.

"I can tell you," he continues, settling onto the floor with his back against the wall. He splays his hands out, palms up. "I knew your mom when she was young and wild."

Slowly, tentatively, I sit down, though I remain a good distance away from him. Katy warned me. She did.

But she also told me to trust her, and all she has done is hide the truth from me for years.

"Katy," Arthur calls from the counter again. "Katy, I can help you. Did you want to pick out a book? I'll check in the back for the Poirot—"

"It's all right," Curtis tells him firmly. "Lucy? Shoot."

So I ask him what her favorite color was, and what sports she played, and if she went to football games on Friday nights with her friends, and who her friends were. I ask him what kind of person she was, because I'm beginning to think I don't know who she is *now*, let alone then.

It's all the pieces of me that never fit right. All the things I didn't know, couldn't imagine my way into.

And Curtis tells me as the afternoon wears on toward evening that Katy loved green and used to garden with her dad but never did after, that she was better than he was at smuggling alcohol in Gatorade bottles into the football games.

That once he and Katy and Blake and Langley had all thrown a rooftop party, and Cliff's predecessor, some stuffy sheriff named Williamson, had chased them and nearly caught him.

"I thought we'd never see her again," Curtis says finally, tipping his head back against the wall. "Not after what my mom did to her."

At this, my head snaps up again.

He is looking down at me sadly. "I haven't been perfect," he says. "Not to her, or to my own kid, or any of my shitty choices. I'm sure you heard about the argument I had with my dad before they cut me off from the family, and there's nothing I regret more." His gaze looks distant, but the sadness in his face is the most genuine I've seen from any Anselm. "I ran when I should have stayed. But your mom? She had this dream of being a private investigator ever since I can remember. And Veronica almost destroyed that for her."

"What are you talking about?" I fold my hands tightly, watching him carefully. The conversation had felt easy, simple, like talking to someone who had known my mom and cared about her. But there in his eyes, suddenly, is that Anselm look: like he *wants* something.

"One of the only things that could have stopped her was a felony," Curtis says finally. "And Veronica tried to make that happen."

"What?" I'm on my feet, clutching the newspaper in one hand and my phone in the other. "What do you mean? What did she *do*? Did Veronica frame my mom for something?"

And if Veronica was able to frame my mom, what else could she have orchestrated? Cover-ups for my grandparents' deaths all those years ago?

"I think that's a better story for your mom to tell," Curtis answers. He stands, too, ducking his head. "I'm sorry, Lucy. And I know it isn't easy being back here, so tell Katy—well, tell her I said hello. And if either of you need anything, I'm here."

He squeezes my shoulder briefly, and I jump at the touch.

"I'm sorry," he says quickly, pulling his hand away.

I don't give him anything—not a polite *it's okay* or even a verbal answer of any kind. Instead, I stand in the middle of the room, feet planted, arms crossed, staring after him long after he nods his goodbye to Arthur and disappears through the double doors.

"Lucy."

Arthur is speaking to me, his eyes sharp and his tone hard.

And he's saying *my* name. He looks clear eyed.

"Don't go digging, Lucy Preston," he says firmly. "Some things are better left buried."

I begin my long walk toward the edge of town. I could wait for Mom to pick me up. I *should*. But there's something reckless and furious in my chest, a whirlwind that's finally been unleashed.

I had imagined Mom from a bright, brutally cold city like Minneapolis, or a crowded, raging city like San Francisco, or from bustling Atlanta or Chicago or any other city we've traveled through.

But now I know. She's not just familiar with these people; she *is* these people.

There's no bright, vibrant city in her past. Nothing exciting or glamorous.

There's just this, the silent, waiting little town at the edge of the forest. This tragedy that has been clinging to my skin my whole life, even if I never understood why.

So I walk, because I'm too angry to stay in one place.

Ten minutes later, a motorcycle roars behind me and kicks up dust, gritty on my tongue and teeth.

"Need a ride?" Audrey asks. She has that lopsided grin on her face, but it doesn't reach her eyes. Her cheeks are reddened from the wind, and there's a look, a haunted, hunted look in her eyes that I can't turn away from.

"Are you sure?" I ask her. "Won't both our moms be mad?"

What aren't you telling me about the night Pierce died? I want to ask her. *What did you really see at the park?*

But I don't ask her, not yet. Because I am afraid of the answer. Because I am afraid that my new friend has more darkness in her than I want to face. Because already this town has wrapped around me, invaded me, made me part of it.

Whether I wanted to be or not.

This time, I climb onto the motorcycle without slipping off once. "I found out something about my family today," I say as I settle in behind her. "We were from here. Mom's people. Her parents."

Audrey tenses. "Your mom never told you where she was from? Never talked about this place?" She hesitates, her hand on the ignition, but she doesn't start the motorcycle. "That's weird, Lucy."

"I mean, she hardly ever even talked about college or about meeting my dad. I would ask her questions, but she was always vague and... No, she never talked about being a kid," I say. "I didn't think it was weird. My mom isn't much for sharing feelings and stuff. It just isn't her personality."

"What happened to her... to *your* family sucked," Audrey says. She settles into the seat, and then reaches back and puts a steadying hand on my thigh again. "I'm sorry I was a dick about it earlier. If there's anything you want to know, I'll tell you. My mom and your mom grew up together, and my mom talks about Katy sometimes. She says Katy was strong and fierce and that it was good that she got out when she could. But also that Katy was a bitch."

I laugh at this, but it's a harsh, bitter sound. "Did Veronica try to frame my mom?" I ask her.

Her head swivels to look at me, hand hovering over the starter. "Not exactly," she says softly. "Hold on to me this time, okay? And don't go run off to murder Veronica after you hear this."

"No promises," I say. "On either front."

In a moment we'll be flying down the road at Audrey's pace on this death-trap motorcycle, but if I don't *think* about it first, I don't have to be anxious about it. I get to be anxious about something else instead. A foolproof plan.

"Your mom and Blake and Curtis had all been caught doing some graffiti on a building Pierce and Veronica owned," Audrey tells me. "*My* mom didn't get caught because Katy had told her to run. And covered for her. But afterward, Veronica blamed Katy for getting her perfect kids in trouble. She told Katy not to come home that night. And when Katy did, she had her arrested and tried to get felony burglary charges to stick. You don't even need to have stolen something for a burglary charge to stick. You just have to break in. Or in Katy's case, just go home."

I stagger backward off the motorcycle, jerking away from Audrey's gentle hand and nearly tripping as I do it. "What the *fuck*," I whisper.

"I know," Audrey says, swinging her foot off the motorcycle again and coming to stand beside me. "It's fucked up. Pierce made sure they dropped the charges—she wouldn't have been able to get her PI license if he hadn't—but the arrest record is still there. And I'm sure that fucked up her chances a bit. Anyway, then Katy left and never came back."

She wraps one lean arm over my shoulders, her touch comforting and strong.

I lean into it, resting my head on her shoulder. "That *bitch*."

"Yeah," Audrey says. "She is."

"Why do you think she did it?" I ask.

Audrey shrugs one shoulder. "You'd have to ask your mom or Veronica," she says. "Though neither of them seems like the secret-spilling type. But I'm sorry the Anselm family fucked up your family so bad."

"Yours too," I whisper against her shoulder. "I didn't know... Audrey, I didn't know that we were the same. That both our families died in that park."

"The Anselm family has always been evil," Audrey says bitterly. "And I—I don't know why your mom still speaks to them at all. I don't know why she's doing this for Pierce. If it were me, I'd want to ruin them all."

I lean away from her just slightly. "Audrey," I say, but then I shake my head. "Come on. We can go over our notes at the motel. I don't want to be out here after nightfall."

She shudders and then helps me back onto the bike. She hesitates, as if she wants to say something more, but then the motorcycle roars to life under her hands.

And then we're off, leaving Haeter Lake behind us as we once again take the curving road north of town that goes up, up, up like a roller coaster taking us deeper into the forest.

Mom is still out, so I text her:

Audrey is taking me back to the motel.

Nowhere else, Mom texts back immediately.

Yeah. Nowhere else.

We do stop for muffins from the diner—lemon poppy seed for me and cranberry orange for Audrey—but Mom doesn't need to know about that bit.

I flop down on my bed and pull out my notebook. Audrey sprawls next to me, her body so close she's almost touching mine.

"So," she says tentatively. "Do you wanna talk about the case? Or do you wanna go burn some of the Anselms' shit?"

A laugh bubbles up from my chest despite myself. "Maybe both," I say. "But no. We can. You think that the Anselms killed Pierce and are trying to frame your mom, yeah?"

Audrey's face hardens. "Yeah," she says.

"But why would they kill Pierce?" I prop myself up on my elbow. "If it's Curtis, why *now*? He's already hated him forever. If it's Blake and Veronica, why *now* when Blake is going to inherit the company?"

"Maybe Pierce was going to come clean about all the shit they've covered up?" Her eyes flick to me. She looks like she wants to say something more, and my heart beats a little faster. Then she shakes her head and leans back on the pillow again. "Maybe stuff that went as far back as your grandparents. Definitely the stuff that happened when my dad died."

She takes my notebook and pen, starts writing a list of suspects and reasons and clues.

Curtis Anselm. Disinherited, bitter, angry. Or maybe lonely, grieving, kind. Or maybe both.

Blake Anselm. *Bitchy* is all Audrey writes at first, though when I threaten to steal the pen from her and do it myself, she writes down the rest of it. *Power. The family company. Money. Inheritance.*

Veronica. I stop Audrey before she can just write *bitchy* again, and we write down theories about cover-ups and about what Pierce might have known or not known.

We write down others, too—Mickey, the diner owner who is an ex of Blake's, who never really liked Pierce. A former mayor who lost his seat because the Anselms funded his opponent. But no one with recent rage, no one with any new and pressing reasons to push Pierce from the top of his own roller coaster. Just his family, and Audrey's, and mine, tangled up in one another for three generations now.

Outside, the shadows are growing long again. The wind is blowing and the trees are groaning outside the motel, and the little rocking chair down the way creaks loudly. But in here, Audrey's body is warm beside mine and she looks like she could handle anything that comes through that door.

So I let myself lean back on the pillow. I let my eyes drift shut.

Eventually, I even let myself sleep.

And when I do, I dream of it all. Roller coasters and bloodstains and mansions and a grandmother who has my name.

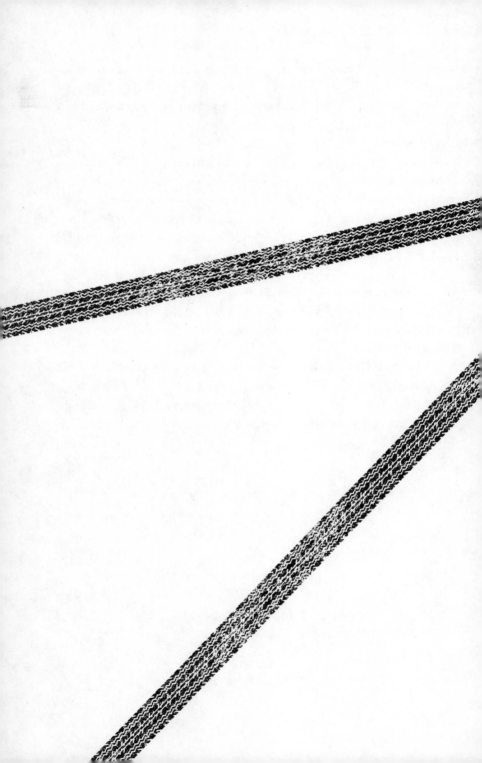

DAY THREE: SUNDAY, MARCH 24

CHAPTER 12

AUDREY

6:03 A.M.

I WAKE WHEN IT'S STILL DARK. PROBABLY BECAUSE I'm cold.

Sundress has hogged all the blankets, is practically burrito-d in them, just her wild red hair spilling out at the top.

I groan and roll over.

I hadn't meant to fall asleep here.

And—

Fuck.

There are seven missed calls from Mom. Way more texts.

Sorry, I text. *Stayed at motel with Lucy.*

The dots appear immediately.

Get your ass home, she responds.

Lucy's mom lifts her head when I slip toward the door. "Be safe," she says softly.

I acknowledge her with a nod, but by the time I'm out the door I have another text from Mom.

Never mind. Stay where you are. I'll facetime.

Mom looks exhausted when I answer her calls; still in her scrubs, still looking as if she hasn't had a decent night's sleep in weeks.

"What the hell?" she snaps. "I was worried *sick*."

I shove my keys into the pocket of my jeans. "I'm sorry," I say. "Mom, I am. I'm sorry. I meant to text. I just fell asleep."

Mom's brow furrows, and with horror I realize she looks closer to crying than she does to yelling at me. "And you were there all night, baby?" she asks. "Do you promise? And Katy and her little girl can vouch that you were?"

"Yeah," I say. "Yeah, of course, Mom. Why?"

"Do you promise?" A single tear streaks down her face. "You can tell me. You can tell me if you weren't."

"Mom." I shove my hands uncomfortably into my pockets. "What's this about? Where do you think I was?"

"There's another body," she answers after a beat. "Baby, there was another body and I think they're gonna try to pin it on us, too, and I don't know how yet, but they will—"

"Mom," I cut her off. "Mom, whose body? What's going on?"

"They found Arthur Joyce, the librarian." She drops into a chair in our tiny kitchen and puts her head in her hands. "On the dam. They found him just after midnight. Some kids who were out having a bonfire by the river found him. I was at the clinic when they brought him in."

"Jesus."

Mr. Joyce has always been kind to me. Even after all the shit I did, even after everyone started looking at me as nothing more than that little shit from the trailer, the girl with no future but this, he always had a smile and a book recommendation if I wanted one. I wasn't even much for reading, at least anything that didn't have pictures. But he'd find a graphic novel or recommend one I could order.

And he's—

He's dead.

"What happened?" I drop onto the curb, my legs feeling suddenly too wobbly to keep me standing.

Mom leans closer to the phone, her voice dropping. "Cliff will probably be back around asking questions," she said. "But first, you need to tell Lucy you want to talk. When you're in person, and Katy isn't around and listening—and only then—tell her to make sure she tells the cops you were with her all night."

My face warms, and I duck my head to hide my blush. "Okay," I say. "Yeah, okay. But why—what happened to him? Was it an accident? Why would they come after us for it?"

Mom sighs, her eyes shutting for a brief moment before she opens them again. She glances over my shoulder toward the motel rooms, where the curtains are still drawn tightly. "Last night, Katy took Lucy to the library. And Lucy asked questions about her family. And after *that*, Arthur called Cliff and said he had some information."

Mom's face twists the way it only ever does when she's thinking about Dad.

I gasp. "Mom."

"Not about Dad," she says. "About the old accident, with Katy's parents. Cliff's deputy—the new girl, Annika—told me this morning. She has the recording from the nine-one-one call, where Arthur mentioned there was something he should have told Katy a long time ago. And if there was something about that park, something about Katy's family—then we were probably right about your dad, too."

"Of course we were right about Dad," I snap. "So you think—"

My words are cut off when lights flash, red and blue and harsh all around Mom, bleeding through the window. I don't have to see to know that it's Cliff pulling up in front of our trailer, his sirens off, but those horrible lights flashing the way they have on all the worst days of my life.

"The Anselms are powerful," Mom says urgently. "And I'm going to keep us both safe, okay? Just keep your head down. Don't tell Cliff anything. And trust me, all right? We're going to get some answers, baby. For us. And for your dad."

LUCY 6:14 A.M.

My alarm goes off for the third time, but this time when I reach to snooze it, my phone is gone, and Audrey is nowhere to be seen.

I groan and drag my eyes open. Katy is sitting on her bed in the motel, already impeccably dressed in her navy-blue pantsuit and heels, holding my phone and letting the alarm ring and ring and ring, growing in volume as it does.

"Ugh, *Katy.*"

But the expression on her face stops me.

She looks paler, more tired than I've ever seen her.

"No more of the snooze and reset game, Lucille," she says. She pastes on a smile, something that's almost convincing, and finally silences her alarm. "Come on. Up, up. I have a meeting at seven with the sheriff, and you need breakfast first."

"Breakfast is a human need, Katy," I tell her, shoving the thin, fraying motel quilt off me. I stand, groaning again as I stretch. "I refuse to let you make me feel bad for it, just because *you* consider coffee a meal."

We both hesitate, the weight of everything I learned—everything she lost—hanging between us, unspoken as it has always been, but heavier now.

Then Katy tosses my phone back to me and takes a long sip of her coffee, waggling her eyebrows at me as she does it. "I also have meals," she teases when she finally sets her disposable coffee cup down. "I just prioritize coffee sometimes. Hurry and get dressed. We'll grab breakfast from the diner. Though if you take a hundred years to get dressed, that breakfast is going to have to be to-go."

So we're not talking about it, I guess.

Not talking about any of it.

"To-go is fine," I say, shoving down the flash of anger. "As long as I can hang out with Audrey afterward."

Katy grins, and my blush is automatic. "I like your new friend," she says. "She's outside, by the way. On the phone and pacing like a tiger."

I disappear into the bathroom to splash water onto my face and change into a dress, a soft blue thing with yellow daisies that ends just above my knees. I consider the leggings and T-shirt in case the motorcycle is our mode of transportation again today, but who is there to see me if my dress blows around a bit? Besides, I know I look cute in this, and that's the most important thing here.

I tuck my notepad and pen into the pocket of the dress and lace up my Converses. I love the look of it, the soft dress and the fiercer tone of the sneakers, but as I'm lacing them up, I catch Katy watching me, a small, amused smile on her face.

"Who would've guessed that it would be Langley's kid?" she muses, almost as if to herself.

I huff impatiently. "Ugh, *Mom*, she's a friend. Anyway, when do I get the full story of how you're connected to this place?" I need a distraction from the conversation about Audrey, which is rapidly veering into does-Lucy-have-a-crush territory.

Even if I do think she's cute.

I mean, I have eyes. Of course I can see that Audrey's pretty.

But we were brought together by some depressing shit, so it's not like I have a crush.

Whatever.

"Lucy," Katy says firmly, her eyes meeting mine. "I know . . . I know you want to talk. *Need* to talk. I'm sure Arthur told you a lot yesterday, and you have questions. And after all this is over, we'll go somewhere warm—beach and Wi-Fi as requested—and sit down and have a conversation." Katy's eyes go distant, and her thumb grazes the tattoo on her forearm, back and forth, back and forth.

Memento vitae.

Remember to live.

"Can't you just tell me *now*?" I ask her. "I'm here. I'm listening. I want to know where we come from, Mom."

I want to know who we are.

I want to know who my grandparents are, to push aside the cobwebs of stories I created for myself as a child and see them. I saw their pictures yesterday. I saw a *glimpse* of them, and I feel more lost than ever.

Were they strong and bold like Katy? Did they make each other laugh? Did they love each other?

Does Katy hate Veronica for the attempted career sabotage? Does she hate Blake and Curtis for being unable to stop her?

"I will," Katy promises me now. "But I can't talk about it here. I— It's all too close. What happened to—to my parents. It was all so awful, and afterward the Anselms were kind to me. Beyond that . . . Beyond that, honey, I can't talk about it here, okay?"

Kind seems like a weird description when Mom has tried to sneak me away from the Anselms twice now in two days.

Again, there's that strange flash of anger. I'm not usually an angry person. I'm pretty chill actually if you ask Jules or Amy or Nora or any of my friends back home. But maybe anger is that missing piece of me. Maybe anger is the thing I was meant to find here.

So I stare back at my mom, my hands balled into fists, because I don't have the words to tell her that none of what she said is *enough* for me.

"I really *do* have to be at a meeting soon," Katy says, sighing a little. "Cliff says we've got an urgent development. But after this investigation is done, you can ask any question you want, and I'll answer. I promise." Katy lifts her briefcase, her gaze snapping back to me. "Are you ready?" she asks. "We need to go."

"Yeah," I mutter. "Can Audrey just take me to the diner instead? She's still outside on the phone with her mom. We can hang out together."

Katy hesitates, but I glare at her again, and she sighs. "Okay," she says. "Yeah, that's fine. I'll give you money for food for today. Text me whenever you go somewhere that's not the diner, okay? Even if it's just back to the library."

I groan, but her look doesn't waver. "Sure."

She's silent as we gather our things, sometimes running a finger idly over her tattoo again. So I'm quiet, too.

If she's not gonna tell me shit, I'm not gonna talk to her, either.

I lean my forehead against the cool glass of the motel window and stare out into the trees as Katy finishes gathering her things.

Audrey is out front leaning against her motorcycle.

Mom presses some cash into my hand for breakfast and lunch at the diner. She rolls down the window when I get onto Audrey's bike. "Both of you be safe," she says. "Stay in town. Text me if you need anything."

"We'll be good, Ms. Preston," Audrey says.

There's something reckless, wild, dark in her eyes, and I want to get closer to it.

I've been such a good girl. Nice and charming and funny and endearing. But I like that Audrey *isn't*. Like with her, maybe I don't have to be, either.

"Was your mom mad at you for staying the night?" I blurt before I can stop myself.

She was there when I fell asleep, her arm warm where it touched mine.

She nods. "Yeah, my mom was *pissed*. She didn't know where I was."

"Oh shit. Are you okay?"

Audrey nods, hands twisting together. "She was more worried about the poor librarian. And the cops came asking us questions about him, too. There's some bad shit going on, Lucy."

I freeze. "The—what are you talking about?"

"Your mom didn't tell you?" She tilts her head. It's only then that I realize her eyes are red, as if she's been crying. "They found Arthur Joyce's body last night, the librarian. On the dam. My mom said she doesn't know if it's a homicide or not, but Cliff—the sheriff—came asking us both what we were doing last night."

Holy shit.

Arthur.

Arthur, who kept calling me Katy and offering me books. Arthur, who unlocked the answers I had been looking for.

Arthur, who told me to stop digging.

"That rich family is guilty as hell," I blurt sharply.

Audrey nods. Her gaze looks almost blank, too overwhelmed by everything that's happened in the last few days. She holds out her hands, palms up. "I don't— Lucy, I don't know what to do. My mom said that Arthur called the sheriff, said he had something he had to tell them about the accident, and then he . . . then he died."

I straighten. "Okay," I say. "Okay, okay. So. My mom is scared of the Anselms. We know that. They tried to blame *your* mom for Pierce's death. Arthur wanted to tell the police something, and now *he's* dead. And both our moms told us to stay away from this case."

Audrey looks pale. "Do you think they—do you think they killed him for talking to you?" Her voice is barely more than a whisper.

A shiver races down my spine. "Holy shit," I whisper back. "Audrey. Do you think— Oh my god. Oh my god."

"Hey, Sundress," she says softly. "Breathe."

I take in a panicked breath, and then another. Only on the fourth breath does it start to feel a little less like I'm on the verge of needing to breathe into a paper bag. "Is it my fault?" I ask her.

Audrey shakes her head. "No," she says firmly. "*No.* Okay? Whoever hurt him, *they* are the ones at fault. Not you."

"What should we do?" I ask her. I'm cold. I'm cold all the way down to my toes, and not because of the weather.

Audrey hesitates. "We could do what our moms asked," she says finally. "We could leave it alone."

"But," I say.

"Yeah," she says. "But if shit is getting intense—that means we're close. Right? We're close to some truth that no one wants us to know."

I draw in another breath. "Okay," I say softly. "Okay."

Audrey is watching me carefully, her head tilted. The sun catches the sharp cut of her jaw, the long flicker of her eyelashes.

"So I think what we should do . . ." The wind teases my hair, lifting it from my shoulders, but the goose bumps at the back of my neck have nothing to do with that, and everything to do with the reckless whirl-wind building in my own chest. "We should break into the mansion again."

Audrey laughs, the sound welcome after the darkness of this morning. "You're not as timid as you look, Sundress," she says.

"But before that," I say. "We should go to the library."

Audrey lifts an eyebrow at me. "It's probably taped off while they investigate."

"If it's locked," I tell her, "I'm good at picking locks. We can just duck under the tape."

Good may be an overestimation of my skills, but I am at least profi-cient. Well, I have knowledge. Some.

Anyway.

"What about Gus?" Audrey asks me, her look guarded. "You let him explore the office with us when we found the bloodstain. And he was going to help us get into Blake's office, but—"

"I don't trust any Anselms," I say, though I feel guilty instantly remembering the sickened look on Gus's face when he saw the blood-stain, and the sadness in Curtis's when he told me about what it was like to grow up with my mom.

"Me neither," Audrey says softly. "But if we decide to let him help, he could be . . . useful?" She reddens a bit as she says it, as if she knows by the look on my face that she sounded like an Anselm when she said it.

"Just us," I say. "So. The library. Are you in?" I meet her gaze with my own.

A grin spreads across her face, slow and sure.

"Yeah, Sundress," Audrey says. "I'm in."

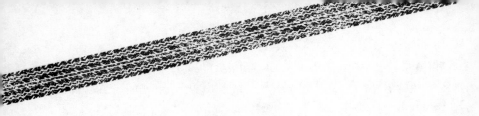

CHAPTER 13
AUDREY
9:43 A.M.

AS IT TURNS OUT, WATCHING YOUTUBE VIDEOS on lock picking is not the same as practical experience, something Lucy discovers as she noisily fiddles with the lock on the back door of the library.

By some miracle, she eventually jimmies the lock open with a pen-knife she had concealed in her dress pocket, and she looks at me triumphantly. "I told you I could do it." Her voice is loud enough to wake the dead.

Jesus Christ.

"You're still so loud," I whisper. "What if the cops are here?"

Lucy was trying to put on a brave face about crossing a police line and breaking in, but I saw the way she had to square her shoulders and catch her breath before she ducked under the yellow POLICE LINE, DO NOT CROSS tape outside the library.

It's endearing to see her commit her very first crimes.

"They're not," Lucy says, but her voice comes out a little high pitched. "Come on."

I follow her inside.

Her eyes have that determined glint she got yesterday when she flipped over the rug and uncovered the bloodstain in Pierce Anselm's office, but they look harder now. Almost angry.

It looks good on her.

It looks powerful.

"What are we looking for?" I hiss.

"Yesterday," she says. "He gave me a stack of old papers—newspaper articles and schematics for the theme park. If there was something wrong with the park—either when my grandparents died or when your dad did—he might have known. I took pictures of everything. But if something's missing, we'll know that's what this is about. Right?"

"Right. Lucy?"

She turns, pausing at a bookshelf full of romance novels. "Yeah?"

"Did you tell your mom about the bloodstain? The one in Pierce's office?"

"Shit," she says. "No, I guess I didn't. Besides, she dropped me off right away. But we should make our own case file, right? We can use the cloud and back it all up. Just in case."

She turns away again, tiptoeing past Arthur's desk, which looks bigger and lonelier in its emptiness, until we reach a table at the back.

"I knew it!" She leans forward, flipping through a stack of news-papers. "One of the schematics of the park is gone. You know, the plans as they're building? They all have to be up to certain codes, and if they took shortcuts . . . well, maybe Arthur realized."

I shiver. If this information has been here all this time, I may never forgive myself for not digging it up before this. "What are we going to do if it's missing, though?"

"Oh, I have the picture. But if—if there was something wrong with the park, whoever killed him took that evidence. Or maybe *he* took that evidence with him to the police, and they killed him on the way. Do we think it's Veronica? You know the family better than I do."

"Or Blake."

Lucy shivers. "Blake," she repeats. "The one with the pantsuit and the gun. Okay. So now we go to the mansion? If one of them killed him, the missing schematic could be there."

"This is the dumbest idea," I say. "Right? Like, they're dangerous. This is so dumb."

Lucy grins, but it doesn't quite reach her eyes. "My friend Jules has this saying, when we're about to do something dumb, and we *know* it's dumb but we just collectively decide we're gonna do it anyway. 'Not a heterosexual or a brain cell in sight,' she says, and our friend Amy always gets annoyed, because she doesn't like being the token straight friend—"

She stops abruptly, eyes widening in the dim library as she realizes she just anxiety-rambled her way into coming out to me.

"Oh. Damn. I mean—not that you're not a heterosexual. Or that *I'm* not a heterosexual. Or that you're not smart. I'm sure you have a brain cell. Probably more than one. Oh god. It's all just—just a silly thing we say for the bit."

Lucy is full-on rambling now, and I could stop her with a hand on her shoulder or a word, but I don't want to.

No.

I want to listen to her ramble and wait for her to decide she's done on her own.

"Stop doing that," she says finally, her voice smaller.

"Doing what, Sundress?"

"Smirking at me," Lucy says. "I was rambling. Why didn't you stop me? Oh god. I can't believe I said all that."

"I would like your friend Jules," I tell her. I pat her on the shoulder, just to see if it flusters her as much as putting my hand on her thigh did yesterday. Because now that I *know*— Well. That makes everything more fun. "Come on." I grin at her over my shoulder as I walk toward the exit. "We have a mansion to break into. Not a heterosexual or a brain cell in sight."

Her face turns as red as her hair, and she groans.

"I hate you."

The creak of the front door wipes the grin from my face.

Lucy lets out a little squeak, and I dive at her, covering her mouth with my hand.

"Shh," I hiss into her ear.

We huddle behind a bookshelf in the backroom, but no one flips on any lights or uses a flashlight. Their footsteps are soft.

Someone else is here.

And that someone is trying to walk very, very quietly.

The door creaks open, and Lucy's hand digs into mine so tightly I'm sure she's leaving marks with her fingernails.

I can only see from the knee down, where we're crouched:

Red high-tops with mud on the soles. Designer jeans, scuffed at the bottom.

I shove myself to my feet. "August Fucking Anselm," I snap. "Why are you here?"

Both he and Lucy let out screams that are nearly identical in tone, pitch, and length, neither of them stopping until I cut them both off with a glare.

"Stop screaming," I hiss. "This is a crime scene. Why are you sneaking around?"

"Why are *you* sneaking around?" Gus shoots back, but his eyes dart to the door again. "Are you investigating? Without me?"

"Last time we investigated together you ran away," I say unfairly. We saw an unexplained bloodstain. Of *course* he ran.

"Why are you here?" Lucy asks softly.

And to my shock, Gus Anselm starts to cry.

First silent tears running down his face, and then his shoulders shaking. "I think—I think my dad killed the librarian," he says, and then he starts to sob.

"Oh Jesus," I say, and pat his shoulder awkwardly.

Lucy wraps her arms around him and hugs him, and he cries onto her shoulder for several minutes.

"Okay, spill," I say.

I don't trust an Anselm.

My hand falls to the bracelet Dad gave me.

I'm sorry, I want to tell him.

I'm sorry my anger is bigger than my compassion. I'm sorry I have to wear it so tightly around me that I don't have kindness left for this grieving boy. I'm sorry, I'm sorry, I'm *sorry*.

A hand touches my face, so gently it jars me back into my body.

It's Lucy, her finger brushing away—

Tears?

My tears.

"Fuck," I say. "No. No, I'm not crying."

Gus snort-laughs through his tears, and then we are all laughing for a moment, despite the horror of the whole situation.

"Okay," Lucy says finally. "Okay, Gus, tell us what you know."

He sniffles a little. "My dad got kicked out of the family a while back," he says. "You know most of it, Audrey. My grandparents kicked him out, not because he's a dirtbag—which he is—but because he was bad PR for their companies. But he's back, and he's angry, and I don't know if he's angry at his dad or at his mom or at me or maybe at all of us."

Lucy shifts uncomfortably, something flashing in her eyes, as if she's not surprised to hear that Curtis is known for his anger. Katy doesn't seem like the most communicative mother, but she must have at least warned her about Curtis.

There is a rumor that when he was seventeen, he beat an employee of their family's company so badly the man needed reconstructive surgery. But it's just a rumor, of course, because the Anselm money filled in the gaps, and any charges that might have existed were dropped before anybody could ask any questions.

"But why the librarian?" I cut him off.

Lucy holds up her phone, opening her mouth to tell him what we've discovered, so I settle my hand heavily on her shoulder.

"Let him talk," I say softly.

She gets the message, her mouth snapping closed.

She has been slow to be as mistrustful of these people as she should have been, but perhaps now, finally, she is learning how dangerous they are.

"He was here yesterday," Gus says, his gaze finding Lucy's. "I know he talked to you."

I whirl on Lucy. This, she hadn't mentioned.

She avoids my gaze, stepping away from my touch. "He told me a little about my mom."

I shove the anger down and turn expectantly to Gus. "Why would your dad want to kill Mr. Joyce?"

"I don't know," Gus says uncertainly, which sounds like a lie. "But maybe—maybe if he knew something my dad had done. Mr. Joyce knew *everything* that happened in this town. And if my dad thought Mr. Joyce would talk…I don't think there's anything or anyone my dad cares about in this world except himself."

Lucy is looking at him strangely but still studiously avoiding my look, when the library door opens yet again.

"Hello?" a woman's voice is at the door, and then the bright beam of a flashlight illuminates the other room.

"Cops," I hiss.

More specifically, Cliff's deputy, Annika, who is new to town. Mom said she was the one who took the call from Arthur last night.

"We gotta run," I tell them. "Can you—can you stay quiet?"

She nods, eyes wide.

I grab her hand and pull her after me, weaving between shelves toward the little office at the back. I'm not sure if there is a door, but we can climb out of the window if we have to.

Just as we're almost to safety—almost to the door to the office—Lucy trips, nearly kicking over a bookshelf. Her eyes meet mine, rife with horror.

"HEY!" Annika yells.

I drag Lucy behind me, slam the door shut, and turn the bolt.

"Window," I hiss-yell at Lucy. "Come on."

Gus stops still. "I-I'll go," he whispers, ducking his head. "I'll be in less trouble. My family"—shame creeps up his face in a shade of red, and I want to tell him yes he *should* be ashamed, even if he's trying to do something good now—"my family will make sure I'm okay."

Lucy opens her mouth to argue, but I shove her toward the window as Gus shuffles back to the other room.

The window's painted shut, but Lucy and her pocketknife make short work of the paint.

Lucy's much better at prying open windows than she is at picking locks, which both interests and concerns me. A moment later, she scrambles through the window with an extra boost from me.

She shrieks a little when my hand brushes her ass, and she tumbles over herself when she hits the ground, her sundress tangling around her thighs.

I leap after her, and then we're up and running, hand in hand as we sprint from the cops.

Lucy is breathless by the time we reach my bike, just down the street, but she's giggling, too.

"I've never run from the cops before," she gasps, half-falling against me as she laughs.

I hold her up. "It's why I'm in such good shape," I tell her, and she collapses against me, and now we're both laughing, half high on each other, half high on the narrow escape we just had.

"Let's go," I urge finally. "She'll come this way sooner rather than later. Gus couldn't have slowed her down for long."

"And we have more dumb shit to do." Lucy giggles, though her expression falters at the thought of Gus.

She still shrieks, just a little, when I help her onto the motorcycle, but this time she slides in close to me without any prompting. Wraps her arms around me from behind. Tucks her cheek against my shoulder.

When we're on the road, I chance a look at her over my shoulder.

Her eyes are closed, her cheek still pressed against me, and in my mirror I can see her red hair streaming behind us like we're leaving flames in our wake.

And maybe I can't trust her at all, this girl who tells me half-truths and falls asleep next to me. But the feel of her arms tight around my waist is still the most intoxicating thing I've ever felt.

This time, Lucy helps me hide the motorcycle in the underbrush. This time, she looks just as scared of the forest, but she stays at my shoulder, squaring hers every so often as she decides that this time, this time fear will not stop her.

This time, we wait until we've scanned the windows at the back of the Anselm mansion to make sure no one is currently watching us.

And this time, Lucy picks the lock *fast*.

"Will you teach me to do that?" I whisper.

"Yes," she hisses back. "Now hurry up. This time we're taking the secret passages."

"The—the *what?*"

Lucy tugs me inside. "That first night," she answers, "my mom snuck into my room that way. And that's how she snuck me out the next morning. They were old servant corridors. The family doesn't use them, but my mom knew all of them."

Lucy throws herself against the wall with a thump.

And bounces off it.

Nothing happens.

"Oh god," she whispers. "I was sure it was here. I thought my mom just—" She smacks the wall again, the thump reverberating through the hallway.

"Oh my god, shut *up*."

There are voices at the end of the hallway, just on the other side of the door.

"We should run for it," I tell her. "They're—"

With another thump, Lucy throws herself against the wall, a bit farther ahead in the hallway, and then the wall shifts behind her. Opens.

"Goddamn, Sundress."

I manhandle her through it, because one of the Anselms is almost at the opening now. I pull it shut behind us and cover her mouth with my hand again, to catch the inevitable triumphant squeak.

"Did you hear that?" Veronica is just outside now. "Blake? Is your brother here?"

"How should I know?" Blake is even closer, her voice low and dangerous. "Did you see Katy's face? She's just waiting for an excuse to snoop around the rest of the house. We need to get back to them."

In the dim light of the narrow passage, Lucy looks a little paler.

"Are you sure it's not Curtis?" Veronica asks.

"Again," Blake says impatiently. "How should I know what your son is doing?"

"Please try to get along with him while he's here," Veronica admonishes her. "At least in front of the detectives."

"Curtis left me a business to run and his damn son to raise," Blake says sharply, "who, by the way, Cliff is dropping off because he was snooping in the library just now."

Veronica makes a sound under her breath, and then there's a pause before she says: "Anything for family, baby."

Blake lets out a breath. "Anything for family."

And then they're gone again, their footfalls distant, a door clicking shut behind them.

I follow Lucy up, up, up, until she's huffing and sweating, and even I am feeling the burn in my legs.

"Tell me," she manages as she pauses for breath. "Tell me more about the family. Who's Curtis? How many are there?"

"Blake and Curtis," I tell her. "Blake helped run the parks, though. Curtis has his own business, technically, though I think his dad paid for it. That's what rich people do. And Curtis got kicked out for being a general scumbag, but it sounds like you should be the one telling me about him, since he's your best bud now."

"We're here." She cuts me off by holding up a hand and then pushes with a little grunt.

We step out into the hallway on the second floor.

"Mom's old room is up here," Lucy tells me distantly. "Come on. We still have to get to the third floor. Veronica's office this time?"

But I have to stand still, just for a moment.

It hits me like a wave as I stand there in the Anselms' fancy-ass mansion.

Sometimes grief is like that, a wave that knocks you off your feet. Most days, it's just like a gash in your skin that keeps bleeding—a slow, steady loss. But today, here in the Anselm mansion, grief is a wave.

Whenever Mom and I argued, Dad would joke that someday I'd grow up to be a lawyer, have a successful practice on the coast somewhere, a mansion like the Anselms.

He said he was going to try to save for my college if I wanted to go, pay my way into Stanford or Yale or other big names that only ever sounded like a dream to me.

Dad would grin at both of us, the corners of his eyes crinkling with laugh lines. Just like that, the tension between Mom and me would diffuse. "Audrey Nadine," he would say, "someday you'll be the most fearsome woman in all of Haeter Lake."

My anger never seemed to bother Dad. He matched it with calm, and now, without him, everything is unbalanced. Just my anger, growing, growing.

Growing.

No one ever asks angry girls what they dream, but Dad did.

Dad was like that, though. Dreaming. Always dreaming.

Right up until the stupid, selfish Anselms took him from me.

I clench my fists tightly, the fury so strong I'm surprised it isn't leaking out of me.

I climb the stairs up, up, up. Past the second floor, where I glance down the hallway and see doors open, immaculate rooms. One with bookshelves to the ceiling and a sofa. Their own home library. At the end of the hallway, a bedroom, the covers smoothed over neatly.

The third floor is as I remember it; the rooms so large and spacious I could never belong here, historic wood and new furniture, new money in a mansion old enough to remember days before the Anselms were its owners.

The offices stand waiting for us: VA on one door and an engraved PA on the other.

And this time it's Veronica's turn.

Lucy gasps a little for breath, her hand clutching my forearm as I push the door open.

From Veronica's window, I can see the backyard—arbor, pool, sidewalk...and the footpath. The one that leads all the way to the park.

Could she have seen Pierce leave from here in the gathering dusk on Friday night? Could she have seen *me*?

I shudder at the thought.

Veronica Anselm plays the long game. And if she saw something that night, she is waiting for the opportune moment to drop that knowledge like a bomb.

Her desk is well organized, which is exactly what I should expect, but the desktop monitor is still lit, as if she has just walked away.

Lucy crows with delight.

Only one thing is open on her computer. A video player, one file loaded.

My hands are slick with sweat as I click *play*.

The screen is black, but the file is labeled with a timestamp, beginning THURSDAY, MARCH 14, 2021. 9:17 P.M.

Oh no.

No, no, no.

This can't be happening.

"Look around the office," I tell Lucy hastily. "I'll make a copy of this. We can watch it later."

Or never.

Because I'm going to delete this literally as soon as Lucy turns around.

Lucy cocks her head, confusion on her face. "Oka-ay," she says. "Yeah.

I'll look through the shelves and stuff for the park schematics that are missing from the library."

She retreats a few steps, and I stare at the screen of Veronica's computer. Two years ago.

I remember that night vividly.

"You okay?" Lucy looks up at me from a file cabinet she's trying to unlock.

"Yeah," I say. "I'm fine."

But what the hell is going on here?

That video Veronica has pulled up on her computer, from years ago. What does it have to do with any of this?

I remember the night. Of course I do.

I came to their house, knife in hand. Carved a message into their garage.

But if she has always *known* that was me, why hasn't she said anything before now? Why didn't she ever tell the sheriff?

My hand hovers above the mouse. What is she planning to do with this footage of me?

I erase the video file from two years ago, and then, just to be safe, I erase the rest of the security footage from her computer.

I pull open desk drawers, and the first thing I find is a tape labeled with the same date.

"I'll hide that," Lucy offers, but I'm already slipping it into my sports bra for safekeeping.

The rest of the drawer is pretty innocuous—one drawer of organized, color-coordinated and metallic office supplies, more expensive-looking than anything I've ever seen in our general store.

One drawer contains stationery with her name on it and a pen. Which also has her name on it. I pull open another drawer, and my hand stills on the handle.

There at the bottom of the drawer is a small pearl-handled pistol with *VA* engraved in gold lettering.

A shiver runs down my spine. I know many people in our town own

guns, but most of the ones I know have a shotgun for hunting and nothing more. They don't keep pistols in their desks, don't have their initials
engraved on them.

All this time, I've been angrier at the Anselms than afraid of them.

But this—this is a jarring reminder that I should never forget to fear
Veronica Anselm.

"Sundress," I say roughly. "Look."

She peers over my shoulder, shivering when she sees the pistol.

"She's a bad bitch," Lucy says finally. "Which, like, I mean usually?
I'd be all about that. But I mean she's, like, *bad* bad."

I force myself to keep going, to open the next drawer and the next.
The last drawer has a well-organized array of pens, Sharpies, and pencils, along with a delicate little hand sharpener.

Veronica probably has a staff member whose sole job is to sharpen her
pencils for her with this stupid little tool.

If I could turn around and show Lucy, maybe I would be able to laugh
at this with her.

But because I'm petty, because grief is a wave today, because I'm still
shaken from finding Veronica's gun, because I'm not a good person, not
where it counts, I take the little sharpener out and stamp it under the
heel of my boot.

Feeling peaceful when it cracks.

Feeling something pleasant where anger had been the deepest ache.

Feeling satisfaction.

Just like I felt last Friday night.

LUCY. 11:04 A.M.

Audrey stomps on something so hard it cracks under her foot.

"What the hell?" I stare at her from the file cabinet. "What are you
doing?"

"Breaking Veronica's stuff," Audrey mutters.

There's a sound in the hallway, and both of our heads snap up at the
exact same time.

"Shit," she whispers. Audrey stares at me from behind the desk, her eyes wide with horror. And then I grab her hand and yank her into the closet, pulling it shut behind us.

We're just in time.

The door opens, and Katy and the sheriff and Veronica and Blake enter together.

"Thank you for letting us look around up here," Katy says.

Her voice is so strangely soft, gentle and mellow, nothing of the fierceness I know she has. Everything I learned over the past few days comes roaring back, and I'm torn between anger at her for allowing these people anywhere near her and overwhelming sadness that she ever felt like she owed them.

"Of course, dear," Veronica says. "Would you like some tea?"

"Tea would be lovely, thank you," Katy says.

Her voice sounds warmer than usual, not the firm, businesslike tone that makes her clients feel safe and makes the people she's investigating feel like running away to Tahiti or some other country that has no extradition treaty with the US.

A fact I only know because Katy loves to talk about extradition treaties and how Tahiti is bad for her business.

Anyway.

Her current friendliness is unsettling.

"No cream, one sugar?" Veronica's voice is silk sheets and expensive Pinot, marble, and stilettos. I wrap my hand tightly around Audrey's.

Katy laughs, a sound so bubbly I hardly recognize it. "You remember," she says. There's something like wonder in her voice.

I can feel Audrey's eyes on me.

I lean my head against her shoulder, trying to force my breath to stay steady.

The closet is deep, coats hanging at the back, but not much else.

I jerk my head, try to get Audrey to scoot to the back of the closet with me. She shakes her head, leans forward so she can peek through the slats in the closet door.

"We just have to complete one more interview with each of you," Katy continues, settling into her seat. "I know it's such a terrible inconvenience, especially right now. Is your wife around these days, Blake? Perhaps we could speak with her next?"

Another stiff silence follows.

Finally, it's Cliff who clears his throat. "Ms. Anselm, am I correct in remembering that you and your wife parted ways a few years back?"

"Six," Blake says coldly. "Six years ago."

"Oh, forgive me," Katy says, and she sounds flustered.

No one, *no one*, has ever made my mom sound flustered.

Cold fear whispers down my spine, and I press my side against the wall to hide even further. Someone who can fluster my mom is not someone I want to mess with.

"We'll speak to Curtis next, then," Cliff says. "I understand he arrived home the same day as your father passed, and that he had had a falling-out with Pierce years ago. Any bit of information would help. Veronica, if you could just give us a moment?"

There's a rustle of clothing as Veronica stands. "Of course," she says coolly. "Cliff? Treating my grieving family as *suspects* is ridiculous." She hesitates.

It's like waiting for a rattler to strike.

I grip my pen so hard the plastic nearly cracks.

"Katy?" Veronica says softly. "I trust you to do what's right."

"Always, Mrs. Anselm," Katy says. From here, I can't see the expression on her face.

I reach for Audrey's hand again.

She squeezes mine in return.

"Oh, come on, Mom," Blake says, her tone lightening. "Katy's just doing her job. Katy, do you remember what she was like when we were teenagers?"

When we were teenagers.

"I do." Katy's voice softens. "Cliff, certainly we can talk to them together. I'm sure they have some interesting perspectives to share."

Is she remembering the fun she had with Blake and Curtis and Langley? Or is she remembering what it was like to be arrested just for trying to go home? And why is she *helping* them now?

"Blake, you were saying earlier that you last saw your father at dinner on Thursday?" Katy prompts.

"Yes." Another rustle, as if Blake is settling back in. "He was in good spirits. Completely unbothered. But really, Katy, I have to admit I'm a bit confused about why you're here. Not that I'm not glad to see you. Of course I am." Her voice is half an octave lower, silky and smooth. "But this case seems simple enough to me. And I know you have big cases coming your way all the time now."

Is Blake *flirting* with my mother?

Katy coughs uncomfortably.

Cliff clears his throat again. "Katy and I were actually both contacted by your father's new lawyers after his death. Kipling and Kaur. Apparently, it was your father's wishes that Katy be called in to investigate in the event that anything happened to him. This leads us to believe that he was worried something *would* happen to him. Are you sure there's nothing you can tell us about his mood?"

The conversation stutters to a halt again. But to me, the prolonged, strained silence seems weighted with meaning.

Pierce Anselm knew he was about to die.

Beside me, Audrey shifts. "We have to get out of here," she whispers. Her eyes are closed, and she looks sick to her stomach.

So I do something she won't forgive me for.

I text Gus—who had sent me a message letting me know Cliff had brought him safely home to Blake with nothing but a scolding—with an SOS message.

I can only hope he receives it, can only hope he decides to help us again after the sharp prickliness Audrey has shown him.

"You know," Blake is saying, "I loved my dad very much, but he was always full of himself. You remember, Katy, what he was like on city council? Dramatic at every meeting. I think it's likely that he wanted the attention, even after he was gone. And it's likely he missed Katy and wanted to ensure she'd come back here for the funeral."

"Of course I would have come," Katy protests, but her voice has quieted. "Still, we have to honor his wishes and complete the investigation. It sounds as if it may have been his last wish."

"Blake or Veronica," Cliff says, "either of you can answer this: Is there anyone you can think of who would want to hurt your father?"

"I do have something I feel I must tell you, dear," Veronica says. "But I would rather the boys not be told yet, if you don't mind. Only Blake and I know at the moment."

"Of course." Katy leans forward, hands clasped. "What can you tell us?"

"Well," Veronica says, "it's about that Nelson girl. Audrey."

CHAPTER 14

AUDREY

11:31 A.M.

WE'RE TRAPPED.

We're trapped in this fucking closet, and Veronica Anselm is out there with her pearl-handled gun and her vicious veneer of perfection, and I'm just shit from the trailer park, and she can say whatever she wants. She can say whatever she wants about my family, and she can be believed.

Will Veronica shoot me right in front of Cliff if she finds me here? She could, and get away with it. What if Katy still has some loyalty to her, after all? I know *Cliff* does.

I cling to Lucy's hand.

No, no, Katy wouldn't let anything happen to her daughter. To me, maybe, because I have always been disposable in this town and so has my family.

"What was it you wanted us to know about her, ma'am?" Cliff asks.

"Well, I'm sure my sons are blissfully unaware of the way some people hated their papa. But you see, I don't think my husband jumped from that roller coaster platform. And I think I have an idea who may have . . . well, someone who blamed my husband for certain things," Veronica says.

I bite down so hard on my lip that I taste blood.

The video. The surveillance video.

She was about to show the police. Thank *fuck* I deleted it. Thank fuck I have the other copy stowed securely in my sports bra.

I squeeze Lucy's hand so hard she pulls hers back.

And then everything gets immeasurably worse, because with the softest of clicks the back of the closet slides open and Gus is standing there, eyes wide in the dark.

I bite back a scream and then glare at Lucy.

I'm sorry, she mouths at me.

"You think someone held a grudge?" Katy is asking.

"I think multiple people *resented* my husband, of course," Veronica says lightly. "Great men always face that, you know. The jealous, the wannabes. But this family—well, after that terrible accident, I do believe they blamed us. We did all we could for them, of course."

We did all we could for them?

I dig my fingernails into my palm. I could get out of this closet now, *right goddamn now*, and make her pay.

"Are we talking about the Nelson family?" Cliff asks. "Horrible thing that happened to Grant, of course."

"Of course," Veronica says.

I want to rip open the door and punch her smug face. Cliff's simp face, too, and Blake, just for good measure. Maybe Katy if she tries to stop me.

Instead, I wrap my hand over the bracelet and pray that will be enough.

If Dad was here—

I stop the thought in its tracks. I'd be having dinner at home at our house. Mom wouldn't be working double shifts or be facing harassment from the police. Dad would put on horrible pop hits from the 90s and 2000s and we'd be dancing to them.

I wouldn't be stuck here in this closet with two people I can't trust, listening to Veronica Anselm tell the world that *my* family is the problem.

Lucy must be able to sense that, because she wraps her soft arms around me, even though she knows I'm angry at her for telling Gus where we are. Even though she can feel my shoulders stiffen.

It's comforting, almost. The dim space, her arms around me, firmer than I would have guessed. The fact that she hangs on because she knows I need her to, even if I'm not hugging her back.

Under less horrifying circumstances, I would be more than content.

But right now, Veronica fucking Anselm is blaming my family. Just like she and her worthless husband did years ago, when my father's throat was still bruised and purpled from the seat belt on *their* roller coaster. From *their* mistake.

How can they be angry at me?

Every time I screamed *Choose* at someone in this cursed town, they chose the Anselms. They always choose the Anselms.

So why does Veronica hold it against me when she won? This park may have closed, but all their other parks stayed open. Everyone chose them. Everyone chose their family.

My breathing is shallow, and Lucy pulls me in even closer so that my head is pressed to her shoulder.

To my horror, a tear leaks out of my eye and cuts a path down my cheek.

Gus waves his hand toward the back of the closet, but I'm frozen, and Lucy's arms tighten around me.

"I think both Langley and her daughter, Audrey, blamed us," Veronica says. "In fact, about a year after the accident—I believe to the day—someone carved an unpleasant message into our garage door. We have the security footage, of course. We didn't say anything at the time, because we thought the poor girl had been through enough."

Gus's head snaps up sharply, the suspicion in his eyes hard as he looks at me in the dim space.

Lucy's body goes a bit rigid against mine.

I deleted the video and stole the hard copy, but I didn't think to look for any other digital archives. Does she have it saved somewhere else? The video of me, kitchen knife in hand, raging outside their house?

It's a video that says I am unhinged, furious, dangerous.

And all this time, Veronica has just been waiting to use it against me.

"You mean you think Audrey has something to do with all of this?" Katy says. "Langley's kid?"

I clench my fist, and Lucy gives me a reassuring squeeze, despite the tension I can feel in her body.

But that's her mom out there, sounding more and more suspicious of *me*.

"What was the message?" Cliff asks.

Veronica clears her throat delicately. "Well," she says. "The girl took a knife and carved *die die die* into the front of our home."

Gus sucks in a soft breath. Now he is looking only at Lucy, sharing a look that says *And you trust her? After this?*

Lucy doesn't look sure.

"Holy shit," Katy says.

"You said it was on the year anniversary?" Cliff asks quietly, and I can tell he's remembering what else I did that night. "Of Grant's death?"

I know he's remembering the fight, my fury, and that I was drunk when he finally picked me up. How much damage I caused, in just one single night.

Of course he remembers.

"We thought it was just grief," Veronica says, her voice sickly sweet. "For her poor father, of course."

I taste bile. I might throw up at the sound of her false sympathy. She wasn't trying to give me a pass all those years ago. She was biding her time, waiting to use this against me when it best served her purposes.

Like making sure that now, everyone will believe I am responsible for Pierce Anselm's death.

"But now . . . well, we have footage of her motorcycle in the parking lot outside the old park last Friday," Veronica says. "It's hard to see on the video, because the cameras down there are old, but they did capture some stills. I haven't told Curtis and Gus yet, because Blake and

I didn't want them to jump to conclusions. You know how protective they are of Pierce."

Lucy tenses beside me. She knew, of course. She saw me in the dark, saw my wide eyes and the glint of my knife and recognized me when she saw me later.

But Gus didn't know.

And despite all of it, I didn't want him to find out this way. And I can explain. I really can.

I just didn't know how to tell Lucy that the first time I thought of her as Sundress was that night, when she was in the parking lot staring in horror, when I was hiding in the trees, crouching there in my mud-encrusted shoes. I didn't want Gus to know what it was like to watch his grandpa fall from a roller coaster platform.

I didn't want to describe the sound I heard when he did.

But I *can* explain.

Even though Pierce Anselm deserved to die.

He did.

But all this time, it wasn't my mom they were trying to pin it on.

It was me.

CHAPTER 15

LUCY

11:41 A.M.

I HAD KNOWN AUDREY WAS THERE THE NIGHT Pierce Anselm died. I had seen how scared she was, and based on her fear of the park, it had seemed so unlikely she'd be able to make it any farther into the park than the entrance.

At the park, despite what she has implied about wanting to avoid it at all costs.

She does hate the Anselms.

But the footage. And the knife. And all that raw unfiltered anger.

I can see by the look on Gus's face that he believes his grandma, and why shouldn't he?

I want to burst out of that closet, run straight to Katy. Because this is all too much. Too much.

"It's hard for me to believe that Audrey would do something like this," Katy says uneasily. "She's just a child."

"I agree," Veronica says. "Of course. And I wouldn't imply it if we didn't have the footage. Would you like to see? I . . . Oh, hmm, I thought I had it pulled up on my computer. I'm not as well-versed in these computers as you young folks." She laughs lightly.

I look at Audrey. Her head is still pressed against my shoulder, her eyes squeezed shut, the light falling on her face through the slats in the closet door. Her breathing is shallow, her chest rising and falling fast. She doesn't look like a murderer. She doesn't.

She just looks like a girl, scared and a little sad. She looks like she's holding on for dear life.

She looks the way I felt last night, walking into the forest with all that reckless grief in my chest, grieving the family this town stole from us. So I decide it then.

I decide I don't believe Veronica Anselm. Not even a little bit.

Not even if Gus Anselm does.

"Though," Katy says, worry creeping into her tone, "um, my daughter is spending some time with Audrey today. I—I think it would be best if I call her."

Another tear cuts a path down Audrey's face.

She *can't* be a murderer.

But Katy has her phone out and—damn it.

If she checks my location data, she'll see that I'm right here. And she can't find Audrey, too. I turn to Gus.

"My turn," I whisper. And then I shove her toward Gus and the open door.

I'll run, too.

Or I would.

Except that's when I realize I never turned my phone back to silent. Katy just called my phone.

So now it's ringing. At full volume. In Veronica Anselm's closet.

That bold, angry thing I discovered last night, that thing takes over. I laugh. Just let it out. It sounds loud and bold and carefree.

I shove open the door and step out, hoping that Gus will help us despite what he just heard, and I find that despite it all, I am grinning. Because what else can they do? How else can they hurt me? These people took my family from me. These people turned Katy into this zombie-version of herself that smiles politely instead of asking real questions.

"Lucille Marie Preston," Katy snarls. "What the *hell* are you doing here?"

There, finally, is the fierce mother I know.

But she called me by my grandmother's name, and that name has made *me* fierce, too.

"Um," I say. "I guess this is me coming out of the closet. Hi, everyone, I'm gay." I step out of the closet and into the office, and my laugh follows the truly ridiculous joke, breathy and nervous and high-pitched.

Holy shit.

I'm doing this.

Really doing this.

And I'm keeping Audrey safe, because someone should. Because she deserves to have someone who does.

I just made a joke when I was caught in literal hell. A gay joke.

Jules is gonna lose her shit when I tell her about this.

I find that suddenly I have to hold back a hysterical laugh.

"You're grounded," Katy says tightly, her voice so sharp I can imagine it cutting through the air like a whip. "For the rest. Of. Your. Life."

"I would just like to say," I continue, because it's too late now. And if I'm fucked, well. I might as well let it all out. "That Audrey is probably not a murderer. She doesn't have to be nice to you to not be a murderer. And also she definitely stayed the whole night with me last night when the librarian died so. You're looking in the wrong place for suspects."

The silence that follows my proclamation is deadly.

So you know what?

I should keep going.

I should tell them I think they're cruel and entitled and I hate them for causing my mom so much pain. I should tell them that even if I don't know *why* they did it, I think they're responsible for all that's gone wrong in this town.

"Are you letting your daughter speak to me like this?" Veronica asks, incredulous. "Of all the— This is unbelievable. How did you get back into my house?"

"I just walked in," I tell her cheerfully. "Come on. It wasn't hard. Well, I mean, I picked the lock, I guess. Besides, what else was I supposed to do? I got bored of hanging around this stupid little town. I ditched Audrey and walked here. Anyway, Cliff, you asked some good questions today. You're not as dumb as I thought you were. No offense."

"Stop. Talking." Katy sounds less than a second away from losing it.

For once, I agree with Katy. This would maybe be better if I could just bring myself to *stop fucking talking.* But then again. Maybe not.

"I can't believe I am being lectured on my husband's death by a child who was hiding in my closet." Veronica's voice sounds close to hysterical.

"Oh, I'm not lecturing." I beam at her. It's already too late for me, so I plow onward like a train wreck, too late to stop, impossible to look away from. "I'm—"

I let out a small *oof* as Katy physically drags me out of the room. I was going to say *accusing,* to plow forward and throw out wild, half-formed theories about cover-ups and safety compromises and everything being connected, shit that would make me sound more like a conspiracy theorist than a private investigator. I was going to say all of that, but my mom is scarier than any of them right now and she is hauling me bodily down the hall away from them.

Still, I will cherish the look on Veronica Anselm's face for the rest of my life for what I did say.

But more than that, I will cherish the look on Audrey's face when she realized I had chosen to help her. I will think about that, too, for the rest of my life.

Which, by the look on Katy's face, won't actually be that long.

But whatever.

"I ought to kick your ass," Katy says shakily, her hand still clenched over my arm. "I ought to take you back to the motel and kick your ass."

Katy has hardly ever punished me, even when I was little, even that one time I accidentally lit the back shed on fire when we lived in that little house in Wilmington.

But yeah, okay, right now she does sound a little scary.

I'm still riding the high of watching Veronica Anselm turn forty different shades of purple with rage.

It lasts just until we're outside the gates of the mansion, Jeep speeding down the highway.

Because that's when I realize Katy is crying.

And not just, like, teary.

No, she has tears running in rivers down her face, which is white as a sheet. She is staring straight forward, fingers wrapped over the steering wheel like she's hanging on for dear life.

"Katy?" my voice sounds a thousand times smaller.

"Don't," she says.

We skirt the town, nothing but the rumble of the Jeep and Katy's frigid silence to keep me company.

Well.

This is definitely worse than last spring break, when I told Jules that my mom was gone on a case in New Orleans, and somehow it all turned into a house party.

And worse than the time when I was supposed to be going to Jules's cabin but instead went to a beach in Miami.

Yep.

Worse than all the other dumb shit I've done.

When we pull up in front of the motel, Katy nearly rips the keys out of the ignition. "Out," she snaps.

She still has tear tracks on her face, but now the fury is back, set deeply in the lines of her face.

She stalks toward our room, her heels digging into the gravel that is softening into mud beneath the warmth of the sun.

I notice a few blossoms on the trees, almost-leaves just waiting to open and fill in the space until we can't even see the road from here. I shiver again. The shadows aren't as long here in the light of day, but it still smells like moss and half-rotted leaves, and the silence is too thick, *too* quiet, as if the trees around me are waiting for something.

And I have a feeling I'm about to be left here alone.

I follow Katy into our room, and she wheels on me as soon as we're inside.

"Listen to me," she says, and to my shock she looks as if she's about to be sick. "They will kill you. Do you understand? They. Will. Kill. You."

Well, this is not the way I expected things to go.

"Katy?"

Her hands are trembling, and she wraps one over the doorknob, her knuckles white. "This is not a fucking joke," she says, but her voice nearly breaks. "You don't know what you're messing with. You don't know *who* you're messing with. And the Anselms . . . the Anselms don't forgive and they don't forget."

"Jesus, Katy," I whisper. "Do you think—"

"This is not a discussion," she cuts me off, but she doesn't sound angry, not really. Just rattled. *Scared.* "Listen. Please, Lucy, you have to listen. I'm sorry I brought you. I am. It's been so many years, and I thought I'd be ready to . . . to face them. Maybe I convinced myself I could do this. I don't know."

"Katy," I interrupt. It sounds like begging. "Can't you tell me what's going on? Can't we just leave? What is happening?"

"Nothing," Katy says, and I'm not sure which question she's answering. "Everything. I have to get back, Lucy. I'm . . . I have to finish this. But I called your dad. He'll be coming to pick you up."

"What?" I stare at her. "Mom, no. You're staying?"

"I'm the only chance this investigation has, and you have to stay safe. But make no mistake, young lady, I will have time to be mad at you for . . ." She waves her hand vaguely at me. "Once we're safely home."

A muscle in Katy's jaw jerks, and then she turns so that she's facing me. Her dark eyes look haunted, and she has her hand on her tattoo again, tracing the letters unconsciously.

"Lucille," she says. "I don't know how much you heard of our investigation. I don't know what you think you know. But this is what I need you to know: I don't know if the Anselms killed Pierce. I don't think so. They're . . . They're all kinds of fucked up, but they do love each other.

So no, I don't think they killed him. But I do believe they'll kill anyone who threatens their family."

"Mom?" I ask. "What is it you know about them that no one else does?"

She sighs softly. "I know they'll protect their image," she says. "Look what they did to their own family. And Curtis made mistakes, I know. But cutting him out of the family entirely? I know what they'd be willing to do to you or me or anyone else they thought was in their way."

The air whooshes out of my body. "Do you think Audrey and Langley are in danger?" I ask in a small voice.

Katy bites down so hard on her lip that she draws blood.

I stare at her in disbelief.

"Neither you nor Audrey will be in danger, because you will be staying far away from this case," she says. "And whatever you think I'm doing, or not doing, don't interfere, don't ask questions, don't—"

Her phone buzzes, and both of us jump in unison.

"Shit," Katy says. "Fuck." When she answers the phone, it's Veronica's voice on the other end, though I can't quite make out the words.

Katy does a lot of nodding, a smile plastered on her face even though Veronica can't see her here. "Of course," she says at least three times. "Yes, and I'm so sorry."

When she hangs up, she turns to me.

"What did she want?" I ask.

Anger flickers in her expression, and for a moment I think we're about to go another round because I've had the audacity to ask a question. But she just shakes her head finally and says, "Veronica wants to give you a chance to apologize. So dinner tonight at the mansion is back on, and you *will* apologize for eavesdropping, and we *will* nod, and we *will* smile, and we *will* act like everything is fine. We will not accuse, and we will not ask any questions that *sound* like accusations. Then tomorrow, I told your dad to come pick you up, and you will never come back here. Never. Are we clear, Lucy?"

"Crystal," I say quietly.

"Good," she says. "One more thing."

She holds something out to me.

"Mom?"

"This one," Katy says, closing my fingers around the small black canister, "is Mace. It's a stream, not spray, so your aim will have to be a bit more precise if you want it to truly be effective. Just in case. And this"—she holds out something else—"is a Taser. Don't tase yourself by accident. Do you know how to use these?"

"I—I can figure it out?" I say in a voice that sounds more than a little wobbly. If this situation wasn't so dire, I'd have energy to be a little offended that she offers the Mace and the Taser with so many disclaimers, but 1) she's right and I *might* accidentally tase myself and I *can't* actually aim a stream of Mace, and 2) there are more pressing problems right now.

Like dinner with Haeter Lake's scariest family and an apology I don't mean.

"Good," she says, nodding her head firmly. "Good. Keep it on you, all right?"

"No?" I push myself off the bed, the Taser in one hand and the Mace in the other. "*No*, Mom, it's not all right."

But Katy doesn't wait for me to answer. She doesn't wait for anything.

She just turns and walks away, her shoulders curled in a little as if she's lost something important. And then she gets in her Jeep, and she's just gone, and I feel like I've lost something important, too.

I plop down onto the motel bed, which creaks angrily in response.

Well, I'm all alone at the murder motel, and Katy just had a breakdown in front of me because of what I did, so things aren't great. But on the bright side, I have my phone, a Taser, and Mace. Only one of which I know how to use.

And I have my little notepad full of information on this case, plus the pictures from the library.

My phone doesn't have service out here, not a single bar, and I wouldn't risk texting Audrey, in case she's still making her way out of the Anselm house.

So I gather all the courage I have and set out down the gravel road toward town. Walking. On foot. By the murder motel, through the forest that looks like it might want to swallow me whole.

And I'm sorry that I scared Katy as bad as I did. I'm sorry that I hurt her. I'm sorry that she's overwhelmed and sad. After all this is done, I'm going to find a way to make it up to her.

But right now, I have a case to solve. I have grandparents to find, and pieces of myself to recover from this small town that has cannibalized so much of Katy and me. I have Audrey's name to clear. And I am detective Katherine Preston's daughter.

Besides, Audrey needs me to be brave.

And maybe, just maybe, that's something I know how to do for her.

CHAPTER 16

AUDREY
12:14 P.M.

FOR A LONG MOMENT, I THOUGHT GUS WOULD shove me back through the closet toward his family and the cops. But then he slides the door quietly shut and I follow him through the long, narrow corridors, past old wood and spiderwebs and over creaking floorboards that threaten to reveal us. I am drenched with sweat, both from the heat of the cramped space and from the anxiety that has been swirling through my body like a tornado.

I send Sundress a text that says, *I'm out.*

And then I tiptoe down the stairs, both Gus and I straining for sounds of the family. When I finally reach the hallway to their in-home theater, he stops, his arm braced on the hallway between me and the exit.

"I—" He opens his mouth and then shuts it again.

The sound of Veronica descending the stairs breaks the silence, and Gus looks as if he is deciding.

Whether he believes I am innocent. Whether he is going to turn me in. Whether the friendship we once had means anything to him now.

And then he steps out of my way, the look in his eyes sad. "Run," he says.

And I do.

The shame follows me as I go, because they didn't sell me out, even though I have given them both half-truths this whole time. And Gus had to find out from eavesdropping in Veronica Anselm's closet.

Not your best move, Nelson.

I sprint across the backyard, my hood up over my face, covering as much of my face as possible, though at this point I am more concerned with just escaping than I am with escaping unseen.

Because if they found me in that house, what would they do to me? If they thought I knew something I shouldn't, would they take me out to the abandoned amusement park? Would I fall like Pierce or die like my dad? Would Veronica shoot me with her pistol and leave me in the woods?

There are so many ways for them to kill me.

There are so many ways to die here.

I reach the tree line and I keep running. Running.

Branches whip my face like they did on Thursday night when I ran through the forest away from the park. Pine needles and half-rotten leaves and branches beneath my feet.

Friday night.

When I saw Pierce Anselm's body fall.

When I wasn't sure if I was horrified or sad or relieved.

A birch tree cuts a long line down my face, tracing my cheekbone like a claw.

I keep running, and I don't think I'll ever, ever stop.

When I reach my bike, I ride until I can't feel my legs.

Out of Haeter Lake, south away from town toward Knoxville, and then back again, looping around town.

Ride until I can't feel anything else.

I finally get off my bike at the cemetery, overshadowed as it is by the nearby roller coaster.

I swear I can hear Dad, though I can't bear to go closer to his gravestone this time.

Audrey Nadine. His voice would be so gentle. *My wanderer. Can I keep you company?*

Because he did. Because he wasn't ever scared of my worst. Because he would sit next to me when I was angry or sad and just wait until the emotions had run their course.

Because he's gone, and all the good things I ever had evaporated with him. They're buried here.

I sit down in the damp grass near the cemetery gate; for how long, I don't know.

It's the buzz of my phone that finally jars me back to the mossy earth and parade of tombstones and darkening afternoon sky.

Lucy has texted.

I'm going to the park.

You don't have to come.

I don't expect you to come.

It has always been waiting for me.

I have to face it.

I will have to face it today, and again after that, and maybe again after that.

If I do not, it will remain in my dreams for the rest of my life.

So I text her back.

I'll pick you up.

I pick her up on the dirt road to the motel.

She's walking, determination on her face, though she looks exhausted.

"Took you long enough," she says. She manages a smile.

I don't.

I offer her a hand, and she climbs on, sucking in a sharp breath.

That's the only vestige left of her fear, though. That, and she wraps her arms around me so tight I can hardly breathe.

"You were going the wrong way," I offer.

"What?"

"Park's that way," I tell her. "Remember that first day? I was going to go down that path and see if I could find anything at the park to clear my mom's name. Remember?"

Her arms tighten again, though this time it feels like she's trying to hug me, trying to offer some comfort. "Would you really have gone?" she asks.

"Maybe," I answer. "I was trying to be brave."

"You're always brave," Lucy tells me.

We are silent for a moment, and then she asks, "Are we going that way now?"

A smile tugs at my mouth. "No," I say. "No, we don't have to walk through the forest. Don't worry. I figure I don't care if the Anselms see that I'm poking around this time. Let them know I'm coming for them."

I start my bike, and then its familiar roar covers up any further conversation.

Lucy's arms are tight around my belly, and I am grateful for their comfort. I am.

But if she could see the inside of my mind, the dark corners that I try so hard to hide, would she stay? Or would she drift slowly away like every other friend I had after Dad died? Would she leave, too?

I keep my hand on her thigh to steady her, to steady me.

I take a breath, deep as I know how. And then I turn down the road that will lead me toward the darkness I tried so hard to forget.

The road winds deeper into the forest, the shadows growing longer above our heads.

"The librarian said they drained the lake for this," Lucy says suddenly, as if she's only just remembered, nearly shouting to be heard above the sound of my motorcycle.

I don't respond.

Before the accident, Haeter Lake drew all sorts of visitors from Knoxville, or even from other folks who were road-tripping through our state to get to Nashville or past it, to the coast.

And before the Anselm Amusement Park empire started in the open space just north of town, there was a lake, vast and blue and unfathomable. I've only seen the lake in pictures, but I can imagine the stillness, the occasional ripples. The lake is long gone, and now—now so is Pierce, with my dad and Lucy's grandparents and Mr. Joyce, the librarian who was always kind to me.

What was it like then, the thick unending forest and then the sudden break in the trees, still lake waters shining beneath the sun?

They took that, too, I realize.

The Anselms.

They were like Veronica and Blake stomping through the forest, crushing anything beneath their feet because they didn't care to tread carefully.

I can picture it before we arrive: the way everything in the park slopes slightly down at first, then sharper, pulling you, down, down until you reach the roller coaster at the center. They killed the lake to build it— drained and dammed and destroyed, because that family destroys every-thing it touches. *Pierce* destroyed everything he touched, right up until the moment he finally got what he deserved.

The Anselms didn't care about what they crushed, not even when it was my family and Lucy's beneath their feet.

We round another bend in the road, and then it stretches out before us, a vast, sprawling dead thing that makes my stomach drop all the way down to my toes.

It was only closed a few years ago, but already the forest is trying to reclaim what used to be her territory. The parking lot is wide and eerily empty, a place made for perhaps hundreds of cars.

The park used to bring all sorts of visitors off the main highway—we used to have other tourist attractions, too. At the far end of the park-ing lot stands a weathered gate, its hinges rusted. A padlock holds it shut, but there is a gap in the fence just a bit farther down that a person could easily slip through.

I pull the key from the ignition and hop off, offering Sundress a hand without really glancing at her.

She takes it, leaning hard on me. "Are you okay?" she asks.

I nod tightly, scuffing the toe of my boot against the pavement beneath our feet. I'm sure it used to be smooth, but now I can't remember what it looked like, and tree roots are already buckling the pavement in places, pushing up beneath the cement. Give this place a few more years, and the forest will swallow all but the memory of it.

Beyond the gates, the abandoned amusement park is brightly lit beneath the sun. The space slopes down, just like the lake it used to be. The land drops off sharply after the ticket booth, the path leading downward past empty sheds that probably sold kettle corn or cotton candy.

Beyond it, at the center of the park, the roller coaster looms, twisting toward the sky like the skeleton of a falling monster.

I shiver.

The sight is all wrong: everything around us cloaked in the shadow of the forest, except the sun beating down on the rusting metal of the roller coaster.

"That's where he died," I say dully. I pull my hand away from Lucy.

"Pierce?" she whispers.

"My dad," I answer. My voice sounds distant, even to me. "We were on the roller coaster. Me and Mom and Dad. Something went wrong with his seat while we were all upside down. He fell, and his seat belt caught him by the neck."

"Oh my god," she whispers. "Audrey. I'm so sorry."

"They said he died right away," I continue. I am standing still in the center of the path beside the ticket booth, my eyes fixed on the metal beast before us.

Around us, the whole place is silent except for the whisper of branches at the border of the park. The occasional flutter of wings. The brush of dead vines on worn buildings.

"They were wrong. It took eighty-eight seconds," I continue finally. "I remember. I remember every single second." A shudder runs through my body from head to toe.

"My god," Lucy says softly.

"And then we had to finish the ride," I say finally. "Mom was screaming the whole time, and the people behind us were, too. They could see it happen. But I . . . I just sat there and stared at Dad. I couldn't do anything. I couldn't do anything at all."

For a moment, Lucy looks like she's going to try to say something comforting, but I can't—I can't.

Then she steps forward instead, wraps her arms around me, and pulls me close. My body trembles, but I don't make a single sound, just let her hold me as the shadows lengthen all around us.

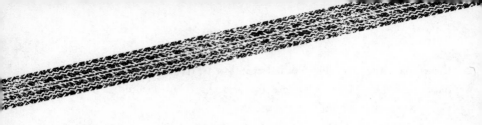

CHAPTER 17

LUCY

4:17 P.M.

I DON'T KNOW HOW LONG WE STAND THERE, BUT the shadow of the roller coaster falls across us as the sun dips lower toward the tree line. I don't know at what point Audrey's grief seeps out of her body straight into mine, but at some point I find that my whole chest aches with it.

With her.

With this place, where my grandparents died.

Asa and Marie. Marie and Asa.

Above us, the sky is still cloudless, but the sun does not seem to reach through the thick trees.

Was the sky this blue the day my grandmother fell to her death here? Marie.

The thought nearly knocks me to my knees.

Mine, and I never knew them. They never knew me.

I am not as close to my grief as Audrey is to hers, but the grief is there all the same. Grief and anger, too, anger that has been here, waiting for me to find it. And I do. I find it on a cracked cement path overtaken by weeds, under the shadow of a forgotten carousel, moss growing over the wide, staring eyes of the horses.

"Do you want to look around?" Audrey asks me finally, her voice muted. "I'm sorry—" Her voice cracks.

"Do you want to wait at your bike?" I summon all the bravery I have. "It's okay if you don't want to do this. It is."

Audrey tilts her head to one side, the barest teasing smile clinging to her lips. "You're okay being here by yourself?" she asks.

I square my shoulders. "Audrey Nadine," I say. "I can do this myself." I pull the notepad from the pocket of my dress. "I can be brave."

She snorts, a sound I'm growing increasingly enamored with. "You are brave," she says. "But I am, too. I can do this."

She reaches out and takes my hand in hers, threading her fingers through mine. "Together?" she asks.

"Together."

The path steepens as we reach the roller coaster. I glance around, take in the other rides. The spinning teacups are frozen forever, paint peeling, the ghost of the last customers' laughs clinging to the wind. One of the cups groans gently, shifting on its rusted wheels.

We move past the carousel, where the faded horses creak in the wind, staring at us out of age-blackened eyes. The ones covered with moss are worse, hiding their faces from us. At the base, in the long brown grass of last year, something rustles.

I bite back a scream.

"A squirrel," Audrey soothes. But her hand is still slick with sweat.

It rustles again, and I see it.

Yellow eyes. Narrow. Watching us. Brown fur. A few sharp teeth. Too large to be a squirrel, I think? Its fur is strangely matted.

But it's gone before I can be sure.

I force myself to keep walking, another step forward and then another.

For my grandparents Asa and Marie. For Audrey and Langley and for Audrey's dad. For my mom. And for Arthur, who was kind, who was caught up in all this somehow, who died because of a rich family and their park.

"Do we know where he fell?" I ask Audrey. "Pierce?"

"Base of the roller coaster," she answers. "Heard Cliff and Veronica discussing it after you were dragged away and before Gus and I got out. How was your mom, by the way?"

"More scared than mad," I say. Katy's reminder to trust no one echoes in my head.

The Taser Katy pressed into my hand, and the Mace after it.

The tear tracks on Katy's face.

Did she mean Audrey, too, when she said *trust no one*?

Because I'm holding Audrey's hand in mine.

"Really?" Audrey drags her gaze away from the roller coaster and looks at me. "I heard her when she pulled you out of the closet. She seemed pissed."

"She was," I say. "But I expected it to be a lot worse. She's really just scared of Veronica Anselm, I think."

"Everyone is scared of Veronica," Audrey says.

"Not you," I say.

"Well," she says. "There isn't much more she can take from me."

We reach the base of the roller coaster, and Audrey goes dead still beside me.

It is a horrendous thing, gaunt steel that groans against the wind, rust stealing its way up from the damp earth, reddening the bars that still glint in the dying sun.

At the base, there is a red stain on the concrete. I can see the moment when Audrey notices it. She gags and stumbles.

This time, it is my turn to catch her.

We don't stay long, after that.

There's too much death here, too close to both of us.

So I snap some pictures to add to our shared case file on the cloud later, and then I take Audrey's hand and we walk back to her bike.

The walk feels long, though the park isn't as big as some I've visited. Something—another squirrel, maybe?—runs down the old carnival piano in the distance, strange, discordant notes sounding here and there as it does.

"Are you gonna be okay?" I ask Audrey, and she just... doesn't answer.

Instead, she stares back behind us at the Tilt-A-Whirl forever off kilter, at the corpse of a lake warped by a family who wanted too much for their own.

She drops me off at the motel, tucks a strand of hair behind my ear, and says she has to go ride for a while.

"Can I see you tomorrow?" I ask hesitantly.

"Of course, Sundress."

And then she leaves, and I'm alone, poring over all that we know, all that we don't, Katy's assurance that the Anselms would never have killed their own, despite what Curtis experienced, that Veronica who said *anything for family* would never have murdered her husband.

LUCY. 6:45 P.M.

Katy arrives in the evening, her eyes still haunted with fear and worry the way they were when she left me here. "I'm sorry I was gone so long," she says. "Come on. We're going to Veronica's for supper."

"Did you learn anything?" I ask, looking down at the floor. "About— about Arthur?"

Katy runs a hand down her face, pinching the bridge of her nose. "I learned that my daughter won't leave well enough alone."

I scuff my toe against the floor. "He was so nice to me," I tell her. "Yesterday? When you left me there? He was kind."

Katy looks at me wearily. "I'm sure he was," she says finally. "All right. The medical examiner ruled it a homicide, Lucy. You won't get more details from me or Cliff or anyone else you ask, so leave it alone."

She turns on her heel and walks out of the motel, and I trail after, thinking of the kind, wrinkled face looking at me from across stacks of books.

Arthur didn't deserve this.

Neither did any of the rest of us.

The ride up into the mountains is much smoother in Katy's Jeep than it was on Audrey's bike. And while I may not have much sense, I do have the good sense not to comment on that.

Katy is still frigid, speaking in monosyllables.

We pass the turnoff to the amusement park, and I suppress a shudder.

I want to tell Katy that while I'm angry, it isn't that I'm angry at her, not entirely. I want to tell her that I know why she loves this family, why she left them, why she fears them. Or at least I know the beginning of it now.

But we have to go and face them, and pretend it's all fine and normal, and now doesn't seem like the time to burden Katy any more than I already have. Or maybe, maybe I'm too angry to fix it for her this time. Maybe I'm not sure I know how to do that.

"Are you okay?" she asks me finally as we pull up to the gate.

I nod quickly. "Yeah," I say. "A little nervous? I think I should probably apologize to Veronica."

Katy's eyebrows shoot up. "You *think*?" She shakes her head. "You know that regardless of the circumstance or reason or the person in question, I would make you apologize for breaking into someone's house. Do you understand that, young lady?"

I redden. "I mean," I say, "yeah. Of course. But also I could apologize for lecturing her about the case? If that would help you?"

"It's not your job to worry about me," Katy says. "But it *is* your job to apologize for breaking and entering. How *did* you do that, by the way?" She is trying very hard not to sound *too* interested in my answer, but I hear curiosity in her voice. Maybe even a tiny bit of pride.

"Picked the lock," I say. "I saw a YouTube video on it once."

"Of course you did." She sighs as the gates slide open in front of us. "Well, that's a skill that takes a lot of practice, so it's concerning that you were able to do it today so easily. Is there anything else I should know about? Any other cases I've worked on where you've hidden in the closet and eavesdropped?"

I make an executive decision not to tell her about the Fallwell case. Which was interesting, damn it. But Katy doesn't need to know about the hiding-in-the-vent thing.

We pull up in front of the mansion, and I shrug. "Must have been beginner's luck. How do *you* know anything about lock picking?"

Katy grins, maybe for the first time today.

I follow her up to the doorstep. "I don't usually come in this way," I comment before I can stop myself.

The corner of Katy's mouth twitches, but she just turns away from me and knocks on the heavy oak door.

A woman in a black-and-white uniform opens the door and ushers us inside.

She takes our coats and then leads us through the ornate entryway, past twin lion statues.

"The family is in the dining room," the housekeeper says. Her voice is barely more than monotone, her expression neutral and blank. "Shall I show you in?"

"Oh, Katy, darling," Veronica's voice floats through the hall, and then she enters.

She is wearing a black silk dress and a gauzy black wrap. Her silver hair is twisted around her head like a crown.

She looks down at me, one perfect eyebrow arched.

"Hi, Mrs. Anselm," I say. "Um, I'm sorry. I'm sorry I hid in your closet earlier? That was rude of me. I was curious about the case, but that's no excuse."

I had rehearsed the words in my head and practiced not telling her I think she's a horrible murderous bitch. If Audrey were here—

I stop the thought.

Veronica nods once, though her eyes are still a little bit cool. "I should have expected Katy's daughter to be rambunctious," she says. "I'm sure you were just . . . emotional. Well, come in, dear. Have you met my son yet? He's here for supper."

Veronica Anselm leads us into the dining room, and a flood of longing washes over me.

How many times did Katy walk through this hall as a kid—as a new orphan? How many meals did she eat with them? Was she always scared of them?

Does she love them anyway? Even after what Veronica tried to do to her?

Curtis looks at me, barely hiding his smile. "Oh, *she's* the kid you found hiding in the closet?" He looks as if he's trying not to laugh. "Hi, Lucy."

Katy's gaze snaps to mine, confusion and then something darker crackling in her eyes. "Oh," she says softly. "I didn't realize you two had met."

Blake looks at me out of those ice-blue eyes, her expression perfectly calm. "Your daughter seems to have many plans of her own these days," she says, but the look she gives me is very interested.

Curtis shoulders forward, looking very different from the man I met in the library—now he's wearing a button-up and dress shoes, his hair tied neatly back at the base of his neck. On his hand is a gold band around his ring finger. "Katy." He smiles at her. He has the same smile as Gus, charming and wide, full of perfect, straight teeth.

Gus is watching it all unfold carefully, his eyes wide.

Curtis kisses Katy's cheek and then hugs her, and she lets him. Returns the hug, even.

He's kind and charismatic and funny until he's not, she had said, though she's hugging him now. *He's smart and pretty and good until he's not.*

He's smiling at her, something that should be friendly, something that *is* friendly but unsettles me anyway.

He turns to me.

"Hello again, Lucy." His eyes twinkle at me as if we are old friends.

"I'm glad we get to meet again over dinner. I can't believe Katy kept you from us all this time."

I laugh nervously and glance over at Gus, who is grinning.

"They're all jealous that I got to meet you first," he says, his look knowing.

Blake holds out a hand to shake mine, though, her grip firm. "Good to see you again. And so glad you decided to use the front door this time," she adds dryly.

Something flashes in her eyes as she turns to Mom. Like Curtis, she kisses Mom on the cheek. "Sit with me," Blake says, her hand lingering in Katy's.

What were they like as teenagers growing up in this mansion side by side? Somehow I can't imagine Blake ever being a kid.

Or Katy, for that matter, even now that I've seen the picture of her, wide-eyed and small, in the old newspaper, and heard the stories about Gatorade bottles and break-ins and the night that almost ruined her.

Katy jerks her head to the chair on the other side of her and drops into the high-backed mahogany seat. She smiles at Veronica as we take our seats at the long dining table.

"Our chef had the lobster brought in fresh," Veronica says. "Lucille, do you like lobster?" She lifts a long, serrated knife and smiles at me with perfect, even teeth.

"Um," I say. "Yes?" I glance at Katy beside me.

We lost our family to these people.

Katy's smile is frozen on her face. Her hand rests on the sleeve of her blazer, hovering over the tattoo beneath.

Memento vitae.

I lift my knife, too, and I meet Veronica's eyes.

She smiles at me, and this, only this, makes Mom shift.

She lifts her knife. Pauses, knife in hand, and looks first at me and then at Veronica. "Veronica," she says softly. "I'm so glad you invited us. I hope we can move forward from the unfortunate nonsense of this afternoon." Her eyes find mine, the expression a very clear message to *apologize.*

"Of course," I say. "I'm—like, I said. Yeah. Very sorry. It was rude of me."

"I am sure you're curious," Curtis says easily. "After all, your family is as much a part of this as ours is."

Blake's hand clenches over her own knife, her wedding ring clicking gently against the steel. *"Ours?"* she asks icily. "Did you want to be an Anselm again, then?"

I look at Gus, seated next to me in one of the high-backed dining chairs, who is staring down at his plate.

Impulsively, I reach over and place my hand on his arm beneath the table, squeezing it gently before I let go. I haven't ever grieved someone like this—I grieve my grandparents now, but it's not quite the same—and I can't quite imagine doing it while my family tears itself apart.

"I wasn't the one who changed the locks," Curtis shoots back, his eyes firmly on Blake now. "Or told someone to stay away from their own damn kid."

Gus's head snaps up, and mine does, too.

This is news to him, apparently. That Curtis was pushed out of this family so firmly.

"That might have had more to do with me," Katy says. Her eyes meet mine, giving me the smallest shake of her head, perhaps a message not to involve myself. She has a light in her eyes now, that sharp, hungry look she gets when she's *close* in a case, when she's about to crack something open and get the answers she's been waiting for.

And for the first time I think maybe she still *is* in control. Maybe she still is investigating the way she always does. Maybe the timidity—at least some of it—has been almost a cover.

The doorbell chimes pleasantly before anyone can respond to Katy.

"Who the fuck," Blake says, enunciating each word with a polite but firm jab to the food on her plate, "is it *now?*"

"Blake, please," Veronica cuts in. She gives Blake a look not too different from the one Katy sometimes gives me. "I invited Cliff, remember?"

"Who's next?" Blake asks. "Shall we also invite the entire sheriff's department? Maybe Curtis's band?"

"It's a musical adventure experience," Curtis says, grinning when Blake's face reddens further.

Gus meets my eyes for the first time, masking a snort with a cough. "I'll get the door," he says.

"No, Lucy and I will," Blake says. "Come on, Lucy."

"You need help opening a door?" Curtis says. His eyes are hard, the mischievous twinkle of a moment ago evaporating.

The doorbell chimes again.

"Oh, for heaven's sake," Veronica says. "Must *I* get the door?"

"You did send your housekeeper home early," Blake says.

Curtis snorts. "God's sake."

I set down my knife. "I'm on it."

I leave them all behind glaring daggers at each other while Katy watches them with a look that is careful but also somehow eager. I disappear down the long hallway, only to realize Curtis is at my heels.

"I'm sorry," he says. "I made an excuse about needing my sweater that I'm sure no one believes."

"Um," I say. "Should I let the sheriff in?"

It has begun to drizzle again, and I do consider leaving Cliff out in the rain for a bit longer, but Curtis is uncomfortably close to me now. *He's good until he's not.*

The smile on his face makes the hair at the back of my neck stand up now. *He's friendly until he's not.*

Curtis backs up as soon as he sees my look. "Sorry," he says again. "My family—I'm sorry you're caught up in this. You can see what they think of me. But there's something I think you should know about my father."

"I—" My back is pressed against the wall now. "What should I know?"

"Why I came back," Curtis says softly. "He wanted to make amends, in the end. He sent me a letter and then a text. I asked if I could apologize and we could talk, and we had a phone call—just one."

"Have you told the police?" I ask shakily. And if he hasn't, why *me*?

"I told Cliff," Curtis answers. "But my mother and sister—they didn't agree with my father's decision. They—"

"*Curtis,*" Veronica's voice cuts him off. She's at the end of the hallway, suspicion on her face, though quickly masked by that same polite smile. "I need your help bringing in dessert."

"No one wants dessert." Blake's voice echoes from behind Veronica. "It's okay, Mom."

I pull open the door.

Water is dripping from the brim of Cliff's hat—the one with the sheriff's badge on it—and he takes it off and nods to me. "Hi there, Lucy-Luce," he says as easily as if he really does know me, so well we're on a nickname basis.

"Hi, Cliffy-Cliff," I respond. "You should invest in an umbrella."

Curtis snorts but reaches past me to shake Cliff's hand. "Glad you could make it, my friend," he says.

Now *this* is an interesting development. Officer Bad Vibes being friends with the black sheep of the Anselm family?

Curtis waves us in down the hall, and when we rejoin the others at the table, Veronica is placing dessert next to Katy.

Katy nods to Cliff. "Cliff."

"Katy."

Cliff kisses Veronica on the cheek before he sits down, and then he lifts his knife and looks around the table at us.

I lift my knife, too, just because it seems like everyone at the Champagne Problems table is into clutching utensils tightly. All my life, I've been good at reading the emotions in a particular room, because I had to get so good at reading Katy's—what annoys her, what would be too much for her, what would be too overwhelming or loud and make her shut down and send me out.

And okay, sometimes I use that ability to be helpful.

And other times I use that to be a pain in the ass. Because when you can see the tense emotions swirling around you, you can either choose to be helpful and patch up the situation or you can decide to tug on a string and see what happens.

Ever since I saw my grandmother's dark eyes staring back at me from that picture in the newspaper, I've wanted to keep choosing the second option.

"So," I say, my voice just as calmly polite as everyone else's. All around me are sharp, serrated knives, the Anselms with their perfect, straight teeth and identical ice-blue eyes; a sheriff whose loyalty I cannot be sure of; and a mother I'm not sure I know at all. "Terrible what happened to poor Mr. Joyce at the library."

Blake makes a soft noise in her throat, and all eyes turn to me.

"Yes, of course," Veronica says. "How terrible."

"We had just spoken that day," Curtis says. He's watching Veronica carefully.

Blake is watching him, and Gus is trying and failing to hide that he's watching both of them.

Cliff is looking at his plate.

And Mom is watching him.

"It's so shocking," I continue, because that anger beating against my rib cage is pushing harder and harder, and it says push harder still. "To have two horrible crimes happen in such a small, safe town."

Katy's eyes snap to mine.

"We probably shouldn't discuss any of the details while we're here," Cliff says mildly. "But yes, what a terrible situation."

"It seems like he was such an important part of this town," I say. Katy is watching me intently, but I find that the anger wants to burst out of me at her, too. "Not that I know anything about Haeter Lake, of course." I laugh lightly, like this is funny, like I'm being polite, like I could fit into this horrible family and this horrible place. "Since my mom never talked about you all."

Blake's eyes turn on Katy, who shakes her head slightly.

"I'm sure we talked about it from time to time," Katy says, waving one hand in dismissal.

"Tea?" Veronica says in a choked voice. "Lucy, maybe you can help me bring it in?"

I follow her into the kitchen, Katy's eyes digging into my back as I go. The second the kitchen door shuts behind us, Veronica settles a hand on my shoulder. "This must be so hard for you, sweetie," she says. Her voice is soft, coaxing, her head tilted to look at me. It would sound almost *safe* if I hadn't heard so much from Audrey—and even from Curtis—about the kind of coldness she's capable of. "I just wanted you to know that if you have any questions, or want to talk about this with anyone, you can tell me."

"What should I tell you about?" I ask innocently, taking the teacups she hands me.

That voice in my head is pulsing louder, and it's saying *Push harder* and *Break, break, break it all*. I am named for my grandmother. My family was stolen from me. I have no history and no one who knows me. I am alone in this house with its secret passageways and painful history and a family who could be mine but isn't.

"You're going through so much," Veronica says. "I'm sure your mother tries to keep you from the gruesome details, but as you know—" Her voice cracks, and for one moment she looks like the grieving widow she is. "My husband died so horribly. And whatever you've had to hear about it all must be so upsetting."

"I heard about Grant Nelson," I say.

The teacups rattle in her hands, just for a second. "Oh?" she says softly.

"Yes," I tell her, squaring my shoulders the way I imagine my grandmother doing. Fearsome women.

"My son seems to have been chattering away about the family," Veronica says pleasantly. "But his version is always a bit... well, one-sided, so if you have any questions, I thought I'd make myself available, dear."

"Are you asking me to tell you what Curtis told me?" I ask her bluntly.

You're here to apologize.

But I don't have any left. Not apologies or the same caution I've clung to all my life.

Fury wraps itself around my rib cage, so tight I can hardly breathe. I am not a toy to be played with, a piece in a complex game the Anselms are playing with one another. And neither is my family.

"Veronica," I begin, "I—"

And then the door swings open, and Cliff is there, smiling genially. "Thought I could help carry everything," he says. "Come on, Lucy."

What is with everyone in this house trying to interrupt each other? Does *no one* here trust one another?

I follow them both back into the dining room, where Katy is talking to Blake about something very innocuous—I catch something about high school graduation.

When we sit down again, Gus makes his own attempt at keeping the conversation from turning south. "What was the wildest thing you all did together?" he asks. "Back when you were young?"

"Oh, your father was a bit too busy to do much with his own family," Blake answers, her eyes still shooting daggers at Curtis.

Curtis grins back at her, though his eyes are crackling with anger. "And you were too busy trying to use Katy and Langley for your own bitchy ends. When we—"

"No one used me," Katy cuts him off in a voice that is so deadly I stop to look at her. "I don't regret a single one of the choices I made."

I have never heard that tone.

Not even the time I was out all night on our trip to San Antonio with a bunch of kids who were three years older than me.

But I can be fearsome, too. Fearsome and fed up.

"Of course not," I say. "Not even the one you made not to tell your own daughter anything about our past."

Katy takes in a sharp breath as if I have struck her. "Lucille," she says warningly.

But it's too late.

I'm being unfair, I know I am, and that this is hard for her, probably impossible, and that she didn't deserve the way the Anselms treated her. But it's all spilling over now.

"Let the girl speak," Blake said. "I, for one, am curious, since we can't seem to get through dinner without half a dozen private conversations occurring. I think some honesty would be good for this family."

I snort. "When have *any* of you been honest?"

It's too late now. I'm not Katy. I can't mask for these people, or pretend I'm not furious with them, or with myself somehow, or with her. God, with *her*.

"I don't know which of them you're investigating for all the murders," I say sharply, pushing back my chair, "but good luck, Mom. Have fun with your family."

I stand.

Knives rattle and teacups shake and instead of the easygoing, good-natured girl I am supposed to be, I am a whole fucking earthquake.

And then I walk out that door and leave them all behind, down the driveway in the dark toward the forest, and the looming park beyond, and the graveyard where my family is buried.

DAY FOUR: MONDAY, MARCH 25

CHAPTER 18

AUDREY

12:07 A.M.

AS SOON AS I GOT HOME FROM THE PARK, I stretched out on my narrow bed in the little bedroom. I have been here for hours now, staring at the pockmarked ceiling, unable to sleep.

Mom got home late from her shift, only about an hour ago, and I heard her puttering around the kitchen and then the sound of her bedroom door, so close to mine I can hear every sound she makes in our little trailer home.

It's late—I'm not sure how late—when there's a knock at the door.

It's Lucy, looking desperately out of place in our little trailer park, her hair wild, her eyes hard with anger. "Hi," she says. "Can I come in?"

I nod and step out of the way.

Mom emerges from her room, but she takes in Lucy's state with one glance and then just nods her head. "I'll make some tea."

"I'm fine," Lucy says.

Mom doesn't say anything; just fills the kettle anyway and sets to work.

"Did you walk all this way?" I ask Lucy.

She has the same look in her eyes as I had in the park earlier today.

She shakes her head. "I walked down the road and hitched a ride," she says, and then she looks a little like herself again because she shudders. "Her car was gross and she smelled like peppermints. Which I *hate*."

I step forward and wrap my arms around her tightly.

"Does your mom know where you are, honey?" Mom asks, pushing a mug of tea into Lucy's hands.

All our mugs are mismatched—the sunflower-yellow one I loved when I was little and refuse to let Mom throw out now, even though the corner is chipped, the Christmas one Mom insists on keeping out year-round, the Tallahassee one Dad brought back from an airport on his last business trip because it was so ugly it was funny.

Lucy is holding the sunflower-yellow one tightly, her hands trembling. "No," she says finally. "I think she's been calling me."

"I'm going to let her know you're staying the night," Mom says firmly. "Audrey? You make sure she has what she needs? There are extra blankets in my closet."

I nod and tug Lucy with me toward my room. Usually, I'm conscious of just how *small* the space we live in is, even sometimes when my friend Chris is over, but Lucy looks so small and shaken that I don't have time to think about it.

"Hey," I say firmly. "Sundress, look at me."

She shrinks into herself, shoulders hunched.

"Lucy."

Her eyes find mine.

"Stay with me," I tell her.

A tear tracks down her cheek, and impulsively, I reach out and brush it away.

"Come on," I tell her. "Let's rest. Tomorrow will suck less."

Lucy crawls into bed next to me, curling into the crook of my arm, and we lie there together for what feels like forever.

"Curtis wanted to make amends," she says finally.

I sit up slightly in the darkness. "What?"

"He wanted to make amends," she repeats softly. "With his dad. Does that change everything? Or anything? I don't know anything anymore."

"Shh," I tell her, though my mind is spinning at this revelation, spinning toward possibilities about Blake, or even Veronica, about power and inheritance. Lucy goes quiet against me, her body growing heavy in sleep, and I lean my head against hers.

My eyes are finally drifting shut, when I hear a slam of metal on metal, and then a crunch.

From outside.

Not in our little home.

Outside, something, *someone* outside.

I sit straight up and pull the curtain that functions as my bedroom door aside. "Mom?" I croak into the darkness. "Is that you?"

She's at my shoulder suddenly, her hand firm on my arm. "I heard it," she says quietly. She switches on the flashlight in her hand. In her other hand is a kitchen knife.

Lucy lets out a small scream, clapping her hand over her mouth.

"Do you sleep with that thing?" I hiss.

"Go back in your room." Mom's voice is quiet, deadly, and it chills me to the core.

"Mom," I protest.

"Now," she whispers. "I'm sure it's just a raccoon."

But she wouldn't have the kitchen knife in her hand if she thought that, not really.

"Should I call the police?" I ask, my voice wobbling just a little.

She hesitates and then nods.

I dial the police—really, it's just Cliff and the deputy, Annika.

Cliff answers, because we don't have a dispatcher for Haeter Lake. Or anywhere in this county, probably. "Hello?" He sounds sleepy. And grumpy.

"It's Audrey," I say. "Audrey Nelson."

"Audrey?" he asks. "Is everything okay?"

Our door creaks open, and then the screen door slams.

Please be okay, I think as Mom disappears.

"Um, I think someone's outside our house," I say, reality sinking in as I say the words out loud. My voice is shakier as I continue. "Can you—can you please come? *Now?*"

And that's when Mom screams.

Lucy is huddled at my shoulder, and her scream echoes Mom's.

I race outside, my motorcycle keys clenched in my fist like a knife.

But no one is outside but Mom, her face haggard in the sickly light of our lone streetlight. "Get back inside," she snaps when she sees me, keys still clenched in my fist.

"Are you okay?" I ask breathlessly. "I heard you *scream*, Mom. I couldn't just—"

She points inside, but her eyes are fixed on the wall of our house, and I turn to look.

There, in bloodred letters, bleeding down the side of our house, are the words:

YOU'RE NEXT.

The *R* in the middle is running down the metal siding of our house. It's as if our home is bleeding.

Fuck.

Fuck.

Someone was here, just now, painting this just a few feet away from where Mom and I and Lucy slept. But who the fuck would do this?

For the second time in twenty-four hours, I'm trembling violently.

"Inside," Mom repeats, raising her hand to point at the door. Her hand is shaking, too. "Now."

I do as I'm told, Lucy at my heels again, but Mom doesn't follow.

I watch her, framed beneath the dying yellow glow of our streetlight, her brown hair curling loose over her shoulders, the kitchen knife still clenched in her fist.

And then a few minutes later, she's framed by flashing red-and-blue lights as Cliff pulls up in front of her.

He surveys it all—the message, Mom, the knife, and Lucy and me pressed against the window.

Is he thinking of what Mom told Pierce Anselm last year?

I'd rather watch you die.

I think of Pierce Anselm's body falling toward the concrete.

I squeeze my eyes shut until I can block it out.

Lucy places a hesitant hand on my arm, and I'm so focused on shutting out the images in my memory that I jump at the touch.

Outside, Mom and Cliff talk for a few minutes, and then Cliff takes a few pictures. Finally, he puts a hand on Mom's arm as if he's trying to reassure her.

"I wish I knew what he was saying," I mutter.

Beside me, Lucy is focusing intently. "Shh," she says in that bossy tone I have begun to find so endearing.

"Can you hear them?" I ask in amazement.

"I can lip-read," she says, biting her lip as she concentrates. "If I try really hard. He said something about *her history* and maybe *plea for attention*. I couldn't focus on the rest when you were talking."

No.

Cliff can't think I did this. But by the furious expression on Mom's face as she comes back inside, it sounds like Lucy interpreted correctly.

"Pack a bag," she says curtly. "We're going to stay at the motel. Whoever did this might come back."

"What?" I stare at her, open-mouthed.

She puts a hand on each of my shoulders. "Those fucking Anselms," she says, and I see it finally.

A fury, barely contained. She leaves the kitchen knife on the table, but I stare at her, at the knife.

Wonder how she has managed her rage after Dad died. Wonder how she manages the memories she must have, because she sat on the other side of him on the roller coaster on that last, horrible, endless day.

Did she manage her rage? Did she manage her memories? Or is she like me, letting them build and build and build until they destroy her?

Mom shoots a look at Lucy, who steps back.

"I'll give you a second," she says, a little shakily, before she withdraws to my room and closes the door.

Mom turns back to me and settles her hand on my shoulder.

"They're trying to rattle us," she says. "And I won't let them, do you hear me? Cliff said he'd send the deputy by to process the crime scene, see if she can lift any DNA."

"Mom?" I say. "Does Cliff think I did this?"

She gives me a look that says she's annoyed I overheard somehow. "He says I should consider the possibility, and I insisted that Annika come down here and process the scene. She can clean off the paint, too, he said. But I don't want you anywhere near here while they do that. I don't want you looking at that horrible message."

I flinch, thinking of the words I carved onto Pierce Anselm's garage two years ago, worse than this:

Die die die.

Because I wanted him to.

I did.

I wanted him to.

And when I saw his body plunging from the top of the roller coaster platform on Friday night, I didn't feel one speck of sadness.

CHAPTER 19

LUCY

3:23 A.M.

IT'S WILDLY SELFISH OF ME TO BE DISAPPOINTED that we're going back to the motel, where Katy is definitely waiting—and definitely furious with me—but I bite my lip and get in the car with Audrey and her mom.

The sheriff follows, his car tailing hers closely.

When we reach the small motel, Mom throws open the door, still dressed in the blazer and pants she was wearing earlier. Langley startles, and then her face hardens.

"Katy." She turns away from my mom.

Audrey looks back and forth between me and Katy.

"Are you okay?" Katy asks them, still not quite looking at me. "What's going on?"

Cliff gets out of his car and lifts a hand to Katy.

"What's going on?" she presses.

"Staying here a while," Langley answers. She unlocks the door to their room and steps inside without looking back at us. "Lucy? Are you staying here?"

Katy looks stricken, her dark eyes wide in the darkness.

Audrey looks at me apologetically. "Luce," she says softly. "Up to you."

"Audrey," her mom calls sharply. "Come inside. Lucy?"

I shake my head, drawing in a deep breath. "With my mom," I say.

The door shuts firmly behind Audrey, and Katy and I are left standing out in the cold staring at Cliff.

He sighs. "Keep an eye on them for me, won't you, Katy?" he says. "They're . . . well, Audrey's a good kid at heart. I'm worried about her."

He leaves, too, and I turn to Katy slowly. "Um," I say. "Mom?"

The lines in her face look deeper, as if Haeter Lake has aged her in just a few days.

Katy looks down at me for a long moment and then sighs deeply. "Come inside please."

We sit down inside our motel room, me sitting on the edge of my bed, shifting uncomfortably.

She sits on her own bed, and then finally runs her hands down her face. "Lucille Marie Preston," she says. "You will never, and I mean *never*, do something like that again. I don't care how angry you are. Running off in Haeter Lake is—" She stops, shaking her head.

I look down at my hands. "I should have told you where I was going."

"You should have," she says softly, but then she gets up and sits down on the bed next to me. "And Luce, I'm sorry, too."

I have the sudden urge to grab on to Mom's hand, something I haven't done since I was about eight years old. Because back then, Mom looked me in the eyes and said, *We are fearsome women*, and then let go of my hand.

"Mom," I whisper. "Were you ever going to come back to this place?" *Were you ever going to trust me?*

She shakes her head slowly. "I . . . I don't know, Lucy. I don't know if I was ever going to come back. I love the Anselms. You were right when you called them my family tonight. They are. They raised me. Loved me. Took me in as their own. But they were also . . . Well, I was never theirs. Not all the way."

A tear spills down my cheek.

Katy reaches out hesitantly and wipes it away with her thumb. "Oh, sweetheart."

"I know what they did to you," I manage. "I know they weren't always kind."

She withdraws a little, twisting her hands together. "They had expectations, and Pierce wasn't happy when I pursued investigative work. He wanted me to help in the family business, and Veronica thought I owed it to them. That whole thing with . . . with the felony charges. They've been supportive since, though. They've asked to meet you, more than once. But the thing about the Anselm family—well, everything they see belongs to them. And I think I wanted you to be just mine."

The words—the fear in the words—make my skin crawl.

"That's weird," I say.

"That I wanted you for my own?" she asks, quirking an eyebrow at me.

In the distance, an owl hoots. The wind makes the trees outside creak and groan as if they, too, are mourning a loss.

"No," I say. "That whole family. They're weird and possessive, and a lot of people have died at their park."

"That's what I'm trying to say," she says seriously. "You were right yesterday. And I know you're curious about me, and my past here, and I know I keep begging you, but please, *please* stay away from this current case."

"But I have some ideas," I offer tentatively. "I've been looking around. I know you didn't want me to, so I didn't tell you, and I should have, I know I should have, but—oh shit, Mom, okay, that first time when we were in Pierce's office? There was—I keep forgetting to tell you. I'll send you the picture of what we found."

"I'm sure you have lots of ideas," Katy says quietly. "But I won't involve you in this anymore than I already have."

"Well, I have case notes," I say quickly. "I mean. You know, nothing formal. But I have a list of persons of interest, and I created a timeline of where everyone was on the night Pierce died, and—"

"Lucille," Katy cuts me off. "This town has become too unsafe, and there is more going on here than Pierce's death that I need to get to the bottom of. For me, for you, for Pierce, for all of us. There's someone out there who killed two people, Luce. Remorselessly. They're here in this town, and they aren't going to stop. I'm not doubting that you're smart, or that you have good ideas, or that you're *capable* of helping me. But you need to stand back. Stay out of harm's way. Dad will get here soon. And backup, too. Cliff said he called and asked for a few extra people from the Knoxville police to come and help out."

"Mom, I do want to know about...about my history," I finish. "I want to know about my grandparents. I mean. You don't have to tell me everything now, or even while we're still here in Haeter Lake, but I want to know about where I'm from. About *who* I'm from."

Mom sighs. "When we're back home, Lucille," she promises for approximately the four millionth time. "You can ask me whatever you want." She hesitates and then gives me a weary smile. "And we will be talking about your tendency to hide in closets and eavesdrop."

She leans over and hugs me close.

"I am sorry I ran away tonight," I whisper.

"I know," she says, and kisses the top of my head. "When this is all done, we can make it up to each other. Deal?"

I nod fervently. "Deal."

CHAPTER 20

AUDREY

9:18 A.M.

I SLEEP FITFULLY AND WAKE LATE, LONG AFTER
Mom has left for work.

I stumble into the pair of black jeans I wore yesterday and shrug on a wrinkled T-shirt that I shoved into my bag late last night—or earlier this morning, I suppose—when we rushed from our house. I don't want to think about the bloodred words scrawled across my home, running down the side in little rivers.

You're next.

Die die die.

I stumble outside to knock on Lucy's door.

She'll make sense of this with me. I think she could make sense of anything.

We can talk about what we overheard Veronica say, and I can tell her what I know about the Anselm children—Blake and Curtis—and she can show me her case notes, and we can talk about our plan. What we'll do next, what we'll explore. Maybe more breaking and entering. Definitely more time on my motorcycle, her soft, freckled arms around my waist.

I raise my hand and knock.

Lucy pokes her head out a moment later, her red hair wild and tangled. She looks charmingly disheveled and sleepy, and I can't help the grin that tugs at my mouth. She's wearing dinosaur pajama pants and a flannel shirt.

"Morning, beautiful," I say.

She blushes beet red.

"Who," she says, then stops herself. "I mean yes. I mean hi? Whatever. Just come in."

Lucy is charming every way I have seen her—in floral dresses or dinosaur pajamas, flustered and fearless all at once.

"Is your mom here?" I ask.

"Nope," she says. "Come in and sit on my bed. Or, you know, the floor's okay. You don't have to sit on my bed or anything, just that you can. If you want. *God*. Let me get my case notes."

I grin at her again, and her blush deepens, redder than the roots of her hair. I think about her coming-out-of-the-closet joke yesterday, delivered at the most inappropriate time for a joke in the history of inappropriately timed jokes.

"Lucy," I ask as she sips from her glass water bottle, which is covered in stickers from various art museums, "did you mean what you said yesterday? The *not a heterosexual or a brain cell in sight*. And also the coming-out-of-the-closet thing?"

Lucy spits water out so hard she drenches her mom's pillow. "Shit," she says. "I— What? Uh. Is it okay if I am? A non-heterosexual with absolutely zero brain cells?"

I inch closer to her.

She scoots back, eyes finding the floor.

"It's definitely okay," I tell her. "Haeter Lake decided it was okay with gay people when its favorite family had a gay daughter."

"Oh, I heard them mention Blake's wife." Lucy grins. "Of course she is. She had a vibe."

"Are you saying you believe in gaydar?" I tease her.

"I can say I have gaydar because I *am* gay," she tells me. "It would be different if I said that you—"

"If I what?" I lean forward, until I'm closer to her face than I had planned. And oh. She has exactly eight freckles, one at the very end of her nose. "If I was gay?"

"I didn't want to assume anything," she says.

"Your gaydar was right." I poke her playfully in the ribs.

This is better than thinking about my blood-drenched house or Pierce's falling body or the knife in my mother's hand. I know Lucy isn't thinking about her shitty day, either, and that's enough for me.

She squeals, batting my hand away. "Sometimes my gaydar is wrong just because I'm *hoping* someone is—I mean, not that I was hoping *you*— whatever, are you *trying* to throw me off my game?" She glares at me.

"I would never," I say. I lean forward, drop my hand on her thigh, knowing my hands always make her fall apart. "We should look at your case notes."

I don't know what the hell is wrong with me.

Everything is crumbling. Everything.

This town, my mom, my whole entire life. It's coming crashing down around my ears, and still I am perfectly content to flirt with this girl on the shitty motel bed.

To my complete shock, she leans forward, closing the gap between us. "The hell with the case," she says, and then kisses me.

The kiss lasts less than a second, though, because in her enthusiasm she misjudges many things, including her distance from me and the balance required to stay upright. She tumbles to the floor before I have the chance to catch her, sending her case notes flying.

She pops up again, scarlet down to the roots of her hair, and turns away from me so fast all I see is her auburn hair.

"Shit," she says loudly. "Goddamn. Where is my case notepad?"

I stand more slowly. "Are you okay?" I reach out a hand to grab hers.

She lets me take her hand, and then she squeezes it in return, but she doesn't turn to look at me. "I'm great," she says too cheerfully. "My notepad—"

"What happened to *the hell with the case*?" I ask her softly.

She still doesn't look at me, but she releases my hand and steps past me. "I didn't mean it," she says, her voice still too loud. "Also, I fell off the bed. It's better if we just forget *that* ever happened."

I spin her around so she's facing me, until we're inches away from each other again.

"*I* don't want to forget it," I tell her fiercely. "I don't want to forget any of this."

This time, when she leans in to kiss me, I make sure I have both hands braced on her hips. Just in case.

LUCY. 11:44 A.M.

Okay, so there was some kissing.

Maybe a lot.

We kept trying to work on the case, to sort out all our notes, but there was this other thing to do that seemed more distracting.

Even though I fell on the floor the first time I tried to kiss her.

Jules and Amy and Nora would die laughing if they knew that, but Audrey didn't even smirk at me.

Not that I mind when she *does* smirk at me.

Anyway.

She has a shift at the diner, so she took us there on her motorcycle, but everything felt different. Everything, including wrapping my arms around her waist. I wanted to keep kissing her, and also have my arms around her waist, and also, maybe, do a few other things. Things like kissing, but with less—

"Lucy?" Audrey is staring at me.

And okay, so I'm still sitting on the motorcycle, staring dreamily off into space. And okay, so maybe I'm a little distracted.

Because Audrey is a *good* kisser.

She takes my hand and helps me hop off so that I don't kill one or both of us doing it myself. She knows me well, even though we met only a few days ago. Is it stupid, to go this fast with someone you've only just met? To be this smitten by someone you're going to leave behind at the end of spring break?

But it feels like I've known her forever, like we've been bound together by something more than just chemistry. The way this town is wrapped around both our lives, the way the Anselms thread through them, the way the park and the town and the loss have shaped us. I don't believe in fate or destiny, I don't think.

I do believe in Audrey—and the way her hands and the corded muscle of her forearms look in those fingerless gloves she wears when she drives the motorcycle. Yeah. That's something.

She doesn't let go of my hand, not even when she pushes open the door to Mickey's diner and guides me through.

We pass under the flashing neon sign that reads MICKEY'S. The bulb in the *M* is burnt out, so it actually just says ICKEY'S, which seems more appropriate anyway.

I like letting her lead, I realize. Even though I'm definitely the one in charge of this case we're solving together.

It's exactly the way I imagined based on the outside, and if I had to guess, it has been exactly this way for the last fifty years. It is a narrow room with off-white walls that look as if they were probably white before the layer of grime, a few booths with torn leather seats, and stools at the bar with aged red leather.

I plop into a booth on the east side. Sunlight streams in through the dusty windowpanes, and I draw a breath, letting the warmth of the spring sun seep into my skin.

Gus looks up from the counter, and his expression turns into a scowl when he sees Audrey. "Nice of you to show up," he says. "Hi, Lucy."

I lift my hand in a little wave at him. "Um?" I say. "Hi?"

"Hey, it was fun seeing you at dinner," he says, sliding into the booth next to me despite Audrey's glare. "But I didn't get the chance to ask about you snooping around my grandma's house yesterday."

"You don't hate me?" I ask him. "For making family dinner terrible?"

Audrey shoots me a look, and I realize I had never actually told her.

"I mean, it's usually me picking at my aunt or my grandma, or them nagging at me," Gus says, a flicker of sadness in his eyes. "But you made both my grandma *and* my aunt mad. And that part was kind of awesome."

"Oh," I repeat. "Gus? Are you okay?"

He hesitates and then shakes his head, his eyes looking suddenly wet. "They all hate one another," he says softly. "Especially my fucking grandma."

"Do you not get along with your grandma?" I ask stupidly. It's not as if *anyone* in that family seems to like one another.

"Does anyone get along with my grandma?" he asks. "Not even my grandpa gets along with my grand— Oh. I mean, he didn't used to."

Not for the first time, Gus looks gutted. But he shakes his head as if clearing the emotion away. He scuffs the toe of one of his running shoes against the floor of the diner, and a little piece of caked mud tumbles off onto the linoleum. "Do you want food?" he asks me. His lip curls when he looks at Audrey. "And you. Are you here to work or just to be an asshole and then ditch me again?"

"I'd be happy to do both of those things if you'd like," Audrey tells him. "But no, actually I am here to work. Because I have a shift. On the schedule. Which you'd know if you bothered to read it. I forget, can you read?"

I press my hand over my mouth. "Both of you stop," I say.

They ignore me, Gus rolling his eyes at Audrey. "As if I care about your schedule."

"Can I get something to eat?" I call after him as he turns back toward the kitchen.

"Maybe," he calls back. "If you're nicer to me than Audrey is."

She grins at me as she ties her apron on. "Veronica used to complain to the school that I was *bullying* her precious little Gussie," she says. "But I mean, maybe I kind of *was*."

"Seems like he's into it, though," I say, and then my own words make me pause. "I mean, actually, maybe he *is* into it."

She shrugs. "We were friends, like I said. But I also kissed him once," she says. "Before—before everything happened."

I sputter on my water bottle, though at least this time I don't spit it halfway across the room. "You kissed—*him*? A boy?"

She shrugs again. "Everyone makes mistakes," she says. "I didn't know I was gay until I kissed him. That still pisses him off."

I snort with laughter. "Okay, go work, or harass Gus, or whatever you usually do for a living," I tell her. "I'm going to sort through my notes, and then I'm going to go sneak around town a bit. How late does your shift go?"

Audrey sighs. "Seven," she tells me. "I'm sorry. If I can get part of it covered, I will, but I really have to be here for the lunch rush. I need the tip money."

I lean in and kiss her cheek. She blushes just a little, and it's satisfying to see that I have some effect on her, too.

The thing I don't tell Audrey is this: I am going back to the amusement park.

Yesterday, when we went there together, she told me about the worst day of her life. She let me hold her. And I was grateful, for the chance to know her and the chance to support her.

But I still have a case to solve. A case that involves her and me and so much more. And I need to visit the scene of the crime if I have any chance of solving it.

And there's that nagging memory of what my mom said about the Anselm family. That no matter who they might hurt, they would never, ever, ever hurt their own. No matter how angry they were.

Anything for family.

But Curtis, nice as he is to me, wasn't really treated as if he was part of the family.

They all have their own story about why: his band, his abdication of responsibility, his refusal to fit in with the family image. But he was rejected by his family, whatever the reason. And he *was* one of the last people to see Arthur alive at the library.

And then of course, there's the person the police have interviewed.

Langley is furious, too. Of course she is. She *deserves* to be.

It would only hurt Audrey to know that I'm even considering her mom.

The park is almost three miles outside of town, but I don't dare ask anyone else to drive me—not Audrey on her motorcycle, and certainly not Katy. The hike up there takes me almost two hours in the increasingly windy weather, and I am by no means the most fit person in the world. Audrey would probably get here faster even without her motorcycle.

I'm still so damn scared of the forest, the way the trees seem to be constantly reaching for me. And if, say, for instance, a branch brushes against me and I turn around and spray my Mace, in a panic, that's no one's business but my own.

The tree probably had it coming, anyway.

When I arrive in the parking lot, I am struck again by the strangeness of this place. The forest around this area is so thick—around the town, too, even in the middle of it, like the forest is just waiting to take everything back.

A chipped sign advertises cotton candy, and my mouth waters automatically in response. In the bright light of day, I notice the carnival piano, the keys rusted and mossy.

Like yesterday, the roller coaster looms large above me.

I force my feet forward, fighting the dread spreading through my body. As I draw closer, I can see the yellow crime scene tape around the base of the roller coaster. Wooden steps lead up, up, up, winding around and around until they reach a platform high above me. On the concrete below the platform is a dark red stain.

My stomach flip-flops again.

Because suddenly that bloodstain isn't just Pierce's.

It belongs to him, but to Audrey's dad, too. To Arthur, who tried to warn me. To my grandparents.

This place is fucking cursed.

I almost turn to run. But then a ray of sunlight hits something on the ground near the place where Pierce's body landed, something that glints and shimmers.

I force my feet forward again and dig in the pocket of my dress for the plastic bag I brought. Evidence collection. I pull on plastic gloves because I know at least a little bit about preserving evidence.

It's an earring. A small, delicate gold stud with a diamond at the center.

Veronica's, maybe?

It looks a bit conservative for her taste, but I'll chase down any lead at this point.

I don't want to think about any other possibilities, or any chance that this earring could belong to Langley, or even Audrey.

Or could all this be about something else entirely? Could there be other deaths covered up by this family? Audrey did say they have parks all across the country. An empire, born here. But if this park has been shadowed by four deaths, isn't it possible that their other parks are, too?

I nudge the earring into the bag and stare up again at the imposing wooden platform, the winding metal bars of the roller coaster. It makes my head spin, even imagining being up that high. What was in Pierce's mind when he walked up those stairs for the last time? What was the last thought that ran through his mind?

A tear cuts down my cheek, and then another.

What did Audrey's dad think about, high above me on that roller coaster with no one to help him?

What did my grandma think when she fell? My grandpa?

I want to take a match and light this whole thing on fire. I want to get in my mom's Jeep and drive and drive until this whole horrible town is far behind us. I want to chop down the dam they built and let the old lake reclaim this place.

I wish we had never come here.

I try to summon the determination I had just a moment ago to solve this case, to clear Audrey's name, to find my own family. But most of it has slipped away, bleeding into the stained concrete.

I just want to go home.

Mom tried so hard to escape this town but ended up right back here to solve a case that might break her heart. I think of the look in her eyes, sadness and secrets, when she turned away from me this morning. I think of Audrey, standing paralyzed beneath this roller coaster just yesterday, telling me about the worst day of her life.

So I keep going.

Because this is more than just a spring break trip, more than just the boredom and curiosity and selfishness that I started with.

This is the history of my family, the history of *me*. It's like this place, this empty, haunted park, filled an empty place beneath my ribs that no spring break beach trip ever could have.

I circle the base of the roller coaster, though my gaze keeps drifting back to the bloodstain on the concrete. On the opposite side, the concrete is almost entirely corrupted by roots, leaving behind thick, packed mud in the widening gaps.

I know Katy and Cliff must have already been here, studying the scene, but I snap pictures with my phone anyway. There are lots of footprints, though apparently local kids hang out here often.

I can see why—it's a good place for dares or drinking or hooking up. Not that I would ever be brave enough to do any of those things, but most teenagers probably would. Or maybe I would, here. Maybe a version of Lucy Preston who grew up here, who knew her roots, maybe that Lucy Preston would do those bold things.

Maybe I would have been like Katy, smuggling vodka in Gatorade bottles and getting in trouble with my friends.

Maybe the person I'm becoming, a person who gets angry—maybe that person could learn to be bold.

A fearsome woman, the kind Katy has always wanted me to be.

Still, I pore over the footprints, careful to balance on the remaining concrete islands and not to add my own to the mix in the mud.

There are a few similar to the footprints on the footpath to the Anselms' mansion: the heavy sole of a man's dress shoe, the lighter imprint of a woman's narrow boot. But there are more than that, too, and it is impossible to tell which of these prints was from the night of the murder, and which were here earlier. Even if I were to check when it last rained, there are too many to differentiate.

One of the footprints looks like running shoes—a man, maybe a teenage boy. Another is flat like a sandal. The rest are far too scuffed to tell.

Except—there.

There at the edge of the sidewalk is one deep indent, circular and sharp. Like someone jammed a stick down deep—or the spiked heel of an expensive shoe.

Perhaps it was Katy, slipping off the sidewalk and regaining her balance in the mud as she studied these footprints.

Or maybe not.

I snap a picture and think of Veronica's heels, clicking against her living room floor.

She has to be smart enough to wash her shoes if she *did* step in the mud at her husband's crime scene. Still, I have the picture. It's not proof, but it is something. On the other side of the base is the red stain where Pierce Anselm fell, but he would have had to start climbing from this side, would have had to walk through the mud here to reach the first step.

I stare more closely at the footprint of the man's running shoe, at the footprints I have been assuming were Pierce Anselm's. There is a clean line of him walking from the edge of the concrete toward the steps. Was he found wearing running shoes? I had imagined him perpetually in a suit.

I shrug my jacket tighter around my shoulders, staring out at the lengthening shadows. It's nearing the evening, and there is no freaking way I'm going to be in this creepy place after dark. I haven't learned much—the earring and the footprints are all clues that lead in different directions, footnotes in a story that remains too broad for me to grasp.

The earring haunts me as I begin my long walk back to Haeter Lake. I don't have answers, real answers, from Audrey, about Friday night. Maybe it's because I don't want them.

I hunch my shoulders under my jacket as clouds obscure the sun and the first few drops of rain begin to fall, the earring as heavy as a boulder in my pocket.

AUDREY. 5:31 P.M.

Despite the fact that it's the dinner rush—if you could call what we see in Mickey's Diner in Haeter Lake a *rush*—I find myself glancing out the window every five minutes to see if Lucy is walking down Main Street toward the cafe.

Where the hell is she?

It started to rain, slow, steady droplets about thirty minutes ago, and I expected her to dash in, hood up over her shoulders, maybe to trip over the front step and stagger in, blushing furiously when I catch her.

And I *will* catch her.

But she isn't here.

And I'm beginning to worry.

I pull my phone out of my apron pocket and shoot her a text. *Everything okay?*

It doesn't deliver.

If she was in town like I assumed she would be, she would have service, even if it's only one bar.

So why hasn't she seen my text? There are only two other places she could be—well, three, but there's no way she would go back to the murder motel, as she calls it. The park or the mansion.

And both of them are dangerous, especially after what she did last night. Gus had told me in a tone of something akin to awe, but I had listened in growing horror. Because anyone who pisses off the Anselms the way she *must* have pissed them off last night pays the price.

LUCY. 5:45 P.M.

A bar of service appears on my phone and wavers as I round yet another bend in the trees. I must be approaching town by now. How many more curves do I have to round to find more trees instead of the familiar, dilapidated buildings of Haeter Lake? I must have been walking for at least a hundred years by now.

The rain is falling more heavily now, large droplets landing on my hood with a *slap-slap-slap*.

Maybe that's why I don't hear the car pull up behind me until it's right beside me. Maybe that's why I hardly notice that it slows until it is nearly blocking my way, until the window rolls down and a familiar voice says firmly:

"Why don't you get in, Lucy? It looks like you need a ride."

CHAPTER 21

LUCY

6:07 P.M.

LANGLEY STARES AT ME, HER FACE UNREADABLE.
I climb into her car slowly, dripping onto the worn seats of her Civic.
"Um," I say. "Hi?"

She raises her eyebrows at me. "What are you doing all the way out here by yourself?"

I could ask her the same question, because as far as I know the park and the mansion are the only things on this road.

"I was . . ." I begin. "Um, walking?"

Yeah, I'm very bad at this.

But why is Audrey's mom out here, and what does she want with me?

Haeter Lake is turning me into a suspicious person. Up until this week, if a friend's mom offered me a ride because of the rain, I would have blithely hopped into the car without a second thought.

I buckle my seat belt with cold, shaking fingers.

"Are you okay?" she asks.

"Yea," I say. "Why . . . Why are you out here?"

She doesn't answer, just puts the car into drive and takes off down the rain-slick highway faster than seems safe. Like mother, like daughter, I guess.

"Where should I take you?" she asks. "Back to the motel?"

"No," I say, way too quickly. "The diner? Please?"

Again, she doesn't answer, and my stomach flip-flops.

Finally, Langley pulls over in front of the diner, but she doesn't turn off the car, and the doors don't unlock. "I hear that you're helping your mom with the investigation." Her eyes bore into mine. "Is that true?"

"No," I say. "I mean, I'm not *supposed* to be. I mean, I maybe am paying attention but—"

Langley holds up her hand, and I fall silent. She leans across the seat so that she's closer to me, and I shrink back. "I want you to know," she says—and though her voice is quiet I feel she could explode on me any second—"that my daughter is not part of this. She *will not* be part of this. Make sure your mom knows that." Her hand closes over my hand.

"I— What?" I'm frozen in the seat, staring back at Langley.

"I'm saying," she continues fiercely, "that Katy does not get to come back to this town and mess with my family. Tell her for me. I have a daughter, too, and I'm prepared to fight for her."

She puts the car into park, and I fumble on the door handle as soon as the doors unlock, launching myself out of her car so quickly I stumble to the ground, staining my knees muddy.

Langley stares at me coldly, unmoved, her eyes the same shade of blue as her scrubs. "I'm not fucking around," she tells me, and then she swerves out into the street so fast her tires squeal on the packed gravel.

Did she just threaten me? I'm staggering with confusion, the clues and leads running through my head in circles. It's like I'm trying to solve a hundred different mysteries at once, some decades old, some recent, all strangely personal in ways I did not expect at the beginning of this strange, surreal week.

I push the diner door open, and I must look half-feral—dripping wet, mud up to the knees, hair matted to my shoulders, eyes wide.

"What the hell happened to you?" Gus asks, wiping his hands on his apron. "Uh, are you okay? Did Audrey find you?"

My heart sinks in my chest. "Audrey?" I ask him.

His eyes narrow, and then he glances down at the phone in his hand. "Shit. She stormed out of here a while ago," he says. "She was looking for you. She looked worried, which is rare for her. Like, too worried to give me shit about anything. You must have just missed her."

"Did she say where she was going?"

"I'm not exactly her confidant," Gus says. He approaches, and then crosses his arms and looks at me, head tilted. "What are you two up to? Are you hooking up?"

I cough and then choke on my own cough and cough harder. "What?" I say stupidly.

"So that's a yes," he says, sighing. "Well, I figured as much. But why would she think you were in some kind of trouble?"

"Did she say she thought that?" I ask Gus.

He shrugs, his blond curls flopping over his forehead. "No," he says. He doesn't quite meet my eyes. "But you're covered in mud and you look like you've seen a ghost. And just a few minutes ago, Audrey ran out so fast she forgot her phone."

Shit, shit, shit.

She doesn't even have her phone with her?

How am I supposed to find her now?

I glance down at my own phone. A text from her had arrived at some point during the fifteen minutes I spent in Langley's car.

Langley and Audrey. Audrey and Langley.

Both of them with as much tying them to that park as I have.

Both with a lot of unexplained time there.

I shake my head. This is all too much for me. I pat my pockets, looking for my case notebook. It's a little damp, but the deep pockets of my dress protected it from the worst of the rain. My hand brushes the small plastic bag with the earring, and I snatch my hand from my pocket as if the touch had burned it.

"Is there anything I can do?" Gus asks.

I know he's an Anselm, but he's looking at me with real sympathy in his blue eyes, and he's helped us so far. It's not his fault he was born into a family who destroyed mine.

Tears prick my own eyes. "Uh, no," I say. "I don't think so. I think I need to call my mom. I can take Audrey's phone."

He hands it to me, and I hesitate.

I shouldn't look at it.

I know that.

But maybe it could give me a clue about where she went.

I type in the passcode I saw her type yesterday—1218.

The phone unlocks, and I scroll through her texts, opening the chain with her mom to see if she had mentioned anything about where she would be going.

There's nothing but a few texts from earlier in the morning, when Langley asked her about her shift at the diner, and one about being home for supper.

Audrey doesn't have many texts, period. There's one text with Chris, the one friend she mentioned from school. One with her mom. One with me. One with Mickey, her boss at the diner.

One with Gus, which appears to be mostly trading insults.

And one with a number that says *unknown*.

I shouldn't click it.

But what if this could help me find Audrey now?

The time stamp reads *Friday 9:31 p.m.*

I'm so sorry, the first text reads.

Who the hell is this? Audrey had texted back.

I swear I didn't know, Unknown had responded.

Didn't know what? Audrey had texted. *Who are you and why won't you leave me alone?*

I'm so sorry. I didn't mean for any of this to happen.

Tell me who you are, or I'm blocking this number, Audrey wrote back.

Meet me at the park tonight, the final text reads. *I'll explain everything then. Please.*

Fuck off, Audrey wrote.

But she didn't block the number, and she didn't delete the text.

I know she went. I *saw* her, at the edge of the park, eyes wide in the dark.

But I didn't know she'd had an invitation.

I shove Audrey's phone in my pocket.

"Everything okay?" Gus asks. He's still there, hanging at the edge of the diner, watching me closely. "You know, I could probably drive you when I get off—"

"No," I interrupt. "I mean, no, it's all good. I can call my mom. Thanks, though."

I pull out my own phone and find Katy's number. With another backward glance at Gus, I step out of the diner, pressing my back against the wall so that I can get as much protection beneath the awning as I can. Rain drips off the edge, splattering my muddy legs.

Katy doesn't pick up the first time I call, but the second time she answers.

"What's up?" she asks. "Everything okay?"

"Um," I say, and then I start to cry.

"Lucille?" Her voice hardens with worry. "Where are you? Are you at the motel? Are you okay?"

"I'm at the diner," I manage. "Katy, I've got to talk to you."

I'm probably never going to be allowed to leave the house after this, but I have to tell Katy about this. About the footprints, about the earring, about Audrey being out there somewhere by herself, about Langley's vague threat.

Maybe not that part.

"I'm on my way," she says.

And then, tires screeching as she pulls up only five minutes later. "I was at the station," she says. "Cliff and I are still putting together a picture of what happened Friday. But—anyway, are you okay? Jesus. You're covered in mud."

"Katy," I say. "I saw some things. About the case."

She raises an eyebrow, her eyes flashing dangerously. "The case I told you to stay far, far away from?" she asks.

"Yep," I tell her. "That one. I. Uh. I went to the amusement park."

She slams her hand down on the hood of the Jeep in frustration, ignoring the rain that is already drenching her perfect hair. "Are you *serious*? You went to the *crime scene* after I told you to stay away from this case?"

"Katy," I say. "I know you're mad. I know. I'm sorry."

"You said that when you were caught in Veronica Anselm's closet," Mom snaps. "And yet here you are, telling me you went to the fucking amusement park afterward."

"But I have something important," I tell her.

She hesitates, her eyes still flashing. "What is it?"

I reach into my pocket and pull out the bag with the earring. "I found this," I say. "A few feet away from the bloodstain. Where Pierce fell."

Katy snatches the bag out of my hand, her eyes widening. She has that look in her eyes, the sharp, bright thing that's almost joy. She gets like this when she's close to uncovering answers about a case. She forgets everything else, even how mad she is at me.

Now Katy lets out a breath, slow and deep. "Do you have pictures?" she asks. "Of this on location?"

I nod and hold up my phone.

"Text them to me," she says.

I do, and then I look up at her. "Do you know who it belongs to?" I ask her.

She stares down at the picture. "That's not possible," she says. "I did a thorough sweep with Cliff when we arrived. I did another one alone afterward, just . . . just in case. And there was nothing there. So whoever dropped this was out there after we were. Still." She hesitates.

"It could still be someone who was involved, though, right?" I press. "Mom, we have to—"

"No." She talks over me, her eyes far away. "Honey, it won't be admissible as evidence if anyone finds out that *you* found it." She hesitates, and she won't quite meet my eyes.

"What are you asking me to do, Katy?" I ask her quietly.

"Just don't mention it to anyone," she says finally. "I'm not saying I'm going to claim that *I* found it at the park during my search this morning. But if we interview a suspect who doesn't know that the evidence is inadmissible, we might be able to use the jewelry as leverage to get a confession."

"Which suspect?"

Katy opens her mouth, and for a moment I think that she's about to tell me, but then she clamps her mouth shut, her teeth clicking. "No," she says. "All right, that's enough. We'll grab dinner and then I'm taking you back to the motel. You can say goodbye to your friend in—"

"She's not here," I say. "Katy, that's why I wanted to talk to you. I found this at the park, but when I came back to the diner Audrey was gone. She left in a hurry—Gus said she was going to look for me—and she left her phone behind. We should tell her mom. We should..."

I pause. I don't particularly want to see Langley again after the strange, threatening car ride.

"I'll call Langley," Katy says. She pulls out her phone and steps under the awning to join me. The phone doesn't even ring once, just goes straight to voicemail. Either Langley has her phone off, or she was just quick to deny Katy's call.

I'd put money on the second option, especially after what Langley said to me earlier today.

My daughter is not part of this. Make sure your mom knows that.

Or maybe Langley is back at work. She was wearing her scrubs, after all.

"Mom, can we please go look for Audrey?" I ask. "Please? She might have gone looking for me at the park. I don't want her to be out there at night, especially because...it's hard for her. You know. That's where her dad died. She would only have gone out there to look for me. She hates being there."

Katy looks at me strangely. "Does she?" she asks quietly. "All right. Let's go look for her. Get in. But then we're going back to the motel and you're staying put all night, you understand me?"

"Yes," I tell her. "Thank you."

But when she turns and gets into the Jeep, I can't help but wonder if I really want Katy to see what we'll find at the amusement park.

Meet me at the park tonight, the text had told Audrey.

And she *had*.

201

CHAPTER 22

AUDREY

6:14 P.M.

LUCY STILL HASN'T REPLIED.

Maybe she's just focused on her investigation. Maybe she's so deep into her discoveries that she just isn't paying attention.

But maybe she's too deep.

Maybe she went so far that she found something she shouldn't. Maybe she uncovered the wrong thing, and the wrong person knows about it. Maybe she was all alone out there, all by herself in that stupid adorable pink dress with the embroidered daisies.

So I toss my apron at Gus, who sighs with frustration but doesn't argue with me.

"It's Lucy," I say. "I have to go."

"Is she okay?" he asks, and if there's mild concern there, I don't want to hear it.

Everyone likes Lucy, okay? Even stone-cold assholes like August Anselm. He doesn't get any special recognition for that.

"She's fine," I say. "I just have to . . . have to go pick her up."

"Where is she?" he asks. "Should we call her mom?"

"She's at the park," I blurt, and his eyes widen. "She got turned around. Went for a walk from the motel." I tack the lies on after, hoping for the best.

"We could still call her mom?" Gus says it like a question. He's looking at me with those sad puppy-dog eyes, and it makes me want to kick him in the shins.

"Why are you always trying to call an adult to come fix a problem?" I ask irritably. "I told you, it's fine, I'm just going to go get her."

But it's there in his eyes all the same, fear flickering like a dull streetlight in the dead of night. "Okay," he says. "Yeah. Go get Lucy."

I'm probably overreacting. I hope I am.

"I hope she's okay," Gus says as I push the door open.

There's sincerity in his voice, but still. Still. I let the door slam behind me.

I swing my leg over my bike and roar off down the road, not caring that the rain is nearly torrential, that it whips my hood back and soaks me to the bone, that I can scarcely see a few yards in front of me.

I drive all the way up the long, winding road to the gate at the end and stare through at the mansion, silhouetted against dark gray clouds. It looks as if the house itself is glaring at me, demanding to know why I'm here, what I want.

Where is she? I want to scream, at the house, at the family inside that has taken so much from me. *Where is Lucy?*

I drive back down the mountain, slowing my pace and staring into the trees as I pass.

As if I would be able to see more than a few feet in on a good day. As if there are any footprints left now that the rain has washed everything away.

When I reach town, I loop around each road, down to each dead end. I pass the diner slowly, peer inside in case I missed her somehow, in case she found her way here by some happy accident.

Nothing.

Lucy vanished, and I wasn't there to stop it.

So then I do the thing that scares me more than anything else ever has.

I drive back up that winding road, higher and higher into the forest, and then, finally, down the abandoned lane that leads to the empty lake, the husk of a park. Alone.

In the rain, at nightfall.

There is new crime scene tape at the edge of the park, near all the old TRESPASSERS KEEP OUT signs, so I walk my bike into the underbrush, where it won't be visible if someone parks in the lot.

It would be worth it if I found her. If I found anything.

And because I am desperate now, I hop off my bike and race across the park, down the uneven path toward the roller coaster. In my head, the memories come alive—teacups swirling faster than they should, carousel horses bobbing manically, disjointed music playing faster and faster. The roller coaster creaking to life.

Lucy, I scream over and over again. *Lucy, Lucy, Lucy.*

I approach the roller coaster, the platform, the bloodstain.

How many more will this place take from me?

Lucy, Lucy, Lucy.

But there's no one there.

Any trace of footprints has vanished, and even the bloodstain in the pavement is beginning to wash away.

Finally, when I have searched in every corner of this damn park, I turn and walk back toward my bike, trying to push aside the small noises I hear in the darkening park. The whisper of something stepping on last year's dead leaves, muted by the sound of the rain. The crack of a twig in the forest, barely audible above the spring storm. The creak of a roller coaster that isn't, *couldn't* be moving.

I'm just about to haul my bike back out to the parking lot when the crunch of tires stops me.

Lucy, I want to shout, but of course it's not.

It's the sheriff's car.

Cliff steps out, looking around carefully.

I crouch in the thicket of trees, keeping myself as still as possible, my heart slamming against my ribs. It's not weird for him to be here, of course, but the way he's looking around—careful, watchful, as if making sure he is unseen.

He walks slowly, still looking around him as if searching for signs of life.

I trail along the edge of the woods, shadowing his footsteps. When it becomes impossible to hide under the cover of trees, I slip behind the carousel, crouching near a molding unicorn whose sparkly harness has darkened with lichen.

It creaks gently, and I bite back a gasp at the noise.

Cliff is at the base of the roller coaster now, searching carefully in the mud. He paces back and forth, back and forth, squatting and then running his fingers through the earth.

If Lucy was here, she'd be inching forward, snapping pictures, chattering my ear off. So I take the picture of Cliff hunched over in the mud, running his fingers back and forth as he searches for something he clearly expects to be there, unsure of what it could mean. And then, my hands trembling, I sneak back out of the park.

But when I reach my bike, the air is leaking from both tires.

A slash mark runs along both edges, deliberate, deep.

Someone took a knife and cut these while I snuck through the park following Cliff. Which means someone was watching us both.

And now I'm stranded here in the dark.

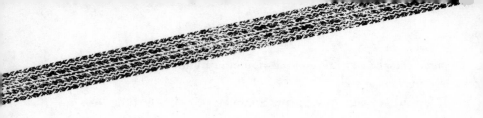

CHAPTER 23

AUDREY
7:14 P.M.

THE HIGH BEAMS OF A CAR CUT THE DARKNESS, their light distorted by the rain.

Maybe the Anselms have come to kill me. To take revenge.

Maybe Cliff has come to arrest me.

I can't bring myself to run, to care, to move at all.

I am crouched on the concrete next to the fading bloodstain, staring up at the roller coaster. The metal beams bisect the rain-black sky.

They are there with me, Dad and Pierce Anselm. Eyes bulging, necks blue. Heads bleeding.

I hear voices, but I can't hear what they are saying. It's as if the lake has returned, filling the hollow, and drowning the old amusement park and me with it. As if I'm underwater, and the people calling my name are far, far above.

Audrey, their voices blur with the sound of the roller coaster, the music from the carousel, the wind whipping through the park. *Audrey, Audrey, Audrey.*

Like I called for Lucy today as I ran through the park. It feels like a hundred years ago.

And then Lucy is in front of me, cupping my face in her hands and speaking to me.

Can you hear me? she shouts. *Audrey, I'm here. I'm here. You're safe.*

And then I can hear everything. Rain on dead leaves. The motor of a car. Lucy's voice. The creak of the old roller coaster above me, a gentle sort of groan.

The cups and carousel are not moving, empty of people, empty of everything. They are not careening down the old tracks, the rusted metal is not creaking and screaming above me like I had thought.

Lucy tugs my hand, trying to reach me, trying to pull me back.

Her mom, standing behind her with a flashlight, looks pale, too.

I'm sorry, I'm telling them, over and over again. *I'm sorry, I'm sorry, I'm sorry.*

And I can't tear my eyes off the bloodstain beside me.

LUCY. 9:17 P.M.

It takes a long time for us to get the whole story out of Audrey. We found her crouched beside the puddle of blood and rainwater where Pierce Anselm died last week.

We take her back to the motel, and after a hot shower, a meal, and a long, long time staring at empty space, she tells us. That she went looking for me. That she saw Cliff at the base of the roller coaster, looking for something.

That her tires were slashed. That she panicked, that she doesn't quite remember a bit of what happened in the middle, but that she does remember sitting at the base of the roller coaster and crying.

Katy is serious and sad and quiet, focused entirely on us for the first time since we arrived in Haeter Lake.

Finally, when Audrey has snuggled beneath the blankets on my bed, Katy stands.

"Langley is at the clinic," she says quietly. "I'm going to go have a talk with her. Tell her—and the sheriff—what happened to you. We'll put the bike in the back of my Jeep and bring it with us. I can talk to the deputy about investigating who would have slashed your tires."

"We know," Audrey whispers.

"Excuse me?"

She looks up, her eyes haunted. "It's the Anselms, Katy," she says. Her voice sounds as hollow as the teacups at the park. "It's always them. You should know that."

Katy sighs. "Well, I think there's only one working camera, so it may not give us what we need. Are you two going to be all right here by yourselves for a while?"

Audrey stares into space again, her brown eyes vacant.

But I nod, and Katy leaves us behind. The hope I saw in Katy's face earlier is gone, replaced by grim determination.

Audrey twists her hands together. "What do you think is going on?" she whispers.

"I think there's more going on than we really know," I say. "I wish I had answers."

I stare at Katy's briefcase, left on her bed. It's closed, but not…not locked.

"Um," I say. This is yet another bad idea, but I plunge onward. "We could look at my mom's case files?"

Audrey giggles a little hysterically. "You're serious?" she says. "Today was…Today was the worst fucking day, and somehow you're still coming up with bold, ridiculous ideas like this? Incredible. What would I do without you, Sundress?"

She's been calling me Sundress this whole time, so why does it make me blush *now*? "Well," I say, "you would probably be pretty bored."

She leans back on the pillows and laughs, that snort-giggle that seems to take her whole body. "Yeah," she says. "You know what? I think I would be."

I nudge Katy's briefcase open. Inside is a thick folder labeled PIERCE.

I've seen her case files before. And okay, maybe I've even *snooped* in them before, but we don't need to talk about the Fallwell case. But my point is that if this was a normal case, it would say something like ANSELM, PIERCE, 03/11/2021 (HOMICIDE).

But this file just says PIERCE, as if that is the only detail she needs to know. As if she will remember everything else about this case, forever, without any help.

This man was like a dad to her.

And, like my own grandparents, I only knew him after he was a body at the base of that stupid, cursed roller coaster.

It's a heavy feeling in my chest, all the missing pieces of our history that I have never had. But how can you miss someone you never met? How can you wish for someone you never knew?

I open the folder and take a breath.

First are the pictures. Crime scene pictures, autopsy pictures.

I flip to the back to read the copy of the autopsy report.

"Wait," I say. I stare down at the next words for so long that they blur together.

Evidence that death occurred before the fall.

Holy shit.

"What is it?" Audrey sits up and scoots closer to me. "What did you find?" She catches sight of the pictures and flinches back. "Oh Jesus," she says. "Lucy, I don't...I can't look at those."

"No, not the pictures," I say. "He...He was dead when he fell. The fall didn't kill him. That bloodstain we saw? *Audrey.* Did he die in his office? Did they throw him off later?"

"What? But why would someone drop him from up high if he was already dead?" Audrey asks, cocking her head at me. "That doesn't make any sense."

"Could they have been trying to make it look like a suicide?" I ask. "But if someone was trying to stage that, they did a shitty job. Cliff and my mom both knew it was homicide right away."

"That was because of the phone, though, right?" Audrey interjects. "Because they couldn't find the phone. And that means someone else has it. But I thought...I was assuming someone pushed him?"

I flip through the folder, to some notes Katy has scribbled across the back inside flap of the folder.

> 9:30 p.m.—Pierce Anselm leaves mansion
>
> 12:30 a.m.—apology text sent to everyone in the Anselm family
>
> TOD could have been earlier? 11:15 p.m.–1:15 a.m.
>
> Who sent the text?

Audrey is pale, but she looks strangely relieved. "Lucy," she says. "I have to tell you something."

I freeze.

"I didn't tell you earlier because—well, we didn't know each other yet," she says. "And I was worried you would think... that I had something to do with the murder. But now that we know that he didn't die from being pushed off the top of the platform..."

"Yes?" I ask her when she trails off and stops speaking entirely. "Audrey?"

"You already know I was there," she whispers. "The night he died, I was there. I saw him fall. But I... he texted me first. He *asked* me to come."

I sit bolt upright, my spine stiff, my stomach dropping down to my toes. It was one thing to have suspected, but another to hear her confirm it. "What were you doing there?"

I swear I didn't know, the text had said. *I'm so sorry.*

"Before he died," she says. "He came to my house around seven thirty on Friday night. Mom had just gone to work, and it was just me home, and he stood there and he looked... He looked scared, and I didn't understand. He kept saying he was sorry, and he kept saying he didn't *know*, and I asked him what the fuck he was doing in front of my house."

She pauses, and I want to reach for her hand. I want to be brave enough to do that for her.

"And he just left," Audrey continues. "But then later I got these texts. Whoever was texting me kept saying they were sorry. And then they told me to go to the park that night and they would tell me everything. It seemed so cruel, you know?" Her voice breaks a little, but she continues. "That he would ask me to meet him there when it was where my dad *died*. He was an asshole. Even at the end, he was an asshole."

"Yeah," I murmur. "Or whoever had his phone was."

"Either way, I think... I think he was trying to do the right thing, after all those years. I believe he was going to tell the truth about what happened to my dad."

Finally, I take Audrey's hand in mine, and she squeezes mine in return. "Did you see him?" I ask. "Did he say anything to you?"

She shakes her head. "I got there too late," she whispers. "I just stayed in the woods, hiding and waiting and trying to feel brave. I was so scared. I didn't want to go back. I didn't want to ever go back there, not for anything. But if there was a chance that I could get some justice for my dad, I had to take it. When I finally climbed the gate and went in, I... I saw him fall. I heard someone scream. I thought it was him, but now that we know he was already dead when he fell..."

Her voice trails off again.

I imagine again the horror of that night, the creaking wood of the platform, the rusting metal roller coaster, Audrey trying to brave the ghosts that waited for her there. And Pierce Anselm, falling and breaking open on the concrete. It is somehow more horrifying that it was his body tossed from the platform. That he was murdered and then broken again. I shudder, but I keep tight hold of Audrey's hand.

"Lucy," Audrey continues in a small voice. "I was... horrified by what I saw. But I wasn't sad. The first thought in my head was, *He deserved it*. What kind of monster thinks that when a man has just been murdered? What is *wrong* with me?"

I don't know how to answer Audrey's questions. But I do know that the girl beside me with tears in her eyes is not a monster. "I'm sorry," I tell her, because there isn't much else to say. "I'm so sorry. For everything you went through. For everything you lost."

This time, Audrey doesn't cry, but when I wrap my arms around her, she rests her head against my chest and just stays there, her body shaking.

I adjust my position so that I'm leaning against the pillows and she's leaning on me, and then I reopen the folder. "I'm going to see what else I can learn," I tell her softly. "You . . . You rest."

"I'm sorry I didn't tell you earlier," she whispers against my shoulder.

"It's okay," I tell her. "It's okay. I understand why you didn't. Did you tell anyone else? Your mom or Cliff or anyone?"

"No," she says. "But I think . . . I think my mom guessed. I think she might even know, somehow. And the Anselms know, if they're telling the truth about having footage of me in the parking lot." She freezes.

The thought hits me at the same time it hits her.

"If they do," I whisper. "If they have working cameras."

Trust no one, Mom said.

"Then they knew," Audrey says. "When we drove there together. When I went back to look for you."

"So they *have* to be the ones who slashed your tires?" I ask. "But *why*? And which of them is it? Curtis hates his family, and they hate him. Blake and Veronica don't get along."

"Do they think *I* killed Pierce?" Audrey asks. "But if they think that, it means *they* didn't kill him. I don't understand, Lucy. I don't understand any of it."

I stroke her hair gently, my fingers tangling in her curls.

With my free hand, I flip through Mom's notes on timeline and alibis. They interviewed Langley after they interviewed the family, and I pause on a note Mom jotted at the bottom.

He wasn't worth oxygen.

Langley had been overheard saying that the week before.

And about a year ago, on the anniversary of her husband's death, she had been heard saying *Someday he'll get what's coming to him.*

And just months after that, *I'd rather watch you die.*

I picture Langley's vivid brown eyes staring at me in her car, sharp and deadly, and I wonder how much we really know about her. If maybe she has been keeping as much from Audrey as Audrey is keeping from her.

"What is it?" she asks.

She must feel the tension in my body, and it seems too late to keep all the truth from her. "They interviewed your mom," I tell her. "Would she have had any reason to be out at the park that night?"

"She was at work," Audrey says. "I told you. She left in her scrubs, and she was gone until her shift was done. I heard her come back in early in the morning."

I snap the folder shut. "My mom refuses to talk about the case, but . . . she's scared of their whole family." I don't say anything about the tab at the back that says *Audrey*. "So you think Pierce was going to tell you something he had learned about your dad's accident?"

"At the time," Audrey says, "they claimed that Dad had chosen not to listen to the attendant who told him to tighten his seat belt and his seat. They said it was Dad's fault, that he had been careless and endangered himself. The Anselms closed this park after pressure from the mayor, but they still have dozens of other parks around the country. They stayed rich, and we stayed broken. But I've always thought—I've always *known* that Dad wouldn't have endangered himself. Not on purpose, not in any way. It had to have been faulty equipment. It *had* to have been. But it would have hurt the Anselms' business to admit that. And it could have even resulted in jail time, criminal negligence. I looked into the charges later. I thought the whole family should have been charged with murder."

"Was there an investigation after your dad died?" I ask.

"Cliff investigated," she says. "And there was an independent commission who came in and looked at the roller coaster to see if it had been faulty. They said it wasn't, but I *heard* the click of his seat coming undone, and then he fell. I *heard* it. And if I heard it *click* open, it must have been clicked shut to begin with, right? It means Dad did what he was supposed to, and that it wasn't his fault. *It wasn't his fault.*"

"Of course it wasn't his fault," I whisper into Audrey's hair. "Of course it wasn't. And it wasn't yours, either. I promise."

And then she's kissing me desperately and I'm kissing her back, and I toss the folder to the floor because the hell with the case and the hell with the Anselms and Haeter Lake and the hell with *anything* that isn't Audrey and her lips and this messy, perfect moment.

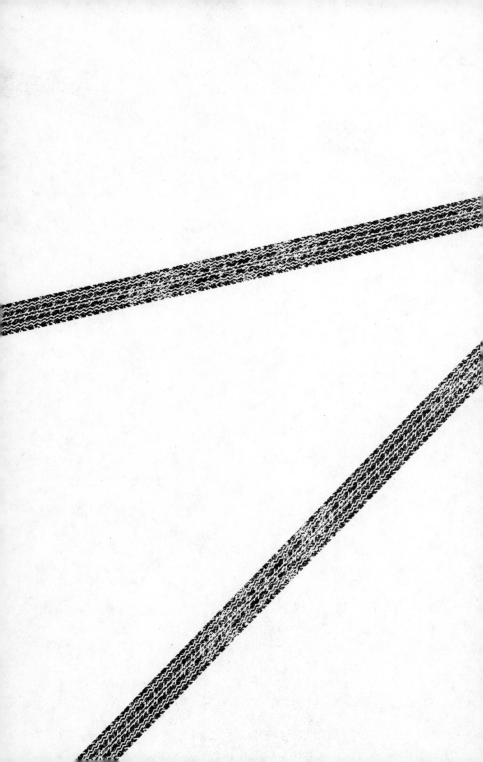

DAY FIVE: TUESDAY, MARCH 26

CHAPTER 24

AUDREY

12:41 A.M.

EVERY BIT OF LUCILLE MARIE PRESTON IS PERFECT.
I should know. I kissed every inch of her skin, found every single freckle from her nose to the few scattered across her torso. I even kissed the one on her knuckle.

And after, we lie there together in her motel bed and giggle and whisper and kiss some more.

It takes us a long time to find the motivation to get dressed, but finally Lucy untangles herself from the blankets and me, dropping one last kiss on my forehead.

"I don't know about you," she says. "But I would rather *not* be found naked by your mom or my mom or, idk, the serial killer probably lurking around here somewhere."

I throw a pillow at her. "There is no serial killer," I tell her.

"This is the murder motel," she retorts. "Didn't you know?"

"The murder motel." I snort. "Why do you keep calling it that?"

She rolls her eyes at me as she pulls her pajama pants—the adorable green dinosaur ones—on and smirks at me. "This is a motel at the end of a dirt road," she says. "In a tiny town. With no cell phone service. And even worse, no Wi-Fi."

"Sounds unforgivable," I say, and she tosses my shirt at me.

It lands on my face, covering my eyes and mouth, and by the time I claw it back off she is dressed in her pajamas.

"I would rather that you're also not naked when someone comes," she says.

"Someone, as in our moms or a serial killer?"

"Exactly." She leans down and presses a kiss to the tip of my nose.

This girl is so adorable it should be illegal.

I grab her wrist and tug her down on top of me.

She kisses me hard, and then nips at my bottom lip before smacking me with my shirt again. "Up," she orders imperiously.

I grin at her lazily. Because despite the horror surrounding us in Haeter Lake, I can still find it possible to smile. Because of her. "But you're sitting on top of me," I protest.

"Whose fault is that?" she says, and swings her leg off.

I reach out instinctively to catch her hand, and I'm glad that I do, because she stumbles the way she does every single time she tries to mount or dismount my bike.

When we are both dressed, she fusses with her mom's case files for several minutes before finally replacing them in the briefcase.

"Should we be in separate beds like good girls?" I ask playfully.

My mom wouldn't be particularly surprised to find me in bed with a girl, but I'm not sure how Lucy's mom would react to us, even now that we're fully and appropriately dressed.

"No." Lucy snuggles in against my shoulder and pulls the blankets up over us. "Shh. I'm going to sleep. And you're staying right here." She cuddles in against my shoulder and then turns her body so that she's on her side and we're spooning.

Sleeping next to someone in their bed seems weirdly even *more* intimate than the moments we shared earlier, and my heart flutters in my chest.

"Lucy?" I ask.

But she's already asleep.

LUCY. 4:13 A.M.

I don't wake up at whatever time Mom comes back to the motel, but I do wake up to a crash much later in the night.

I jerk awake, searching in the dark for any light.

There is nothing.

Not the one single flickering streetlight that usually blinks outside of our window.

Not the red lights of the alarm clock that are usually glaring from the nightstand.

Shit.

I fumble for my phone in the dark and feel Audrey's hand on my shoulder.

"Shh," she whispers. "Someone's here."

There's another crash of shattering glass, and I scream.

"Who is it?" Mom yells, and I hear a thump as she stumbles to her feet, shoving her body between our bed and the door.

I reach for the light switch behind me and flick it. Up. Down. Up again.

Nothing.

There's no power, there's no cell service even if I could find my phone, and *someone is in our motel room.*

And then the clouds move from behind the moon and light floods everything, just for a moment. I see someone, the silhouette of them.

I launch forward out of the bed, past Mom, and grab onto their sleeve, because I am a dumbass.

A hood is pulled down over the intruder's face, but what I can see of the face is vaguely familiar all the same. "Shit—" I say, and then pain explodes through my head and everything goes black.

AUDREY. 4:21 A.M.

For the second time in as many days, I am screaming Lucy's name.

She lunged for the door—for the intruder—before I could stop her, and now she crumples, silhouetted against the moon.

Lucy's mom screams, too, and dives to catch her daughter as she slumps over.

The intruder darts out the door, slamming it behind them. Katy rushed toward Lucy's side, but I—

I run.

I'm out the door, barefoot, sprinting across the dewy grass after the dark silhouette of the asshole who attacked Lucy.

"HEY," I scream. "Who the hell are you? *Show me your fucking face, coward.*"

And then someone else slams into me from the side, and familiar arms are wrapping around me, dragging me backward.

Mom. Fury in her eyes.

"What the hell?" she snaps, dragging me bodily back toward the motel. "Inside, now."

The attacker, whoever they were, is gone, and I'm shaking and seething. So, apparently, is Mom, who hauls me through the door, slamming it behind her.

"You went after someone who broke in," she snarls. "When there's a goddamn murderer on the loose in this damn town. Katy, did you send her?"

Katy is cradling Lucy, and she stares up at my mom with such confusion that I can feel Mom relent. "She just ran," Katy says weakly. "I'm sorry I didn't stop her."

Katy and Mom stare at each other for a long moment.

And then Lucy stirs slightly and groans just a second later, but it's a second where none of us breathe.

"Lucy," I say, jerking away from my mom. "Lucy, you dumbass, what were you thinking?"

"I agree," Katy says, but she is still cradling Lucy and stroking her hair. "What on earth were you thinking?"

Mom shakes her head, her gaze falling on me. "I'm afraid my girl might have been a bad influence on yours, Katy," she says softly, but her touch on my shoulder is gentle.

Katy looks up, her eyes softening, before settling back on Lucy again.

"Um," Lucy answers her. "I'm sure you're both right. But can someone tell me what I did?"

I groan. "You don't . . . remember?"

She shakes her head as if to clear it and then groans in pain. "Um, no?" she says. "Sorry. No. Wait. Oh my god. The lights were out, and there was a crash, and I thought if I could just get a look, I would be able to help us solve the case, but then I remembered too late that I'm not *actually* a badass." She pauses to suck in a pained breath.

"Oh, Luce," Katy murmurs.

"Mom, I really should learn how to defend myself. When we get home, can I take that self-defense class you took a few years ago? The one that was supercool and badass, where you trained with those SEALs and black belts? I don't want to go to the regular karate gym. I'm not the karate kid." She giggles as if she's made a joke.

"Audrey, will you hold on to her?" Katy sighs as she shifts Lucy's head into my lap. "I'm going to get her an icepack and an ibuprofen. She probably has at least a mild concussion."

"I can look at her," Mom says, kneeling beside them on the floor.

They share a look, a long look, and then Katy lets her close to Lucy. . . .

"We should call Cliff," I say. "Katy, someone broke in. Do you think they would have—"

I don't want to finish my own sentence. Were they here to hurt one of us? I have to assume it's related to the case, and though Katy is the private investigator, I'm pretty sure everyone in town has heard about Lucy Preston hiding in Veronica Anselm's closet by now.

Even Chris texted me, from Arkansas, to ask about the new girl who was hiding in closets and messing with the Anselms.

"Shit," Katy says. She's staring at the end of her bed. "They took my notes."

Mom shifts so that her body is between mine and the door, her eyes still watchful as if she is waiting for the attacker to come back.

Lucy tries to sit up and then slumps back on me and presses her hands over her eyes. "They stole all of your notes?" I ask. "Everything?"

Katy nods, looking stricken. "That was everything I had. I had some of it backed up onto my laptop, but not all of it, not today's."

"Doesn't Cliff have his own notes?" I ask her. "It can't all be gone, right?"

"I'll call him," she says tersely. "You three *stay here*. Do not move, you understand? I'm going to call the police." She kneels down and presses a kiss to Lucy's forehead with a gentleness that contrasts with the sharpness of her tone.

"Yes, ma'am," I say.

She tosses the icepack—the single-use kind you have to squeeze and then shake—and a bottle of extra-strength ibuprofen at me. "She needs both," she adds. "Even if she gives you a hard time. Can you handle her?"

Mom nods at Katy.

"I can handle her." I brush auburn hair off Lucy's face and ask her, "Where does it hurt?"

Katy hesitates again. "You can— You'll be okay?"

"I can defend myself," I tell her. "If that's what you're wondering. I have before. We'll be okay. Go."

"Thank you for keeping my baby safe," Katy says. Her voice is the softest I've ever heard.

I nod, once. "It's okay. You can go. I got her."

Katy nods, a pained expression on her face, and then looks at Mom. "Langley," she says, "I—"

"Audrey's right," Mom says, her tone not as cold as it usually is when she speaks to Katy. "We'll be okay here."

Katy lets out a breath and then pulls the door shut behind her with one last look at Lucy.

Lucy touches the left side of her head gingerly.

When I touch it, I can feel the raised bump already, and I press the ice pack to it.

She winces but doesn't fight me.

"I don't wanna take ibuprofen," she says, and it comes out as a whine. "Those pills are too big."

Mom shakes her head. "I can see why you like her so much," she says, passing me the ibuprofen.

I hand them to Lucy despite her protests, helping her sit up and lean against me. I hold the icepack in place for her as she sips water from her water bottle and then downs the ibuprofen I offer her.

"This sucks," she whispers, resting the uninjured side of her head on my shoulder.

"We're gonna catch that asshole," I tell her firmly.

"Uh-huh," she agrees wearily, but she sounds unconvinced. "Audrey? Help me get into bed?"

I help her from the floor and let her lean on me, most of her body weight sagging against my shoulder.

"You're strong," she murmurs, but her words slur together, a combination of sleepiness and head injury that makes her sound almost drunk.

"You are, too," I say. "But next time please don't jump to defend us all from an attacker without...I dunno, a plan? Okay? It could have been a lot worse."

"Audrey Nadine, you are not one to lecture about this right now," Mom says, giving me a look that says there will be hell to pay once we're out of crisis mode.

Lucy grins up at me lazily, her eyes unfocused. "I didn't have a plan," she agrees. "Nope. No plan. Not me. I thought he was gonna get you."

I pause. "He?"

She waves her hand in dismissal, and then lurches and nearly falls when the simple motion sends her off balance. "I always just assume the villain is a man," she says. "Like in *Scooby-Doo*. You know *Scooby-Doo*, right? There's a dog and a guy who smokes weed and there's always an old white man causing trouble."

And with that enlightening summary of Scooby-Doo, she slumps over onto the bed, facedown into her pillow.

I roll her over gently and cover her with the blanket, brushing loose strands of her untamable red hair back from her forehead.

"Goodnight, Lucy," I whisper.

But—once again—she's already asleep.

CHAPTER 25

LUCY

8:04 A.M.

WHEN I WAKE, I AM ALONE IN THE RUMPLED SHEETS, and my head aches spectacularly. I groan and roll over, pulling the blankets over my head to stop the sunlight that is pouring in through the windows.

Fuck. Waking up after a head injury is way too similar to waking up with a hangover.

Which I don't know anything about, of course.

Except for that time on summer vacation, when we were supposed to be having a sleepover at Jules's house, but instead we were at Nora's aunt's cabin and Nora had managed to get the key to the liquor cabinet.

Anyway.

"How do you feel, Lucy?" Katy's voice is too loud.

Okay, yeah, this really *is* like a hangover.

I grunt in reply.

"That sounds about right," she says. The bed depresses and the springs creak as she sits down at the foot of my bed. "Can you drink some water? Eat something, and then take another ibuprofen?"

"I cannot," I tell her. "None of those things. Nope."

This time, she yanks the covers away.

If it was Dad, he would have coaxed me gently, teased me until I laughed, brought the water over to me himself. Babied me, Katy would call it. She's probably right, but I miss him anyway. I miss him always, but especially when I'm sick.

Nurturing isn't exactly in Katy's job description.

Would my grandma have put a cool hand on my forehead? Would my grandpa have brought me the ibuprofen, helped me sit up so I could take it?

"You have to," Katy says firmly. "Head injuries are nothing to joke about."

Fearsome women.

I feel the furthest thing from fearsome right now.

"Urgh," I growl at her. "Where's Audrey?"

Katy's face falls, and she doesn't answer me for a moment that stretches on too long.

"Katy," I repeat, urgency pushing me to sit up, even though my head pounds. "Katy, where is Audrey?"

"She went home," Katy says finally, and then holds up a hand. "But, Lucy, before you talk to her, I need to tell you something. Early this morning, after Cliff and I talked . . . well, Langley is going to be arrested for both murders. Pierce and Arthur."

"Katy, what the hell?" I stand all the way up, and then promptly stagger and fall back onto the bed because, you know, head injury.

She pushes my water bottle into my hands as my head begins to clear. "Come on, drink some water. I brought back some eggs and toast from the diner. You can eat that and then take a few ibuprofen. You probably have a concussion."

"Guess we won't ever know, though," I say sarcastically. "Because you're about to put the only nurse in jail."

Katy sighs. "Honey, *I* am not putting her in jail. You know I don't have the power to arrest people."

"And your pal Cliff would never have done any of that without you.

So spill, Katherine," I tell her, slamming my water bottle down on the night stand. "Why are you going to arrest my—why are you going to arrest Audrey's mom?"

I had begun to say *my girlfriend*, but—well, that would be a mistake. Wouldn't it?

I'm not usually the type to fall this hard this fast, because come on. I'm not some dumbass who believes in fate or destiny or true love. It didn't work for Katy and Dad, and it isn't gonna work for me. But I guess I also don't usually interfere in murder investigations or find that I have long lost family in creepy small towns. Or ride motorcycles. Or, really, have sex.

So I guess you could say that all of this is uncharted territory for me.

"I can't tell you much," Katy says. "I'm sorry. But Langley heard about the earring found at the crime scene, and she came to us herself. She showed us the match to it and admitted to being there the night Pierce died. Then she said she'd go home and wait."

Katy pauses, and I stare at her, open-mouthed.

There is something she isn't telling me. Something more to this, to what Langley said. Something more my mom knows.

"I'm sure it's going to be devastating for Audrey," Katy says, her expression shuttering. "I expect the arrest to happen later this morning, and I would imagine Audrey will need a little bit of space until she has time to process."

"A little bit of space?" I yell at Katy. "You're taking her only surviving family away from her. You made her an *orphan*. Katy. How could you?"

Katy's face hardens, but her voice remains even and calm, as if she is trying her hardest to keep her patience with me. "Lucy, I know this is difficult," she continues. "But I came here to solve this for Pierce, and that's what I did."

"No, you didn't even do it," I say. "I'm going to tell Cliff that *I* found that earring, and I'm going to tell him I found it at the diner, too, not the park. And then I'm going to tell the judge, and the jurors, and everyone else who will listen. I'll go live on Instagram. Jules has a lot of TikTok followers. She could share it there. You are not going to take Audrey's family down for this. What's Cliff's phone number? I'll call him now."

"NO," Katy snaps, and then fear is back in her eyes, the same look she had when she first talked about the Anselm family. She reaches forward and cups my face in her hand. She pauses and then glances over her shoulder as if she is worried someone will overhear her.

Finally, she tosses her phone on the bed next to mine. "Out here." She pulls me out onto the step outside the motel room and leans close, her voice dropping to a whisper. "You cannot trust Cliff."

The wind whips up behind me, swirling leaves in miniature cyclones at my feet.

"Katy," I say breathlessly. "What?"

She hesitates, and then shakes her head. "He said he called out of town for backup," she whispers finally. "But when I called the county this morning . . . they hadn't heard from him. I don't know. I don't know whose side he's on. I don't know whose side anyone is on. And that's all I can tell you, but you have to trust me."

She tugs me back inside.

"Lucy, she said she was there," Katy continues as if we had still been talking about Langley's innocence. "The rest will come out. She's going to be charged, and there will be a trial, and it might get messy. We aren't going to stick around and watch the ugliness start. I'm sorry. I know you're friends with Audrey, but—"

"I can't believe you would do this to her," I say, because that's the only true thing I know. Someone—Langley or the Anselms or maybe even goddamn Cliff—killed Pierce and then Arthur, and my mom, *my mom*, is too scared to do anything about it.

Katy sighs. "This is the best I can do," she says. "Come on. Get dressed, please."

I huff with impatience. It's hard to make a dramatic exit in wrinkled dinosaur pajamas, but I give it my best effort as I stalk into the bathroom, my clothes clutched under my arm.

When I finally reemerge, Katy is standing at the door, her coat already on. "I have a few things to finish up in town," she says, her eyes never meeting mine. "And then pack your bags. We'll be leaving Haeter Lake tonight. I texted your dad. We're no longer needed here, so he doesn't need to come get you, after all."

The words gut me all over again.

It's all over, just like that?

She's leaving Haeter Lake again, despite the fact that she's from here, that these are her people, *our* people. This is our mess.

Or maybe that's why she's leaving.

"Fine," I tell her, though nothing is. "Drop me off at the diner."

"Eat something and take an ibuprofen first," she says firmly. "And then okay. But when Audrey gets there, she might not want to talk to you."

"Well, she definitely doesn't want to talk to *you*, so you're not invited," I tell her. "And fine. Whatever. I'll take the damn ibuprofen."

I swallow the pills dry, in some unnecessary show of recklessness that helps absolutely no one, because I choke and cough one up, and then end up having to drink water to wash them down anyway.

Katy pretends not to see.

And then we both pretend not to look at each other as we get into her Jeep and drive into town one last time.

AUDREY. 8:24 A.M.

Mom is sitting at the table when I emerge from the shower. She is not wearing her scrubs the way I had expected; instead, she is dressed formally in the black blazer and pants she wore to Dad's funeral. Her wedding ring is on her finger, and she looks dangerously calm.

"Sit down, Audrey," she tells me.

"Mom?" I say. "Is this about the graffiti two nights ago?"

My voice sounds almost like a whisper. The graffiti had been carefully cleaned off—it wasn't part of Annika's job as deputy, but she did it anyway, and cop or not, I'm grateful she did.

Mom draws in a deep breath. "In a few minutes," she says, "Cliff is going to come and take me away, baby."

"For more questioning?" I say, but even as I say it, I know that's not it.

She shakes her head. "They're going to arrest me for the murder of Pierce Anselm and Arthur Joyce," she says quietly. "I know, sweetheart, I know." She catches my hand in hers and then leans across the table so that her face is close to mine.

"Listen very carefully to me," she whispers fiercely. "I want you to get out of this town. Today. Do you understand me? I patched your tires, so you just need to fill your bike with as much gas as it will hold and leave. Get as far away as you can. I have some money saved, in an envelope under my mattress. Go in my room and get it, and then get to Atlanta. I have a friend there, and she—"

"Mom," I cut her off, my voice matching her whisper despite the fact that we're alone in our little house. "What are you talking about? I can't leave you. I won't."

"You have to," she whispers back. "*Please.* This is going to get ugly, and I can't—I can't lose you to them. Do you hear me? You have to get out."

A tear slips down my face. "What do they have on you, Mom?" I ask her. "Please. I need to know."

She hesitates, and then leans closer so she can whisper in my ear. "Your earring," she says. "The one Dad gave you. They found it at the park. They . . . thought that you were there, so I told them . . . I told them the earring was mine."

"Holy shit, Mom." I pull back and stare at her in horror. "Are you trying to take the fall for me? Mom, I didn't kill him. I promise. You know he was dead before he fell? Someone killed him and then dragged him up those stairs and threw him over because they hoped it would look like a suicide."

"Jesus." I can tell by the pallor on her face that this is news to her, but relief sweeps through after, immediate and overwhelming. "God. Audrey. I was . . . You saw my shoes. The night I cleaned our shoes? I was there, too. I got a text from Pierce asking to meet me there, saying he'd explain everything, and I had this wild hope that he'd tell me we were right about Dad's death, come clean about everything so we didn't have to live"—her voice cracks—"live like this. But I got there...I got there too late. I saw you run after he fell. And I thought...I thought maybe..."

I take her hands in mine again and hold them tight. "Mom," I tell her. "I hated him just as much as you did. I blamed him for Dad's death. I got the text, the same one you did, but I was too late to save him, too. And I didn't touch him. I waited for him, and I saw him fall, and I ran. But I swear I didn't touch him. I swear."

She squeezes my hands. "I believe you, baby," she says. "And we'll get the truth out of this. I promise. But you still need to get that money and get out of here, at least just until all of this is done, please? Veronica Anselm doesn't fuck around."

"Mom," I tell her firmly. "I'm staying. You're my family. You're all I have left."

Her face crumples. "Baby, you are all *I* have left," she says. "Don't let them take you from me. Promise me." Her hand snakes out, gripping my chin tightly, tilting it up so that I'm forced to look at her. "Whatever it takes, you survive this. Promise me."

I meet her eyes.

I'm going to save my mom, and I'm going to find out the truth about my dad's accident, once and for all. It's who we are: Nelson women, fierce despite the grief. Unstoppable.

"I promise."

When Cliff arrives, Annika in the front seat next to him, Mom and I are standing on the front lawn, hand in hand. I cling tightly to hers, but she pulls her hand from mine and kisses me on the forehead.

"Survive," she whispers to me fiercely, and then she walks toward the cops, her jaw set.

Annika looks at me, her eyes wide, before she ducks her head shamefully and begins to read Mom her rights.

Cliff steps toward me, removing his hat. "I know this must be hard, Audrey," he says.

"Fuck off," I tell him, lifting my middle fingers as a barrier between us.

He sighs. "I'll do everything I can for her, you must know that."

But he doesn't meet my eyes when he says it.

And I saw him in that park, digging around for something as if he *knew* it would be there. As if someone had told him it would be.

Whatever side this man is on, I don't tell him I know or whatever calming platitude bullshit he wants to hear from me. None of this is okay. None of them can make it better. If Dad was here, he would be sorting out this mess, calling a lawyer, reassuring all of us.

But of course, if Dad was here, Mom wouldn't be a suspect in a murder investigation.

"Audrey, we're going to have to talk about long-term care options for you—" Cliff begins.

Mom's head snaps to mine. "Audrey will be staying with some family in Atlanta," she says.

I nod. I'm not actually going to do either of those things, of course. "I have to work today," I say woodenly.

"I can come back and drive you to your shift," Cliff says. "And I'll stop by tonight with dinner—"

"I'll drive myself," I cut him off. "I don't need anything from *you*."

Mom smiles, just slightly, as Annika guides her into the back seat of the car. "I love you, baby," she says. "Remember what we talked about."

I nod, and Cliff stares at me for a long moment once the doors shut behind Annika and Mom.

"If there's anything you know," he says softly, "it could help your mom. So tell me. Please."

"Oh, yeah," I say. "I've got something." I reach into my pocket and pull out my middle finger to salute him with once more.

He sighs. "If you remember anything you've overheard or seen or anything at all, you know where to find me."

And then they're gone, and it's just me. As alone in Haeter Lake as I've ever been.

The jail has three cells, one of which I spent a night in last year on the anniversary of Dad's death. That was the time I painted rude words on the outside of the diner for no other reason than that I was pissed and very, very drunk. Chris had tried to stop me, and we had both been detained by the deputy when Mickey called the cops on us. Chris's family came to get him right away, but Mom was working another third shift, so I spent my night in the jail cell.

Today, though, it's going to be Mom behind those bars.

I won't cry. I *won't*.

Instead, I get on my bike and I ride. Out of town, up the long, winding road to a cemetery beneath the shadow of a park that has haunted my family and Lucy's family for so many years.

I crouch beside Dad's grave again, the overgrown grass dampening my leggings and my boots. And I make him a promise, again.

That I will not let the Anselms win.

That I will not let what is left of my family be destroyed.

I close my eyes and run my fingers across his name.

My Audrey, he would say if he was here, and just the sound of his voice, deep and soft and endlessly kind, would be enough to soothe the sharpest edges of my anger.

But he's not.

It's just my voice left. So I let that anger sharpen into a blade until I am ready to do whatever it is I have to.

CHAPTER 26

LUCY
12:11 P.M.

KATY MAKES ME WAIT UNTIL SHE HAS HEARD FROM Cliff that Langley has been arrested and processed before she even leaves the motel. "They said Audrey left for a while but showed up for her shift at the diner," she tells me at last. "Grab your stuff. Let's go."

I don't speak to her at all as we drive, because I don't think there's much left I could say.

Finally, she pulls up in front of the diner and turns to me. "Don't tell Audrey what I said," she tells me. "About Cliff. I can't have either of you underfoot while we finish up today. I am going to make this right. But you have to trust me."

I don't.

I can't.

But it doesn't seem worth it to tell Katy that now.

The roar of an engine cuts us off. Audrey is on her bike, glaring at us.

She swings a leg over the side of her bike, dismounting with that careless grace I envy. She fixes Katy with a hard stare, and Katy manages to meet her gaze, but just barely.

"Fucking bitch," Audrey says matter-of-factly, and flips Katy off.

I jump out of the car, trip, and stumble to a halt at Audrey's feet. She stares down at me, face unreadable.

"Audrey," I say. "I swear I didn't know that my mom was going to do this. And I know your mom didn't do it. The evidence they have—it's circumstantial, okay? Tell your mom not to say anything to them."

Audrey leans down, takes my hand, and hauls me to my feet. "I know," she says. "I talked to her this morning. She isn't going to say anything, and they don't have anything on her."

"Katy says we're leaving tonight," I tell Audrey.

She pales. "You're leaving?" she echoes.

"I don't want to," I say. "You know that, right? I . . . I want to be here for you. I want to stay until we figure this out."

She doesn't release my hand. "So we only have today to figure all of this out?" she asks. Then she pauses. "My mom mentioned the earring. What do we do?"

Behind me, Katy's car door slams, and I jump at the sound.

"Lucy," she says sharply. "I just got a call from Cliff. His office was broken into last night. Everything he had was stolen."

You can't trust Cliff.

I shiver, gripping Audrey's hand for dear life. "What are you saying?" I ask.

"Pictures, reports, everything," she says. "They left the earring behind. Maybe they didn't see it at the back of the file cabinet. Anyway, honey, I have to go. I want you to come with me, okay?"

"Katy," I tell her. "It's going to be fine."

She huffs impatiently. "Our entire case is gone," she snaps. "What about that seems fine to you? The only thing we still have are copies of the autopsy report because that was digital. Everything else . . . Cliff is old-school. So much of what he had was handwritten."

"I took pictures," I admit. "Last night, Audrey and I . . . um, we went through your case files?" I blush bright red thinking about what we did immediately after, when I tossed the case files to the ground between the motel beds. "And uh, I took pictures of everything in your folders."

Audrey snorts with laughter. "Is that what you were doing?" she asks. "You were fussing over those papers for approximately a hundred years."

Katy sighs and leans back against the Jeep. "Well," she says, "since it appears that no matter what I tell you, you are going to involve yourself in this case, then . . . thank you, I guess. Will you send me the pictures you took? I'll send them to Cliff, and we'll regroup. And, Lucille? I still plan to leave tonight." She glances at Audrey, whose mouth hardens into a thin line.

"You can't possibly think it was my mom," Audrey says. "Two break-ins last night? Do you think my mom did that? She was still at her overnight shift at work when you dumbasses were getting robbed. There are cameras in the lobby at the clinic. You can check those."

Katy doesn't argue with her, but the look she gives us both is heavy with sadness. "Come on, Lucy," she says. "I . . . I need you to stay close to me today. Audrey, you're welcome to come with us if you would like to spend some time with Lucy." She gets back into the car.

Audrey looks after her strangely. "Luce, do you think . . . Do you think . . . No, never mind. I'm going to go back to work for now. Meet me back here tonight after you talk to the cops. I want to run an idea by you. I have a theory about all of this, but I have something to do first."

She lets go of my hand, and I feel suddenly cold. A premonition of sorts, as if this is the last chance I have to touch her. And I am *not* ready to be done touching Audrey Nadine Nelson.

"Audrey, wait," I call after her breathlessly. There's something I have to tell her now, before it's too late.

She turns back at the door to the diner, framed beneath the neon letters on the sign above her. There's a question in her dark eyes.

But I don't say the words.

I don't say them.

And she turns to go.

LUCY. 5:04 P.M.

The evening stretched on endlessly as I answered Cliff's and Katy's questions about each of the pictures I had taken, adding my own observations as they reconstruct their notes.

You can't trust Cliff.

I'd rather watch you die.

Anything for family.

Don't go digging, Lucy Preston.

Suspect after suspect, secret after secret. Generations of secrets. The air is so thick with them that I can hardly breathe.

What the Anselms know, what Arthur Joyce knew before he was killed, what Pierce Anselm was trying, maybe, to reveal.

Across the room, Langley sits unmoving in one of the jail cells, staring straight ahead. She is dressed as if she's ready to attend a funeral.

I try to catch her eye, but she ignores me, her gaze glassy and cold.

The day seems to last forever. Annika brings food from the diner—and the update that Gus Anselm has offered to cover Audrey's shift and she's refused to go anywhere.

It's hours later, at about a quarter to ten, when night has long since fallen around the little precinct, I feel a shiver jolt through me, unbidden. A shiver, and a thought of Audrey.

I'm later than I had planned to be, but I glance at my phone. No texts from her. The fear cinches tighter, and I clench my hand over the armrest.

"Lucy?" Mom is staring at me, head cocked. "Everything okay?"

"I want to go check on Audrey," I say. I jump to my feet, head pounding all over again. Despite the ibuprofen and constant suggestions from Mom to drink more water, my head is still aching. "It's late. The diner closes soon, and she . . . she doesn't have anywhere to go. We have to make sure she's okay."

"Oh, Jesus, it *is* late," Cliff says. "I meant to make sure she got home safe."

Langley is on her feet, watching us silently, her eyes sharp.

I glance over at her again, and the flash in her eyes is deadly.

"You left my kid all alone?" she says loudly, fixing that death gaze on Cliff. "I swear to god, Cliff, I will have your badge for this."

"I'm sure Audrey's just fine," Cliff says soothingly, looking to Katy for support.

Katy's jaw is set, her eyes stony. "You are?" she asks.

"She's just at work," Cliff says, shifting uncomfortably. "She has her own transportation, too, doesn't she? Still, we'll go over and check in. Lucy, I think we've got everything we need from you. Thank you for your thoroughness. Though I think we might need to ask you to delete the remaining information you have on your phone. This is some sensitive information, and we don't want it to—"

"You don't want it to fall into the wrong hands?" I ask, my laugh cracking across the space between us. "You mean like your notes and Katy's notes already did? I'm the reason you have any notes left at all. Can we just go, please?"

Cliff folds his arms across his chest, but he doesn't look mad at me. Just tired. And nervous, too.

Like he knows he's way in over his head with this investigation.

"You seriously only have two cops in this whole town?" I ask him, cocking my head.

Katy sucks in a sharp breath of air, her hand descending on my shoulder in warning.

You can't trust Cliff.

Trust no one.

He sighs. "We've never needed more than the two of us," he says. "And your mom has been a big help, of course."

"I'm keeping the files," I tell him.

"Lucy," he says. "I'm not asking. If you're not willing to delete the files from your phone, I'm afraid I'll have to take it as evidence."

"See, you don't do such a great job of protecting the evidence you do have," I say, taking a step back from him. If he's going to make me delete the pictures I took, I at least have to buy myself enough time to upload them to the cloud. Once everything is safely backed up, I show him. "Fine. Look." I turn the screen toward him so he can see my empty gallery.

He lets out a breath. "Thank you, Lucy," he says. "I'm glad you understand."

I don't understand, though, not really.

Katy must sense that I'm about to open my mouth and ask him, because her hand tightens on my shoulder. "Cliff, maybe I could take a look at the incident report of the break-ins this morning, and we could compare some notes. We still have to finish filling out the police report for the break-in at the motel, but we can finish up later. Luce, let's go." When we reach the Jeep, she jerks her head toward the car. "I need to make a call first, honey. You should have another ibuprofen, okay? And then I'll take you to Audrey."

She paces in front of the Jeep for several minutes, and anxiety builds like a wave inside me.

At one point, Katy lifts a hand in a wave at Cliff, who is standing at the window. His blue eyes are sharp, watchful. He smiles kindly when he sees me looking back at him.

By the time Katy climbs into the driver's seat, my knee is bouncing frenetically, my fingers drumming on the armrests.

"Katy," I begin. "I—"

"Hold on," she says sharply. "Listen. You were right, okay? There aren't enough cops here to prevent something terrible from happening." She glances furtively over her shoulder at Cliff, who lifts his hand in a wave.

I shiver.

"I have a plan," Mom says. "And I want you to know that your instincts are good. They always have been. I've tried to keep you away from this case—this *family*—but you should know that."

Tears sting the back of my eyes. Why did it take this—murder and break-ins and this tiny, terrible town—to bring Mom and me closer?

"Tonight, I want you to stay with Audrey, do you understand me?"

Mom continues. "Find somewhere safe and stay together. Under no circumstances do you separate. I just called someone I know who works for Nashville law enforcement. They're getting a team together to send to Haeter Lake, but I don't know when they'll arrive."

"Mom," I say. "You're scaring me."

"Yeah," she says. "I know. I'm sorry, and I'm sorry I brought you here. I thought things would be simple. It doesn't matter now. We're here, and Mom—your grandma. She was so brave. She would want us to be brave."

My throat is suddenly tight. I don't have the words, so I reach out, my hand closing over Mom's forearm, just above her tattoo.

Memento vitae.

Remember to live.

"But." Katy clears her throat. "I have to keep you safe, too. Audrey is closing at the diner, and it should be safe. The motel was already broken into, and Audrey's home was graffitied, so I don't want you at either of those places alone. But if you're in the diner, you'll have cell service, and you'll be together, and you can lock yourselves in there. Okay? Whatever you do, don't open those doors."

"Mom," I whisper. "What's going to happen tonight? What's going on?"

"There's a lot of secrets here, you know that." She waves her hand in a sweeping motion. "Layers and layers of them, going back generations. I'm close to getting to the bottom of this. I really am. But I need you to stay safe, and I think the safest place might just be next to that girl. She's tough."

"What are you going to do?" I ask softly.

"I'm going to finish this, once and for all," Mom says fiercely. "So you stay safe for me, baby. I'll come get you when it's done."

I lean over and kiss Mom on the cheek. Just like when Audrey let go of my hand earlier, it feels final and heavy in a way that terrifies me. "I'll see you soon."

"Soon," she repeats like a promise. "Listen, you call me if . . . well, call me if you need me. Under no circumstances do you go anywhere else, or you will be handcuffed to my side until you turn eighteen. And you can kiss your phone, and your Switch, and trips with your friends, and anything else you hold dear goodbye. I'm not fucking around."

"I know," I whisper. "I'll be safe. I'll try. You be safe, too, Mom."

But she doesn't promise me that.

She doesn't promise me anything. She just turns the key, the Jeep loud as we make our way toward the diner together, one last time.

CHAPTER 27

AUDREY
9:44 P.M.

I WAIT UNTIL IT'S ALMOST CLOSING TIME TO TEST my theory.

There have been so many ideas swirling around since the beginning of all of this, but I have one now that rises above the rest, spurred by the graffiti and the slashed tires and the fear in my mom's eyes when she talked about how far Veronica Anselm would be willing to go: There was more to Dad's death than carelessness, and the Anselms know more than they're saying.

Pierce Anselm was about to come clean.

And one of the Anselms killed him for it. Killed Arthur, too.

But here's the thing.

It's Veronica's words that very first day that I can't forget. *Anything for family.*

Family.

And who is the only person she ever loved more than Pierce? Not Curtis, the son she threw away. And not Blake, the daughter who makes her life difficult every single day.

No.

I pull out my phone and text back the number, the *unknown* that had texted me apologizing, inviting me to the amusement park on that night that changed everything. Pierce Anselm's missing phone.

The diner is empty of customers, but Gus is wiping down the front counter, his shirt rolled up to expose his forearms. He nods at me and smiles shyly. Lifts his hand in a little wave.

He's wearing jeans and a long-sleeved shirt beneath his apron, and running shoes caked with mud.

I send the text.

I know what you did.

And then the silence of the diner is filled with the unmistakable answering buzz of the cell phone in Gus's pocket.

CHAPTER 28

LUCY
9:59 P.M.

WHEN KATY DROPS ME OFF, I WALK PAST AUDREY'S motorcycle toward the door of the diner, and glance back over my shoulder at my mom.

She watches me go, her knuckles white where they clench the steering wheel.

I enter the diner alone. Mom pulls away as the diner door shuts behind me.

The place is empty.

The lights are still on, and a kitchen rag is still on the counter as if someone just set it down to go to the back.

But Audrey's bike is still here, just outside.

"Audrey?" I call out hesitantly. My voice echoes in the empty room. Above me, one of the lights flickers and then blinks out. "Gus?"

There's no answer, so I duck behind the bar and then poke my head into the kitchen.

The sink is still full of soapy water, a few plates stacked beside it. A broom leans up against the wall.

"Audrey?" I call again.

Another light above me blinks dangerously, and I bite down hard on my lip. Where the hell is she?

Past the kitchen is a little nook where I see one jacket hanging, a jean jacket that looks as if it hasn't been picked up in years. This small space appears to be the equivalent of a break room, or at least a cubby for storing employee belongings, but Audrey is nowhere to be found.

Except for there, sitting on the countertop, are the keys to Audrey's motorcycle.

And that's how I know I'm already too late.

CHAPTER 29

AUDREY
EARLIER. 9:49 P.M.

GUS HAD STARTED CRYING WHEN HE LOOKED AT me across the diner, tears cutting long lines down his face, a steady stream. As if he'd been breaking for days.

I think he was about to say he was sorry. I really think he was.

But then his family stepped into the diner behind me.

Curtis and Blake, identical blue eyes cold. United in nothing, but united in this.

"Why don't we give you a ride, Audrey?" Blake had suggested. I had half expected her to lift the lapel of her designer suit coat to show me that small, ornate pistol we had found in the office.

But instead, she nodded to Gus, and he was crying when he pulled the pistol from the pocket of his jeans.

And there wasn't any other choice.

So now I sit beside Gus in the back of Blake's Cadillac, and he doesn't look at me once.

He stares down at his feet, hands twisting in his lap. As if he didn't want this.

As if he didn't choose this all himself.

As if he wasn't the one who murdered Pierce Anselm with his own hands, and then Arthur, too, to cover it up.

We take the familiar winding road through the trees that choke the road. We climb toward the place I have dreamed of every night these last three years.

Toward the place where my father died.

Toward the place where I will die tonight.

CHAPTER 30

LUCY
10:07 P.M.

I DO TRY TO CALL KATY. I DO. I LEAVE A FRANTIC message saying that Audrey isn't here, that I'm sorry, that I don't know what to do. But Katy doesn't pick up, and who knows where she is? Who knows when she'll be able to check her phone next?

I think of dialing 911, but the only person in this town who answers that call is Cliff or maybe Annika, but she's his deputy.

I clench my trembling hands.

Where would Audrey have gone on foot?

It's unthinkable that she would leave her bike behind. The bike is her pride and joy, and she would never, ever have left the keys behind and run off without it.

Not unless she was forced.

I sprint back out to the counter, opening and shutting drawers looking for any sign, any note. A phone even.

There's nothing but extra rolls of receipt paper, a few notepads and pens for taking orders, and a sleeve of nickels shoved to the back of one of the drawers. And . . . a boy's jacket with a splatter of bright red paint on the cuff. Wrapped in the jacket is a can of spray paint.

It hits me all at once. The bloodred graffiti the night I was at Audrey's, the mud-caked running shoes, the grief that has been pulling Gus Anselm apart at the seams. The way he tried to help.

But it's something more than grief.

It always has been, if I hadn't been too preoccupied with Veronica Anselm or Cliff or Curtis or Blake or even Langley to see it.

Audrey must have figured it all out, too late. That we had been working with a murderer this whole time, and now that murderer—and probably his fucked-up family—took Audrey.

I send Katy one last, desperate text, hoping the service at the diner is as passable as Mom thought, hoping that she has enough service to receive it. And then I shake the can of spray paint and step outside the diner. On the front, I spray-paint a message for Katy.

Gus took Audrey.

Find us.

It's a horrible, unthinkable thing to do to my mom, and she doesn't deserve it. She really, really doesn't.

But it's too late to wait, too late to hope. I have to do something. I have to find Audrey. I have to help.

I toss the can and grab Audrey's keys from my pocket in shaking hands.

Holy shit.

I'm about to drive a motorcycle.

Above me, clouds scud across the slender moon hanging in the sky, jagged branches from nearby trees cutting their own dark scar across its light.

I clamber up onto the bike, staggering and just barely managing to catch myself without crashing to the ground, bike and all. My balance still feels precarious when I gingerly push the kickstand up and insert the key into the ignition.

Audrey makes it all look so effortless. The key is similar enough to a car, but the rest has me guessing: the valve she pushes, the kick start. I am only guessing, and if I break her bike—well, horribly enough, it seems like Audrey won't be here to be mad at me.

Miraculously, the bike roars to life, and I miss Audrey's steadying hand desperately. Her hand on my thigh where my dress has inched up. My arms around her waist. The wind in our hair.

But now it's just me, and I have to be my own courage.

With all the bravery I can summon, I lift my foot off the ground and wrap my hand around the throttle. I accelerate forward faster than I had planned, and then I go wobbling down the center of the road, unable to stop myself from shrieking.

I don't know what my grandma would tell me if she was here, because I never had the chance to know her. But I know I come from courage.

So am I crying in panic as I ride this stupid motorcycle?

Yes.

Am I going to goddamn do it anyway?

Also yes.

I even out on the motorcycle a few blocks later and force myself to bite back another scream when I see a pair of yellow eyes flash in the darkness beside me. There are few streetlights in Haeter Lake, and even those don't pierce the thick forest growing in around us.

Just a deer, I tell myself. *Just a deer.*

There's a sharp flash of movement at my right, and I veer left so hard I drive briefly into the steep, grassy slope down to the ditch.

It *is* a deer this time, as startled by me as I am by it.

Pull it together, I want to scream at myself. How the hell am I supposed to stand up to the Anselm family if I can't even conquer my fear of the forest and the motorcycle and the— Okay, fine, I guess I have a lot of fears.

But they still have Audrey.

And I have to stop them.

The road to the park winds endlessly upward, and I fumble with the lights on Audrey's bike until I find the high beams. I miss the ease with which she operates this bike, her hands deft and intuitive.

Finally, the worn brown bullet-ridden sign saying ANSELM AMUSEMENT PARK looms in front of me, and I accelerate faster, my heart racing.

I'm coming, Audrey. I'm coming.

I planned to pull into the ditch near the entrance and then drag the bike into the cover of trees like Audrey did when we sneaked into the Anselm mansion a few days ago.

What actually happens involves some tumbling. More than I'll admit to if anyone asks me later. And if the bike nearly tipped over on me before I got it halfway down the ditch—no it didn't.

I set the brightness on my phone to the lowest setting, and then use that light to guide me through the trees. Finally, I break into a run.

How long have they had Audrey? What if I guessed wrong, and they have her up at their mansion, not here?

But this place calls to me.

It has been calling to me ever since Katy and I arrived in Haeter Lake on Friday.

Or maybe, somehow, this place has been calling to me my whole life, this missing piece of me. Where my grandparents died. Where Mom became an orphan.

This place bound me to Audrey in some grief-twisted way, but still it calls to me.

I run through the forest, branches cutting into my bare arms, catching on my yellow sunflower dress, drawing sharp lines across my cheeks.

There is one car in the empty parking lot, a black Cadillac near the rusted gate.

Clouds drift past the moon, and the strange, eerie white light of the half-moon floods the park.

I duck through the gate and tiptoe past the old ticket booth, and then I see them.

Past the carousel and the empty-eyed horses. Past the teacups, full of vines and moonlight. Past the moss-covered piano.

The whole damn crowd of them, the Anselms gathered in one place, at the base of the old roller coaster where this began.

Gus and Blake and Curtis and Veronica. All of them together, their whole family, united at last.

And Audrey beside them.

I step out of the shadows and walk down the fractured sidewalk, over rampaging tree roots and cracks in the concrete the width of my arm. It is a wild, barren place, and tonight, I belong here.

A wild orphaned girl with no past and no future but this wild orphaned place.

"August Anselm," I call out, and their heads swivel.

They all turn, looking at me as one.

Identical cold blue eyes. Identical mouths, set in hard, merciless lines.

Only Audrey shows any emotion, her face twisting as she realizes that I have come. And come alone. "Oh no, Sundress," she says tenderly.

She says it like someone familiar with grief, and my stomach nearly bottoms out.

But I square my shoulders.

"I know what you did," I tell Gus. "And I'm here to take Audrey home."

CHAPTER 31

AUDREY

11:04 P.M.

THE ANSELMS' INABILITY TO AGREE WITH ONE another has probably saved my life—or at least prolonged it. They have been arguing about what to do with me for nearly an hour when Lucy arrives.

She's wearing that yellow dress with the sunflowers, one of her endless array of bright floral dresses.

She is pale beneath the moon's light, her freckles standing out against her skin.

"Oh no, Sundress," I whisper.

Beside me, Gus shivers. Another tear traces a line on his cheek, and he stares down at the ruptured pavement beneath our feet. The gun trembles in his hands.

But Lucy tells them, *I know what you did*, so that must mean others do, too, right?

Lucy's mom and my mom and Cliff and the deputy will come roaring in, red-and-blue lights flashing, and it will all be okay.

"Oh, do you, my dear?" Veronica asks idly, folding her perfectly manicured hands together. She steps forward, shielding Gus slightly with her own shoulder.

I'm standing so close to her that I can hear the *click* of her bloodred fake nails on the wooden railing of the roller coaster platform.

"Yes," Lucy says in a voice that shakes only a little. "You're a murderer. All of you are murderers. But especially you, right, Gus?"

Gus whimpers, a sound from low in his throat. "I didn't mean to," he says. "I *didn't*."

"Shut up," Blake says softly. "I've had enough of all this nonsense."

Lucy turns a shade paler, but she keeps walking toward us. "I know what you did," she repeats. "And I'm here to make a deal."

Veronica cocks her head, apparently considering. "What could you possibly have to offer us, little girl?" she asks. "We have everything we need already."

"Such a shame," Curtis says, shaking his head at her. "I tried to warn you, you know. You have spunk. You could have lived, and Katy could have lived. I never wanted either of you to get hurt by this."

Veronica scowls at him. "You always were a sellout," she says icily. "All those years threatening to reveal the truth about the Prestons. You should be ashamed of yourself."

Lucy flinches. "Curtis," she says, a little shakily. "I know you cared about us."

His face hardens. "I did," he says. "I do. But I tried to warn you away. And I made it easy for you, little Lucy. Arthur wasn't around to spill secrets he was meant to keep, and still you kept on looking."

My stomach churns. "Like father, like son," I say.

Blake backhands me across the face.

I don't make a sound, but Gus whimpers.

"Such a shame," Curtis says. His eyes are mercilessly hard when he looks at me. "Such a shame that you couldn't live with what you had helped your mother do. And killing Katy Preston's daughter on top of all that?" He shakes his head at me in mock reproval. "How could you do something like this? Haeter Lake will be talking about your cursed family for years."

I lunge at him, and Blake catches my arm, dragging me backward. "You fucker," I snarl. "Stay away from Lucy. Stay away from my *mom*."

"Oh," Lucy says breathily. "No. I don't think you'll do that, Curtis."

"And why is that?" Blake asks impatiently. "Are you hoping to buy enough time for rescue to come? Because I hate to break this to you. No one is coming to help you."

"Actually," Lucy says, "there's quite a bit more than that. Gus, do you remember the spray paint that you used to tag Audrey's house?"

He flinches, and then shoots a guilty half glance at me. "It wasn't my idea," he mutters, and then fixes his gaze on the ground beneath him again. "I—I didn't want to. I just wanted them to leave you alone. I *told* them to leave you alone. I said we could—we could frame someone else if we had to."

"You're a spineless coward," I tell Gus, who seems to shrink into himself even more.

"I used that paint," Lucy continues, "to tag the diner and tell them exactly where we were and who we're with. So if you kill me, that evidence is my last words, and that's evidence my mom can use. And believe me, Blake, she won't stop until there is nothing left of you or your family or your company but ashes."

To my amazement, Blake pales uncomfortably. "What are you talking about?" she snaps. "This is ridiculous, and I've heard enough. Up. To the top. Both of you. Gus, you started this. You're going up with us to finish this."

"First, though," Lucy says, and then she steps closer, so close that she's toe to toe with Veronica. She's not even looking at Blake or Gus or Curtis or the gun. "I think I want the truth. If I'm going to die anyway, it couldn't hurt. And I really just want to know. About my grandparents."

A muscle in Veronica's jaw jerks. "Oh," she says softly. "I haven't thought about that in years."

"What is she talking about, Grandma?" Gus's brows are furrowed in confusion. "Blake?"

"Shut up," Blake tells him again.

Veronica hesitates, considering.

I struggle against Blake's arms again, and she reaches over, snatches the gun from Gus's hands, and raises it. Points it square at the middle of my head.

The barrel of the gun is cold and dark and round, a single eye staring back at me. Ready. Waiting.

Cursed family.

Dad saw his own death coming for him, too.

"Stop being difficult," Blake snaps. "I can shoot you both and still make it look like a murder-suicide."

"Except you would have to explain how *your* gun was the one we used," Lucy says pleasantly, never even turning to look at Blake.

God, the sheer foolish courage this girl is capable of. For someone who cries about heights and spends more time falling off motorcycles than riding them, she is remarkably cool in the presence of a family of sociopaths.

"So, Veronica," she continues, "tell me about my grandparents."

Something like a smile crosses Veronica's face. "You know what, Preston?" she says. "I like you. Like I liked your mother, and her mother before her. It's a shame what happened. It really is. I've always enjoyed going toe-to-toe with the Preston women."

We wait, all of us.

And it hits me that while Blake and Curtis might know the truth about my dad—and Gus probably does at this point, too—they might not have any idea about Lucy's grandparents. They would have been children when it happened.

"I could answer it," Curtis says bitterly.

Veronica levels her glare at him. "My son tried to tell Katy about this years ago, when she was looking for answers," she says. "We worked out our own deal. Anything for family."

Lucy's gaze finds Curtis, level and unforgiving. "You wanted her to like you," she says. "But you should know she never talked about you once, all those years. You should know that you were a speck in the distance behind her. You mean *nothing* to her."

That, I think, is the worst thing she could have said to Curtis, because his pale face is suddenly blazing red, but he is stopped by Veronica holding up a hand.

"Your grandfather caused a bit too much trouble," Veronica begins, ignoring her son. "Asking questions about safety. And procedures. We had a plan for all that, but we . . . we needed to get the park built on schedule. So I met with your grandfather to discuss his concerns, and I'm sure he never thought *I* was a threat to him. I was pregnant—eight months pregnant—with you, Curtis. I pushed your grandfather off the platform, Lucy."

There is a collective intake of breath as her children stare at her. Curtis is the only one who doesn't look surprised.

Although—Lucy doesn't look surprised, either, just a little sick. A little sad. "You killed my grandpa because he had concerns about the safety of your park?" she asks.

My grandpa.

The words are so raw, so vulnerable in comparison with Veronica's detached admission of her crime.

"Yes," Veronica answers, as nonchalantly as if she were asking someone to stay for dinner. "My business, my home, my *family*. That was all that mattered. His wife—your grandmother—blamed my husband, whom I had not confided in. You remember, children, what your father was like. He wasn't someone you could trust with a secret like that, but I did it for him. Anything for family."

Gus is staring at her as if he'd never seen her before. "Grandma," he whispers. "How *could* you?"

Blake scoffs. "Rich words coming from a boy who nearly sunk our family with his own impulsive crime."

She turns back to me, face hardening again. "Stand still, Nelson," she tells me.

"I did what I had to." Veronica bares her teeth as she speaks. "I asked your grandmother to meet me, Lucy. Wife to wife. Mother to mother. She agreed, and I told her...I told her we couldn't meet at my home and had to meet somewhere at night, because I couldn't risk my husband knowing. She ate the whole story up, that I was the brave wife who was ready to tell the truth despite my husband. I killed her, too. Right here."

Lucy's face doesn't change, but her hands are clenched in fists so tight that her knuckles have whitened. "Keep going," she says quietly. "Tell me everything. You owe me that, Veronica."

I want to rip out of Blake's hold and run to Lucy, hug her until I can take away all the hurt that flashes in her eyes.

I have carried this same grief—facing the person who robbed me of my family and seeing their callous disregard.

"Pierce felt so horrible about what happened to your family," Veronica continues, as if this is a pleasant conversation over mimosas and not the discussion of a cold-blooded double murder. "He took your mother in, and I did care for her, eventually. But those children I bore, *they* were mine. And she was not. But I did right by her. Paid for her college, even. And then she disappeared and never returned. If Pierce hadn't asked, she would never have come back at all."

She skips the part where she tried to destroy Katy for asking questions about her family. And the part where she treated Katy like an outsider who was never quite welcomed home.

"Did Pierce discover what you had done?" I ask. "Or did he only know about what happened to my dad?"

"Ah, yes, your father," Veronica says. "His was an unfortunate accident. That's all."

Hot tears sting the back of my eyes. "That's not true," I snarl. "Did you pay off the commission that said your roller coaster was up to code? Who else did you pay off to make it look like it was my dad's fault?"

"Everyone I needed to," Veronica answers easily. "Everyone has a price. Or a breaking point."

She must really, truly be confident that Lucy and I will die tonight, because she is giving out truth at a staggering rate.

"I kept it a secret all this time," she muses softly, and for the first time I see a trace of sadness. "I would have carried that secret for Pierce always. But he found out, a few weeks ago. He was so cut up by it. And then, last Friday he came back to the house and told us he was going to come clean and disinherit every one of us when he died."

She pauses, her eyes flicking back and forth between Lucy and Gus.

"So, Gus." Lucy turns to him. Her eyes look haunted, but she gives him that annoyingly cheerful smile, as if they are just talking about the weather. "Why did you kill your grandfather?"

He is trembling, holding tight to the wooden base of the platform. "I didn't mean to," he whispers. "I really didn't. Please."

"What happened?" I fix him with a stare, and he cowers as if I were the one with the gun.

"I heard them all arguing," he says. "And then . . . then Grandpa came up to his study, and I asked him if it was true. If he was going to cut us all off from his will, and if I'd still be able to live here or if I'd have to go live with my dad on the road and I couldn't—I couldn't—"

"That's what you were worried about?" I blurt out in disbelief. "You overheard that your family covered up my dad's death, and you were concerned about having to give up your *mansion*?"

Gus whimpers. "I didn't hear all of it," he protests. "I didn't know what they had done. I was just . . . I was scared. Everything was changing, and everyone was fighting, and Grandpa was so mad. He said he didn't want to see any of us ever again, that everyone in this family was rotten, and that I could kiss the house and all of it goodbye. He never liked me. I think he'd have been happy to kick me out like they kicked out my dad, and I didn't think, I just picked up this—this paperweight on his desk—and I hit him."

His words reverberate in the deadly silence in the clearing.

The bloodstain in the office. The already-dead body thrown from the roller coaster. Gus jumping at every noise. His mud-caked shoes. All of it. All of it.

And then Blake's gun clicks as she removes the safety.

"Well," she says softly, "I think we've all heard enough."

She motions with the gun toward the platform.

When neither of us move, Blake's lip curls. "What, did you think rescue was coming?" she asks. "You've stalled long enough."

"The cops are coming," I say, trying to sound confident.

"No," Veronica says. "They aren't."

Fear settles into the pit of my stomach with finality.

Because she sounds as certain of that as she was when she spoke of murdering Lucy's grandparents.

"He— You paid him off," I say dully. The realization is both so jarring and so unsurprising that I have to catch my breath, sharply.

I've known him my whole life. But of course, of *course* he's been paid to look the other way.

"Do you really think one of us broke into Cliff's office to steal those files?" Veronica asks, a small smile curving across her face. "No, darling. When you have enough power, they just leave the door ajar for you themselves."

Lucy doesn't even look surprised.

How long has *she* suspected him?

Because it never occurred to me to think that Cliff, who has known me since I was a baby, would be part of covering up a murder. And framing my mom. Not even when I saw him digging in the park for evidence he shouldn't have known would be there.

"Does the sheriff know?" Lucy asks. "What you did?"

"Not all of it, no," Veronica says. "But when I called him this morning after Curtis broke into your motel, he said the door would be unlocked for a few hours. He didn't ask any questions because he knows better."

I grit my teeth. Did he suspect there was more to my father's death, too? Has he always known? "What do you have on him?" I ask her.

"Oh, that's always my brother," Blake answers. "The petty criminal."

"You hit Lucy?" I snarl, surging forward before Blake presses the gun to my temple again.

Curtis has the audacity to look apologetic. "I didn't kill her," he says, as if he deserves to be lauded for that. "Lucy, you and your mom are important to me." His eyes fall on Gus, a complicated wave of emotion rolling across his face as he looks at his son. "But it's my kid. You have to understand."

"Is that why you tried to cast suspicion on Blake and Veronica?" Lucy asks. "When you told me at dinner that Pierce had been trying to make amends, did you want to push suspicion toward them so that it would be far away from Gus?"

Curtis looks as if he's in physical pain, avoiding everyone's eyes now, but especially Veronica's, which are boring into him.

"I wanted him to be safe," Curtis says finally. "I owed him that much. But I never meant you or Katy any harm. You have to believe that."

As if it matters what we believe now.

Lucy rolls her eyes. "My mom warned me about you." She manages to sound unreasonably sassy for someone currently being held at gunpoint. "I don't care if she was important to you once upon a time."

Veronica lifts one shoulder in a half-hearted shrug. "We are the Anselms," she answers. "We carry this town's economy. We pay Cliff's salary. We were never going to go down for Pierce's death, and he knew it. He arrested Langley this morning so that Katy would have a suspect and leave us for good. And then we'd all be free to carry on as before."

Blake taps her designer flats impatiently. "Enough," she says, waving her gun at me. "Get up there. Both of you."

My feet feel like lead as I take one step forward. And then another.

What will it feel like, to step off the edge of that platform? What will run through my head as the ground rushes up at me?

Will Dad be with me as I fall?

But then to my surprise, a smile unfurls across Lucy's pale face, slowly, triumphantly. "No," she says. "I don't think we will." Her eyes lock on mine. "Anything for family," she says.

She pulls something from her pocket, screams loudly, and—

Well, she maces the roller coaster. Not Blake.

But she does try her best.

Then she whirls to me, yells "Catch," and throws an object at me as hard as she can.

Which, because she is Lucy, is not terribly hard.

I snatch it out of the air. A...Taser?

Lucy kicks wildly at Blake, who is too busy staring at her in disbelief to react quickly enough. Lucy aims for Blake's ankles with the kick, maybe because she doesn't have the balance to kick any higher (we really have to work on that) and then screams *use it* at me.

I jam the Taser behind me against Curtis's rib cage and pull the trigger. "Anything for family," I breathe.

My Audrey, Dad might be saying. They're all around me. I know they are. Dad and Lucy's grandparents and Arthur Joyce. Everyone the Anselms have sacrificed for their family, their power, their chokehold on our town.

Curtis screams as the Taser makes impact, his body flailing as he falls backward against the platform.

And then Lucy grabs my free hand, and we run for our fucking lives.

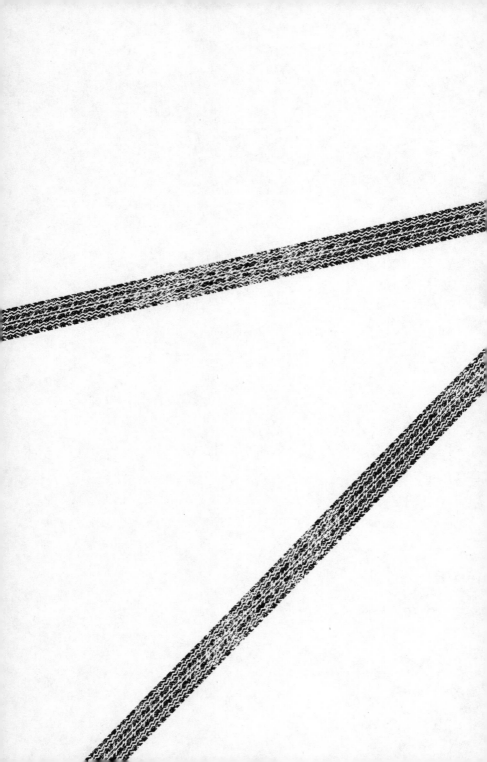

DAY SIX: WEDNESDAY, MARCH 27

CHAPTER 32

LUCY

12:01 A.M.

WE DON'T STOP FOR THE YELLING, AND WE DON'T stop for the crack of the pistol behind us. We just run for the gate and the bike, damn everything else.

"How the hell did you get a Taser?" Audrey shouts at me as we clamber through the gap in the fence.

Another shot rings out behind us.

How many bullets do small guns like that have? I wish I had paid more attention when Mom talked about guns, which she did a truly ridiculous amount of times.

"That's what you're thinking about right now?" I yell back at Audrey.

"I'm also thinking that you standing up to Veronica was kind of hot," she yells back, and I consider whether smacking her would delay us an unreasonable amount of time. "And trying the thing with the Mace, even though you missed."

This girl is unbelievable.

"I hate you," I yell back at her, and she has the audacity to *grin* at me.

"Where are we going?" she yells at me as I narrowly miss running straight into a tree.

"This way," I tell her. "I hope."

"You *hope*?"

"I'm directionally challenged," I tell her as I trip over a tree root. "Your bike's in here somewhere. Do you still have the Taser? Can we use it more than once, or is there, like, a limit? Oh, and Katy gave me the Taser. She said *just in case*. Figured this was one of those cases."

She snorts, something that could almost be a laugh. "Lucille Marie Preston, you better not have lost my bike in this damn forest."

We nearly stumble over it in the pitch-blackness of the forest, but Audrey doesn't hesitate, despite the thunder of footsteps pursuing us. The footsteps are heavy, twigs cracking, and I chance a guess that it's Curtis who is on foot.

Curtis, who is nice until he's not. Who cares about my mom, until he doesn't. Who pretends to be the only moral Anselm, until he isn't.

Which means that Blake, and her gun, are probably approaching from the street.

"Those fuckers," Audrey snarls, hauling her bike back out of the forest with an ease that makes me stare at her in wonder. "Stop gaping and get on, you dumbass." She half drags me onto the bike with her, and then we're off, speeding through the night.

I glance over my shoulder.

The black Cadillac is now bearing down on us from behind.

"Audrey," I scream, because Veronica is driving, and there is no doubt in my mind that she will crush us both if she can.

But Audrey isn't the kind of girl who flinches when she sees an animal in the woods or nearly runs the motorcycle off the road just because she can't balance. No, I can't see Audrey's face but I can picture that look, that small, stubborn smile.

And then she looks back at me. "This bitch," she says above the roar of the motorcycle, "has nothing on me."

She veers a hard left straight down the steep, grassy slope away from the road, and I bounce so hard I nearly fall.

Audrey holds me up, though, as we bump through the grassy gully beside the road, ducking under low-hanging branches.

The Cadillac swerves after us, and I hear the terrible *crunch* of branches snapping forcefully as it crashes through them in its relentless pursuit to reach us.

Audrey is driving one-handed now, the other hand helping me balance as I cling to her.

I'm not chickenshit, I swear I'm not, but all I want to do right now is close my eyes.

Audrey pulls us back onto the road—well, *over* the road and back down into the ditch, and the Cadillac veers after us. I cling tightly to Audrey, resting my head on her shoulder so that my face is pressed against her chin.

We aren't fast enough to outrun it, but with Audrey, maybe we have a chance of outmaneuvering it.

We come to a particularly narrow bend in the road, and I can feel Audrey's grin.

"Hold on," she shouts at me, and then she pulls the motorcycle sharply to the right, until we spin in a one-eighty, facing down the Cadillac.

Every inch of Audrey is illuminated by the high beams, and I see her silhouette, every hair standing up along her bare arms, her dark hair framing her face like a halo.

And then she guns it, speeding toward the Cadillac. Head-on.

I scream, and at the very last second I squeeze my eyes shut, and then—

Sharp swerve as we pull to the side. My body tilting.

Wind and heat as the Cadillac passes us narrowly.

I open my eyes in time to meet Gus's eyes as he stares from the front seat, inches from my own.

His eyes are blue. Ice blue, sad and hollow and wide, wide, *wide* with fear.

I never wanted this.

He opens his mouth as if he's speaking. And maybe he is.

I'm sorry.

And then the Anselms careen past us, unable to make the turn. They crash off the road, straight into century-old oak trees, their car crumpling into silence.

Audrey slows, slows, slows.

Her hand reaches back, finds my thigh.

"You with me?" she asks softly, her voice barely audible above the sound of her motorcycle.

It's an odd, final sort of quiet, just the trees and Audrey and the motorcycle.

Off to our right, the Cadillac is smoking, the glass at the front shattered. It is wrapped almost all the way around one wide oak tree.

We don't wait to see if there are any survivors.

"I'm with you," I murmur.

Audrey drives a bit farther, her hand never leaving my leg. I don't want it to ever leave.

She kills the engine and stays there, straddling the bike, her boots resting on the pavement.

"Do you have service?" I ask. "We should . . . We should call an ambulance. For the Anselms."

She shakes her head. "I don't have service out here. You know," she continues, "we won't have any proof, after this. Not with all the files missing. It's our word against theirs. But at least we're alive."

I shift so that I can reach the pocket of my dress without really letting go of Audrey, even a little bit. Even though I knew she would catch me if I needed her to. "Oh no," I tell her. "I saved the files in the cloud, even after Cliff told me to delete them."

Audrey chuckles softly. "Of course you did," she says. "Still. All those things they told us tonight?"

"Oh, that," I say. "It's on my phone. I recorded everything."

This time, it's Audrey's turn to almost fall off the bike. "Holy shit," she says, righting herself. It's so utterly, utterly silent out here.

Just the whisper of wind in the trees and the murmur of crickets, the far-off hoot of an owl.

And the sound of our heartbeats, beating in time with each other.

"How?" she whispers in amazement, twisting so that she can look straight into my eyes. "I didn't see your phone. I assumed you didn't even *have* it."

"My dress has pockets," I tell her triumphantly.

She grins in disbelief. "Of course it does," she says, and then she leans back to kiss me, just once, slow and sweet.

A roar cuts the silence, a motorcycle approaching, and we both go still.

A second later, Audrey throws her head back and grins.

The bike rounds the curve, and I stare, slack-jawed.

Because there on the motorcycle is Langley, dark hair tucked under a helmet.

And riding behind her, arms wrapped around Langley, is Mom.

I sprint toward Mom before they've even dismounted, and she pulls me into a fierce hug.

"Oh, baby," she whispers against my hair. "Oh, sweetheart, I thought I'd lost you."

And then I'm crying against Mom's shoulder as if I will never stop.

CHAPTER 33

AUDREY

12:53 A.M.

MOM NEARLY LIFTS ME OFF MY FEET IN A HUG.

She doesn't say anything for a long moment, just holds me in her arms and cries so hard her shoulders are shaking.

I'm crying before I realize it, too, and I bury my head against her shoulder. She's still in the black blazer she was arrested in, and now I've soaked the shoulder with tears. "Mom," I whisper. "I'm so sorry."

She draws back and cups my face in her hands. "You're safe, baby," she tells me fiercely. "That is the *only* thing that matters to me."

Sirens sound next, wailing up the road, and then three squad cars pull up.

"Who the hell is this?" I ask. "Mom, what happened?"

Lucy tugs her mom by the hand until they're standing beside us in the circle of red and blue flashing lights.

"Audrey." Katy holds out her hand to me. "I'm sorry that I couldn't tell you. I went along with your mom's arrest because I thought it would buy us time with the Anselms, give me time to get reinforcements here. I couldn't tell you. I couldn't tell either of you. I thought I could keep you both safer that way."

One of the cops—a tall, brown-skinned woman with close-cropped dark hair—strides toward us.

"That's them," Katy says, pointing to the crumpled Cadillac up the road. "The Anselms. Do you have an ambulance on the way?" She hasn't loosened her hold on Lucy, not even a little bit.

The cop nods. "We'll brief in a moment, all right? I'm glad your daughter is safe." She moves past us, up the road toward the smoking Cadillac.

Katy stretches out her hand toward me again, and this time I take it.

"Katy told me after she dropped off Lucy at the diner," Mom tells me. "She came back and just... shoved Cliff into the open jail cell without an explanation. And then locked him up, let me out, and we worked out the details of the case together."

Another uniformed officer approaches us. "Are these your daughters?" he asks Katy.

"This is Lucy," Katy says. "And Audrey."

The cop nods. "I'm glad you're both okay," he says. "We saw your message outside the diner. That was quick thinking—Lucy, right?"

"Audrey was kidnapped from the diner by the Anselms," Lucy tells him. "I came to rescue her and then we escaped together. We got away on her motorcycle, and they tried to run us down, but they crashed into a tree. Just down the road. I'm not sure... I'm not sure if any of them survived."

The cop's eyebrows shoot up. "That's quite the story," he says. "And my partner and I will be happy to hear more, but is there anything we should know about the Anselms? We're trying to extricate any survivors, but we'd like to know if there are any weapons we should know about. We've got an ambulance two minutes out, but we'd like the scene to be clear when they arrive."

"One of them has a gun," I tell them, and Mom's body tenses. "Blake does. A little pistol. They showed it to me when we were in the diner. It's why I got into the car with her. And then they took me to the park, and she pointed the gun at us and told us they were going to make it look like a murder-suicide."

The cop steps away from us and speaks into his radio for a moment. His eyes are crinkled with concern when he turns back to us. "I'll take your statement whenever you're ready," he says. "But first I'd like to make sure neither of you are hurt. Ma'am—Langley, is it?—I'm sorry, but I believe you're the only medical professional here with us at the moment. We'll need the whole EMS team for the folks up the road. Can you see to the girls while the private detective and I talk about some elements of this case?"

"Katy?" Mom says. "We'll head back to the diner, if that's okay."

Katy doesn't look as if she wants to let Lucy out of her sight ever again, but Mom places a hand on her arm.

"I've got her," she says, and miraculously, Katy nods.

"I know you do."

They stand like that, shoulder to shoulder, for a long moment.

"I'm sorry," Katy says finally, and something passes in the look between them that I don't understand. "We…we should talk. After this is all done."

Mom nods, and the look between them lingers for a moment until she finally ushers us back toward the bikes. "Honey, are you okay to drive?" she asks.

I nod wordlessly, and Lucy climbs on behind me. Tucks her face against my shoulder, her cheek soft and reassuring.

Mickey will have a fit that his establishment is being used after hours without telling him, and he will also probably have a conniption over the electric bill from having the lights on all night, and the thought makes me giggle, a little hysterically.

"You okay, honey?" Mom asks, but I just giggle again, and then suddenly I'm crying and Lucy and Mom both wrap their arms around me and wait.

In the end, Lucy gives the cops her phone and tells them to listen to the recording, and our moms tell them we'll give a statement in the morning.

And then we go back to the motel all together, the four of us plus a police escort, and no one says anything when Lucy and I climb into the same bed together and curl up to go to sleep.

There will be time to ask and answer questions tomorrow, to learn about the final fate of the Anselm family, to talk about what the future will bring. To grieve the ones we lost to Haeter Lake's amusement park and the Anselm family.

But tonight, we just curl up, Lucy and I, fingers entwined.

Our moms stand at the door, talking, their voices low and melodic, watching over us just in case.

So, Sundress and I?

We fall asleep side by side.

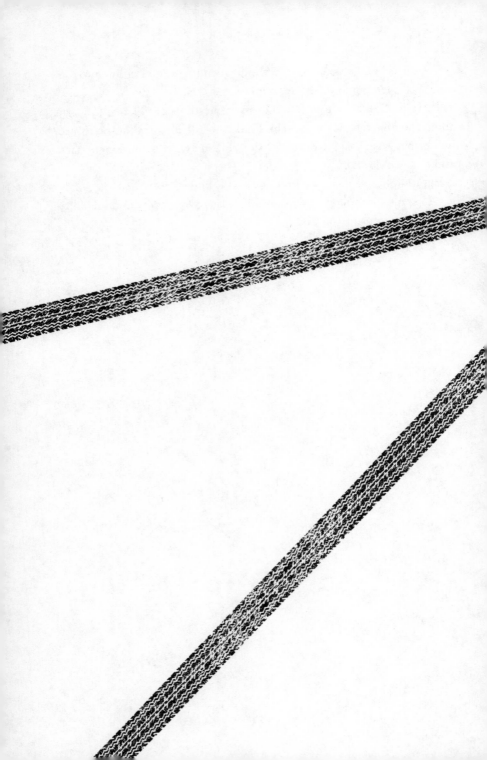

TUESDAY, APRIL 9. TWO WEEKS LATER

CHAPTER 34

LUCY
4:15 P.M.

WHEN WE ARRIVE BACK IN HAETER LAKE ALMOST two weeks later to meet with Pierce Anselm's lawyers about his will, the sun is shining brightly. Spring has crept up on this town since I last saw it, small green leaves dancing gently every time the wind rustles the trees. Mom reaches over and tucks a strand of hair behind my ear.

"You okay?" she asks softly.

I nod.

I am, mostly.

Audrey and I have been messaging nonstop since I went back to Atlanta, when we both had to go back to school after spring break.

I tried to explain what happened to my friends back home, Jules and Amy and Nora, but how could I even begin?

I met and lost my grandparents here.

I met a girl who changed my life.

I rode around on a motorcycle *way* too many times.

And I solved a murder. A few of them actually.

The details of the case had trickled in slowly. Mom stepped aside from the investigation without being asked, something she has never done before and will probably never do again, so the information came to us in bits and pieces.

The cops found two people in the crumpled Cadillac.

One was Gus.

He hadn't been buckled, and he had been thrown into the windshield. They had pronounced him dead at the scene.

The other was Veronica, who was securely buckled and protected by the airbag. She had been in critical condition when we left but has been recovering nicely as she awaits trial.

Because of course she is.

The cops found Curtis farther up the road, still on foot, and he is in the county jail, not here in Haeter Lake.

Investigations had been reopened into my grandparents' deaths, and Audrey's dad, too.

The deputy has been promoted, and Cliff is still in jail, too, keeping Curtis company.

They found Blake's gun, too, abandoned in the Cadillac just outside of Haeter Lake.

They never did find Blake, though.

Just a trail of blood leading off into the forest, and then the trail disappeared entirely.

Mom squeezes my shoulder. "Are you sure about this?"

"Yeah," I tell her. "I'm sure."

When we reach the attorney's office, Audrey is waiting on the front steps.

She's more dressed up than her usual ripped black jeans. Today, she's wearing pressed dress pants and a collared white shirt, complete with a tie that looks a little too big for her.

I almost stop breathing.

Katy chuckles. "Oh, honey," she says, glancing over at me as she pulls up in front of the courthouse. "You got it *bad*."

I really, really do.

I jump down out of the Jeep and launch myself into Audrey's arms, nearly knocking her off her feet.

But she's solid, my Audrey, and she rebalances both of us.

"I'm amazed you survived this long without more previous head injuries," she teases me, and then pecks a kiss on the tip of my nose. "I missed you."

"I missed you, too," I say, and then because her tiny little kiss was nowhere near enough, I press in and kiss her on the lips, even if it isn't quite appropriate for an event as serious as a will reading.

She wraps an arm over my shoulders, which she can do easily because the world is unfair and she is taller than me even when I'm wearing heels. "You ready, Sundress?" she asks me.

I nod. "You? Are you okay?"

She squeezes me closer to her and we pause there, leaning against each other.

"Mom's been making me see a therapist," she says. "And it's a little awkward, because there's actually only one therapist in town, and it's Chris's dad. Chris has been good about all this, too, though I don't think he can ever really understand."

Katy called it a trauma bond, this thing Audrey and I share, and maybe it is. I've been going to therapy, too, and I'm going to make sense of it. I am, someday. But for now, all I know is that Audrey and I shared something special before we ever faced the Anselms.

"I'm glad things have been good with Chris," I say. "Jules and Amy and Nora are trying, too. But I think maybe it's something only you and I will ever really *get*."

She nods, and then she removes her arm from my shoulders and threads her fingers through mine. "How have things been with your parents?"

Dad came back to Atlanta after he heard what happened. At first he stayed at a hotel nearby, but lately he's been sleeping in the guest bedroom so he could be closer. "They've both been overprotective," I tell Audrey. "He couldn't come today, but he wants to meet you. And

Mom wants to spend the weekend in Haeter Lake. She said…She said she'd take us to see where my grandparents are buried. That'd be nice, I think."

Closure, Katy had said, and maybe that's what it is for her. She grieved her parents all those years ago, and she had to grieve them again when she listened to the recording of Veronica Anselm admitting to their murder. But even still, she's lived with this loss a lot longer than I have.

For me, it'd be nice to see where they're resting.

"The cemetery is peaceful," Audrey says softly. "I go there in the summer a lot. Sit and talk to Dad. I went there the night Pierce died, too. To talk to him before I met with Pierce."

I lean my head against her shoulder.

We stay there, hand in hand on the steps as our moms catch up in the parking lot.

It's a perfect moment, sunny, quiet.

"Should we go in?" she asks me finally.

I nod. "Together?"

"Together."

AUDREY. 4:30 P.M.

Pierce Anselm's attorneys are waiting inside, along with the detective we met the night Gus Anselm died. She's taken over the investigation since Cliff went to jail, and she steps forward to shake Mom's hand.

Pierce Anselm's attorneys, Kipling and Kaur, wave us over to the table.

Kipling, a woman about Mom's age, smiles at me. "I've heard all about what you girls did to help solve this case," she says warmly. "Won't you sit down? This will be pretty informal."

"I was kind of hoping for a dramatic reading," Lucy says as she drops into a chair beside me. "Loudly, with a few twists and some juicy reveals."

Kaur, the junior partner at the firm, a young man with jet-black hair and brown eyes, grins. "I'm afraid it isn't really the way it happens in movies," he says. "We have the will right here, and we asked you both here because you are beneficiaries."

Lucy exchanges a glance with me. "Holy shit," she says, and then claps a hand over her mouth. "Sorry, swearing in here kind of feels like swearing in church." She glances guiltily over at her mom. "Not that I ever swear in church."

Kaur chuckles. "No worries," he says. "I'll give you your copies, and I've made some for your parents as well, because the inheritance you receive will remain in a trust until you're of age. Your parents will oversee that trust until you both turn eighteen."

"You can read for yourselves, of course," Kipling says as Kaur hands us the documents. "But I thought it would be easier if I went through it a bit, as sometimes the legal jargon is a bit dense. It's taken us some time to sort out, given that Mr. Anselm passed away under such unfortunate circumstances, but now that the case has been resolved we've been given the go-ahead to move forward with all this." She hesitates and exchanges a look with Mom.

Mom puts a hand on my arm, her touch gentle.

"The first thing you should know is that when Mr. Anselm found out what had happened to both of your families, he was devastated," Kipling continues quietly. "He spoke to us, though not about specifics, but he was truly heartbroken for the pain your families have suffered because of his. He expressed the feeling that Katy and Langley might not be open to receiving anything from him, and that he understood, but he hoped he could offer something to their daughters instead. He has left his estate to you girls in its entirety."

"Well, damn," Lucy says. "Next time we won't even have to break in to get into the mansion." She looks guiltily at her mom again, and Katy rolls her eyes in return.

I can't quite bring myself to laugh with Lucy.

I don't think I'll ever want to go in the mansion where Veronica Anselm lived and schemed and plotted. I don't want to see the office where Pierce was killed or look out the window from Veronica's study and see the park, the roller coaster, the footpath.

"Can we sell the mansion?" I ask quickly.

Lucy puts a reassuring hand on my knee under the table, and my shoulders relax.

"You absolutely can," Kipling answers. "But when I said estate, I didn't mean just the house and grounds, though that's all yours, of course. He also owned twenty-seven different amusement parks around the country. Those belong to you now, though they will continue to be managed by the board of directors until you come of age. You can, of course, sell those off if you wish. The one stipulation in his will was that the park here in Haeter Lake be destroyed. He suggested bringing down the dam and letting the place become a lake again."

"That sounds ideal to me," Lucy says. "I would like to never see that roller coaster again. Or any roller coaster, maybe."

"Understandable," Kipling continues. "Mr. Anselm also had a great deal in the way of liquid assets, and that money has been divided between the two of you and placed into trust funds that you will have access to when you reach majority."

"Um," Lucy interjects again. "Sorry, I feel like I'm interrupting a lot. But trust fund? That sounds like something you need a lot of money for."

Kipling slides identical sheets of paper across the table toward us.

I stare down at the number, my eyes widening. "Holy fucking shit," I say. "Mom, *look*."

That many zeroes in a row can't be real, but Kipling is nodding and smiling and assuring us that they are. And I'm thinking, *Shit*. Mom is never gonna have to choose between rent and replacing work shoes that are so worn they have holes in them. She's never gonna have to eat just peanut butter for dinner because there's no money for anything else.

Lucy jumps up, knocking her chair over, and grabs my hands, pulling me up with her until we're spinning around right there in the law office. She stops, her face suddenly serious. "You know what I'm gonna buy first, Audrey?"

I grin at her, breathless. "What?"

"A *goddamn* motorcycle helmet."

LUCY. 6:04 P.M.

We go to the cemetery together, Katy and Audrey and Langley and I.

We linger at the bottom of the hill, and Katy looks over at Langley. Both women hesitate, the weight of years hanging between them.

"Langley—" Katy breaks off, holding her palms up.

"You left," Langley says. Her voice is soft, as if she speaks too loudly she might break something.

"You stayed," Mom says. Her voice is just as soft, just as sad.

"Yeah," Langley says. "I've missed you, all these years you've been gone. Maybe that sounds silly now."

"I needed to go," Katy murmurs. "I'm sorry. I had to leave because I couldn't live when I was that—that furious every day."

"And I couldn't let that fury go." Langley looks at Katy for a long minute. "Do you think this is something we can move past?"

Katy's eyes shine suddenly. "I'm the one who should be asking that," she says softly. "I hurt you when I disappeared. I'm sorry, Langley."

Langley steps forward and wraps her arms around Katy, and this time, Katy hugs her back.

Well, *that* is another story I will be asking Mom for as soon as I can corner her, but first there is someone else I must see.

Audrey and Langley split off to go visit Audrey's dad, and Mom and I find our way up the hill toward two moss-covered tombstones.

"Here they are," Mom says softly.

I crouch down, brushing dead leaves out of the way. I trace my fingers over their names, their years. MARIE. ASA.

The caption under their names:

MEMENTO VITAE.

Mom's tattoo.

Remember to live.

Grandpa and Grandma.

If they were here, I think they would be happy to know that I have.

And maybe they have been with me, through all of it. Maybe they were right beside me when I snuck through the mansion's secret passageways to find answers, when I raced down winding roads on the back of a motorcycle holding tight to a girl I really, really liked. When I reached and found both anger and bravery, when I gathered my courage and confronted their murderers.

Now, when I close my eyes, all the stories I created for them are gone, replaced by this.

I can imagine them here—the man with the bright smile, the woman with the determined set to her jaw. I can imagine their laughter, their hands on my shoulder, their courage within me.

I open my eyes. The sun is golden, the shadows in the cemetery lengthening. My mom is beside me, tears in her eyes, and Audrey and Langley are coming up the hill toward us.

There are so many things I still don't know. How Audrey and I are going to manage all we've suddenly inherited. What we'll do with a legacy that comes with a lot of painful memories. What will happen with Blake, or with Cliff's trial, or with Veronica Anselm's.

But for now, I have today. *Memento vitae.* I have Katy. *Mom.* I have Audrey and Langley. I have friends at home, and friends here. Home there. Home here. Memories to sort through, and people who love me.

Maybe even a girlfriend.

I set off down the hill toward Audrey, the sun warm against my back, my hands outstretched to meet her.

ACKNOWLEDGMENTS

Bringing Audrey and Lucy to readers was a tremendous endeavor that involved so many people, and I owe so many my thanks.

First, my biggest thanks to my dream agent, Claire Friedman, and the whole Inkwell team. Claire, thank you for fighting for me and for this story. I can't wait to keep kicking butt and selling books together.

And to Kelsey Sullivan, my incredible editor at Hyperion, who plucked me out of the trenches and said that Audrey was her favorite character, too. Thank you for getting my girls—even my grumpy one.

To Colin Verdi and Phil Buchanan, for the cover of my dreams, and to the entire team at Hyperion for carrying this book across the finish line. Thank you for all you do.

To my family, for being there every step of the way. To Dad, for the summer reading challenges, and to Mom, for reading aloud to us (even when we made fun of Elsie Dinsmore). To John, Jojo, Grace, Paul, Daniel, and the babies: bartledo. I am the sum of all of our adventures and all of our stories, and nothing without all of you. To Grace, especially, for believing.

To my grandparents—Grandma Pat, for the blueberries and the laughter. To Grandma Jean, for grandma days and wisdom written on envelopes. To Grandpa Jack, for making the Roach family what it is today through dedication, hard work, and caring for all of us so well.

For my entire extended family, thank you for all your support over the years, but especially to Molly, my very first coauthor. That book must never see the light of day, but I'm proud of us for doing it anyway.

To all my early readers who suffered through the typo-ridden first draft, the biggest of thank-yous: Adrienne Tooley, Lillie Vale, Christine Jorgensen, Cat Bakewell, Cyla Panin, Meryl Wilsner & Carolina C. And to Courtney Gould—thank you for leaving memes throughout, and for attending the most unhinged PowerPoint presentation anyone has ever created.

To Jenna Voris and Brit Wanstrath: Thank you for all the Zoom talks (sorry for the time my phone died and you thought I'd been kidnapped) and publishing tea and for letting me read your brilliant, brilliant books. I love our hot tub witchcraft more than words can say.

To my entire mentee family—Cat, KC, Libby, Morgan, Rachael, Katie, Elizabeth, Shaina, Jenna & Brit—thank you all for being the best hype squad in existence.

To my Pitch Wars slack friends—Lyssa Mia Smith, Chad Lucas, Jessica Lewis, Rochelle Hassan, Meg Long, Elvin Bala, Rachel Morris, Nanci Schwartz, Alexis Ames, Jacki Hale, Jen Klug, Marisa Lynch, Ruby Barrett, Susan Lee & Rosie Danan. You are the best writing group. Thank you all for late night writing sprints, banding together for every member of our community, and showing up for me and each other.

To my Llama Squad, my AMM & Pitch Wars mentor chats, and the many writer friends I have made along the way: Thank you, thank you, thank you for cheering me on, commiserating over publishing, and keeping the flame lit. And to Isa in particular: Thank you for every wild DM conversation. You and our boy Izzy sustained me.

To Jackie Lea Sommers, Elyse Kallgren, and Stacey Anderson: my first writing group. Thank you for believing in me all these years.

To my hapkido family, who had nothing to do with the book but have shaped the person I became in so many ways: Thank you to everyone who has shared the mats with me, but especially Corey Ninneman, Kris Ninneman, Rick Anderson, and Sherri Gregor Anderson. The community you built is unlike any other. A thank-you to all the other black belts at CSD Hutch, with a special thanks to Marc Remhof, for the flights, the daily support with the metro hapkido team, and especially the sword.

A particular thanks is owed the staff of the Barnes & Noble café in Roseville, Minnesota, where I revised this novel, but especially to Lizzie, for making the most excellent iced chai that sustained me through many revisions.

To Ana Franco, for cheering me on at every step. I wish you were here to hold this book in your hands, because of all the projects I've written, this one was for you. I'll see you in the next one, my friend.

To J. Elle, especially, for Getting This Book. You are the reason this book has wings.

To Emma Warner—thank you for being my best friend. I'm so glad the feral hogs and a certain municipal leader brought us together.

And to Arynn, my very best guy for every adventure, for all the Bipple trips and morning swims and adventures in places old and new (and wherever we can find trouble). Here's to all the stories we make along the way.